For my family

Preface

My great grandmother was seven years old when the Civil War ended. She lived on a tobacco plantation in southern Virginia, which her family lost, probably because it was destroyed in the war or they were unable to farm it without enslaved people. She married a former Confederate soldier and ended up in Lynchburg.

When I was a child, my grandmother and my mother told me Great Grandmother's stories about plantation life, the war, and the Reconstruction period. They surely added their own points of view and embellishments. Some of the stories were nostalgic fantasies of a bygone time of graciousness and elegance. Some of them were bitter tales filled with resentment. And others revealed times of poverty they endured with pride.

From these fragments I have woven a tale of fiction. All of the characters are fictitious. I have tried to ground my story in place and history, however. Public events and conditions during the war and the Reconstruction are based on historical accounts, as are the depiction of the Freedmen's schools and the cities of Lynchburg, Richmond, and Philadelphia. Where dates conflict, such as those for the repair of railroads, I use the ones that fit in my story.

In trying to convey how my characters thought and spoke, I have used some language that is offensive today. I have avoided the most offensive of the terms used for Black people, unfortunately knowing that my readers will be aware of what would have been said.

Legacy

Louisa

Southern Virginia

April 1865

Louisa sat rocking on the veranda, soaking up the slight breeze that blew across the bare fields in the late afternoon. She was tired after a day's work that began at dawn. It was her forty-third birthday, and she was just as glad that no one had remembered. She was feeling old right now and had noticed some new lines in her sunburned face that morning, along with a few strands of gray in the brown curls she tied back with a string. But that was not what was on her mind as she sat and rocked. She was thinking back over the last four years, taking stock of things before Sidney returned from the war, and that could be any day now.

Louisa had gotten used to being in charge of everything. She actually liked it now, she thought as she rocked. But when the news of Fort Sumter had reached them, and Sidney told her he was enlisting as a lieutenant in the Confederate army and would be leaving as soon as he could get his affairs in order, she was scared. Until then a war had seemed like a faraway thing, a fine and noble cause, but not something that would affect her as the wife of a Virginia planter, living on a busy tobacco estate, and mistress of forty-six field hands and five house servants. Oak Hill, the Turner family plantation, was beautiful; everyone said so. The large brick house with the wide veranda all across the front was welcoming, and the mahogany furniture inside was elegant.

She liked to stand at the tall front windows and look out beyond the stable and fields to the rolling hills beyond. And in back of the house, a forest of ancient oaks lent an air of permanence.

The day after Sidney enlisted he had ridden over to see his lawyer in Chatham. When he returned, he sat down in the study with their overseer George McCann and went over the books. A few days later Sidney had held Louisa and kissed her tenderly before he rode off and was gone. She had missed him every day and worried about him being hurt in battle. It was a good thing that she had listened to his conversation with McCann, because it gave her at least a sense of the financial side of running their plantation. Up until then, she had only been in charge of running the household, directing the servants, and had simply asked Sidney for money for expenses.

She and McCann had never gotten along to begin with. He disgusted her, with his uncouth manner and crude way of speaking. She hated thinking about him even now. She had wanted Sidney to replace him, but he said McCann was effective, even if rough. It certainly became clear that McCann could not abide being told what to do by a woman. When three slaves ran away soon after Sidney left, he worked the rest harder. Longer hours than Sidney would ever have allowed. And no break for food at midday. Sidney believed that if you treated slaves well, let them raise some vegetables for themselves, and avoided separating families to sell them unless you had to, they would be content and good workers. Of course you had to discipline them out of their laziness, but that was why you watched them so closely. When Louisa told McCann to shorten the field hands' work days that first summer, he sneered at her and spat his tobacco juice on the ground before he answered. "Missy, you don't know the first thing about darkies. They lazy." And he kept right on making the field hands work from sunup to sundown.

Louisa knew Sidney did not approve of whipping slaves, and neither did she. She also knew he had left McCann with clear instructions not to whip, unless one of the field hands ran away. But right away McCann had put up a whipping post in the stable. He started whipping field hands who were not working hard enough to suit him. And to make matters worse, he seemed to like doing it. When Louisa had called McCann aside and reminded him of Sidney's instructions, he smirked. "Missy, you still ain't learned." In September of '62, word spread of Lincoln's Preliminary Emancipation Proclamation and Louisa's heart sank. What would become of them without slaves? Before long more field hands ran away. After three strong young men got away at once, McCann hired the slave catchers. He paid them to find the runaways, punish them and bring them back. It was horrible, too horrible to think about. And so Louisa did not.

More and more slaves ran away. Then McCann helped himself to whatever salary he figured he had coming, leaving little behind. He told Louisa he had no lust for the war and was heading west over the mountains to get away from it. "Good riddance," Louisa had thought. "Not even a real Confederate. A coward and mean as a snake."

By the time George McCann left, most of the field hands had run away anyway. Only a few had stayed on. Joseph, the groom, was old and crippled. As she watched the clouds grow red in the sky, Louisa thought it was strange how grateful she was to him, a slave. When it came right down to it he had saved them, he and May Belle. But really, Joseph had to stay, she thought. He could never have run away with that leg of his. She remembered what he did as if it were yesterday. It was right after George McCann had left. Four Yankees came galloping down the road and right up to the stable. There were five good work horses in there, exactly what the Yankees were looking for to pull their supply wagons. When Joseph had heard them coming he stuck a pebble between the shoe and hoof of the youngest horse, so that it would limp. The Yankees cursed the horse and then they cursed Joseph. Then they rode off with the other four horses tied behind them.

With some instruction from Joseph in hooking the horse to the plow, and more instruction in how to steer it, they were able to plant a large garden and twenty rows of corn, using seeds that May Belle had saved the year before. It turned out that May Belle knew a lot about growing things, and not just about cooking them. Who would have thought it? They had even put in several rows of tobacco in the second field. The corn did fine, so they'd put in a whole field of it the next year, and then more after that. The tobacco was hopeless, since they did not know how to cultivate and cure it properly.

Her grandson Wally came carrying a lit candle, concentrating the way a six-year-old does on his mission. "Mama says to tell you supper's ready Grandmama". "Tell her I'll get something later," Louisa replied. "I need to sit here now, honey." It was getting dark. Louisa took a deep breath and smelled the wisteria, especially pungent after the morning rain. She went on thinking about how hard things had been the winter of '62, how hungry they were, and how they worried about the children. By the spring of '62 she had gotten her daughters Mary and Ellen to work daily in the house, the garden and the fields. At seventeen and eighteen, they were unused to physical labor and objected at first. "You have no choice, it's work or starve," Louisa said firmly. The girls' eyes widened in shock at the firmness of her tone and they began to become aware of the gravity of their situation.

Now they all were capable gardeners and passable cooks. Their cook May Belle had taught them right along with her daughter Sally, who had been a housemaid up til then. The three girls had played together comfortably all the time when they were little, but as they grew older there was tension when they were together. Louisa knew it was because they all recognized the undeniable family resemblance between them. Of course it was never mentioned. But Louisa had seen Sally's resemblance to Sidney the first time she had seen her as a newborn. She was leaning over the basket, wondering that the baby's skin was so much lighter than her mother's dark skin, when she saw why.

Louisa would never forget how she had felt in that moment of recognition. Her heart had dropped to the pit of her stomach. "Please don't let it be true," she prayed, knowing that it was. She looked at May Belle's face. It was defiant. May Belle picked up baby Sally and held her protectively to her breast. Mumbling some excuse, Louisa ran from the kitchen and up to her room, where she threw herself on the bed and sobbed. She moaned and ground her wet face into the quilt, aching to disappear into the soft mattress. She had heard women gossip about some of the planters they thought were impregnating their female slaves. But Sidney was different. And theirs was a love marriage—they really cared about each other, or so she had thought. She had known he was disappointed when she refused him during the last month of her pregnancy with John. But she had been afraid after she saw the blood. That must have been when he sought out May Belle. Louisa had had no idea at the time. How could he? With May Belle! And how dare she look defiant!

When John was born, Louisa was delighted to be able to present him to Sidney. Sidney was as proud as if he had borne the child himself. His heir to the Turner estate. When baby John was not nursing, Sidney liked to carry him around. He even carried him cradled in his arm when he rode the fields on his horse, behavior which Louisa found very endearing. Now her heart ached whenever she thought of John. Kind, serious, young man. Trying to make his father proud. Killed at the Battle of Sharpsburg in '62. She had never thought she would lose him.

Eight months after Louisa bore John, Sally was born to May Belle. Sidney paid no attention to her, still enamored with his little son and engrossed in running the farm. But of course he knew. If he even noticed that Louisa was a bit teary for a while, he certainly never let on.

Sidney was intent on having another son quickly, so Louisa stopped nursing John at a little over eight months. She swallowed her jealousy and had May Belle nurse John right along with Sally, one at each breast until John got too big to share. The sight of those two babies together with May Belle in the kitchen, looking exactly like the brother and sister they were, made Sidney so mad he demanded that John stop nursing. He said that John was too old. But they still did not talk about his fathering Sally. Not then. For Louisa, the pain of Sidney's betrayal remained, a heavy lump in her stomach. She kept looking for signs that Sidney was still bedding May Belle, but nothing seemed to be going on between them. Then May Belle had a son, Jamie, who was the spitting image of her husband James. Then Moses was born and he looked almost like Jamie's twin. Louisa stopped worrying and let herself love Sidney. He seemed grateful for her love and that resulted in Ellen and then Mary.

Louisa smiled as she thought about those days. She and Sidney were close and happy, enjoying their young family. He continued to dote on John, but made room in his heart for his two little daughters. As soon as the children were four, he taught each of them to ride, and when they were all old enough, he and Louisa would go riding with them, stopping for picnics or swimming in the river. Louisa and he joined enthusiastically in the social life of Pittsylvania County, and loved to entertain in their beautiful home. Louisa was grateful for Sidney's skillful management of their plantation, which made their life easy and pleasant. He was proud of his pretty wife, who presided so graciously over their home. Those were good times to remember.

All along May Belle remained a reliably good cook. She also managed all the food preservation and storage they needed, so that Louisa could really depend on her while she was so busy with John, Ellen and baby Mary. Louisa didn't understand why May Belle was not pleased when she complimented her on managing the food preservation and cooking so competently. Negroes were just hard to figure out. Another thing that puzzled Louisa was that, while May Belle brought Sally up from the quarters to play with John, Ellen and Mary, for some reason she did not bring her little boys. When Louisa asked her about it, she mumbled something about how Jamie and Moses liked to play down in the quarters with their cousins. "Well", Louisa mused, " May Belle always was peculiar."

It was not until Sally was fourteen and becoming a woman that it all came to a head. Louisa had been directing Sally in doing housework for a couple of years. She was strong and quick to catch on. Usually she would be alone in the room she was cleaning. When he was fifteen, John had taken to following her and watching as she worked.

When Louisa came upon him one day and saw the longing and fascination on his face, she knew it was trouble. She needed to speak to both Sidney and John right away. No more ignoring the obvious.

When Sidney came in for dinner that day she confronted him quietly on the veranda. Her jaw was tight and her voice tense." John is lusting after Sally. I know she is your daughter, Sidney. It has to stop. Now."

Sidney was taken aback to hear his wife speaking so decisively, and he was astonished that she was actually bringing up the issue of Sally. He was aware that Louisa knew of course, but assumed their tacit agreement not to mention it would continue unchallenged. He had liked that about Louisa—she could ignore the things she needed to ignore.

But when Sidney responded, he showed that he understood what was at stake. "Well, we don't need any more light skinned babies on this plantation. I will speak to John. Then I'll get him more time with his tutor. It is time he helped me more with the farm too."

They went in to dinner and did not speak of it again.

The next day Sidney engaged Mr. Williams to teach lessons in academic subjects three days a week, mornings and afternoons, instead of just the two mornings a week he had been coming. Ellen and Mary had been included in lessons all along, even though Louisa's mother Lou had said it was quite unnecessary for girls. But Louisa had insisted on it, since her father Charles had allowed her to be educated. Charles had confided to Sidney that educated women were more interesting. It was lonely business being a planter, he said, much more palatable when your wife was someone you could talk with. Charles knew from experience. Lou read hardly anything. Charles enjoyed reading Shakespeare and had been delighted when Louisa got to the point where she did too. Literature did not interest his sons at all. But Louisa had cherished her evenings with her father, taking roles reading Julius Caesar and MacBeth.

It was interesting how education had turned out with Louisa's children. All three had readily learned to read and John and Mary enjoyed mathematics. John was fascinated by nature and plants and Ellen liked to write and paint. Only Mary showed real curiosity about history and literature. She became an avid reader like Louisa herself, and they had shared many happy hours reading Shakespeare together, when they still had the leisure to do so. Their favorite play was As You Like It, because of the daring Rosalind. They had laughed and wondered at her cool head and bold tricks.

Louisa and Sidney had enjoyed reading novels by Sir Walter Scott together before they were married. The picture Scott painted of feudal England seemed enticingly romantic to them. She was disappointed when their shared reading stopped after the first year or so. There was so much work running the farm, and that only increased as they acquired more land. That meant buying more field hands and selling more tobacco. Then, with northern criticism of the institution of slavery being discussed wherever he went, Sidney became obsessed with states' rights and the property rights of slave owners.. He started spending most evenings reading and writing about these issues. When they gathered with neighbors for social events, the men all went off to smoke and argue earnestly about self-determination and secession from the union. Sidney didn't talk to her about such things.

When Louisa asked questions about issues like secession, he told her not to bother her head and not to worry. He would protect her and the children. He said he just wanted to enjoy himself when he was with her and the children. But he spent less and less time with them. He was growing and curing a significant crop of tobacco by the late '50's, and was teaching John the business of selling it. John had been excited by this. Who knows how his life would have turned out?

Louisa heard the soft voices of her daughters getting the children to bed. Mary was reading the old nursery rhyme book to her nephews and they were laughing at the pictures. "Hey diddle diddle, the cat and the fiddle…" Ellen was singing to her daughter. Louisa knew that Mary wanted children of her own some day, and was glad she enjoyed her sister's children. Mary had thought Ellen was "settling" to marry Walter, and told her so before she married him. She said Walter strutted about as if he were master of the whole county, instead of a small estate a few miles down the road. When he had inherited the place, people said he had no business sense at all. But Ellen was smitten and there was no dissuading her, even though she was only seventeen at the time. That was back in '59, when the war was still a talking point. Louisa had seen Walter's arrogance herself and had asked Ellen to wait to marry, hoping the infatuation would wear off. But Walter had insisted and Ellen had too, so they married. Their first son Wally had arrived seven months later, so that explained why Ellen was so adamant. She seemed happy with the baby, but kept saying how she missed the rest of her family, once she was living at Walter's. Walter spent many afternoons and most of his evenings drinking whiskey and playing cards with his friends. Ellen soon became pregnant again and had another boy, Henry. That kept her busy, but she was still lonely.

Then Ellen asked Mary If she would come to live with them for a while. Mary was hesitant because she did not like being around Walter. And she would have to give up her lessons with Mr. Williams and her brother John. She loved the lessons and it was practically the only time she saw John, since he was so busy learning the tobacco business. But when Mary rode over to see her sister one day, and found Ellen sitting in tears on the floor in her bedroom, still in her nightgown at three in the afternoon, she changed her mind. Both babies were squalling in the nursery. Ellen looked up at Mary with dull eyes and said, "They never stop. Ever."

"Where's Lizzie?" Ellen asked.

"Walter sold her and five field hands to pay off debts. And Lula has too much to do with all the cooking and cleaning." So Mary changed the boys' soiled diapers, brought little Henry to Ellen to nurse, and put Wally on the floor to crawl. When Walter came home, he was so relieved to see his wife dressed and his sons not crying, he nearly cried himself. Mary told Louisa it was the only time she had seen him without a trace of arrogance. So when he asked her to stay, she agreed.

As Louisa was thinking of her, Mary appeared with another candle. She lay her hand gently on her mother's shoulder, "Papa will be home soon, Mama." "Yes," Louisa said softly. And she thought to herself, "That's why I can't stop thinking and worrying. Everything is completely different now from when he left." She returned to thinking about her daughters. Until recently, Mary and Ellen had seemed about as close as two sisters could be. They recognized their differences and accepted them. They said what they had to say and could then let things go. Walter had been grateful for Mary's help, so she did her best to ignore his pompous ways and pronouncements, such as when he said a Confederate victory was "a foregone conclusion." Unbelievably, the situation had worked. When Ellen got pregnant again, she and Mary worried privately that it was too soon after Henry's birth. But Walter was puffed up and proud that it was proof of his "colossal virility", as he said to Sidney.

And then the war broke out. When Walter heard that Confederate forces had attacked the US forces at Fort Sumter, he was ecstatic. "The war will be over before you know it," he told Ellen. "The Yankees have no idea what they are up against." He left to join up in a matter of days and promised he'd be back before the baby was born. But five months before Laura was born, Ellen received a letter from Walter's captain. He had lasted three months before he succumbed to typhoid.

Louisa was getting chilly in the cool night air, and pulled the shawl hanging on the back of the chair around her. Sidney's experience in the war was very different from Walter's. He'd been in some major battles, but his infrequent letters said little of that. Instead he was sometimes affectionate and sweet, like he'd been when the children were little. In later letters he was curt and angry. She had not gotten a letter for a long time though, and wondered how he would be when he returned. Would they be strangers to each other?

She knew Sidney was alive because the Stanton boy up the road had just returned, and said he had seen Sidney since Appomattox. He could not remember where. Last Sunday at church in Chatham, Reverend Mason had announced that on April ninth General Lee had surrendered to General Grant at Appomattox. There was silence, and then the sounds of the sparse and mostly female congregation weeping. Tears of sadness that they had lost the war, loved ones, and the life they knew. And tears of joy that the killing was over. Then Reverend Mason had another announcement. President Lincoln had been shot and killed on April 15. Silence fell, and the minister said a prayer, asking God to show them all mercy. Louisa held her daughters and they held the children. All of them were quiet as they rode home in the wagon.

Sidney had never even seen his granddaughter Laura. Wally was barely two and Henry was a baby when he left for the war. Louisa hoped they would bring him comfort in the midst of all this loss. She was glad she could not have any more children, and hoped Sidney did not still wish to. He had been much more upset than she was when the doctor had told them she could not have any more after Mary was born. It had been a hard time for them. Louisa had been sick for weeks and started to worry that Sidney would turn to May Belle again when he seemed to avoid her. But he said he was afraid he would lose her and did not want to disturb her convalescence. Gradually they found their way back to each other and became comfortable in their life together, including in bed. At least she thought so.

She and Sidney had not talked about John's death yet, except for one agonizing exchange by letter, that left her feeling empty. Nothing had eased the pain of losing John. But she could not give in to grief—she had to be strong.

How would it be to be with Sidney again now that everything was so different at Oak Hill? No field hands, no tobacco, not even a groom now that Joseph had died. No house servants…

The remarkable thing was that May Belle and Sally had stayed on for several months after everyone else had run off. Louisa was sure she knew why—it was the typhoid. Shortly before the war there had been an outbreak of typhoid down in the slave quarters. Sidney had forbidden the house servants to go down there for any reason. But May Belle's husband James was one of the sick, so she went down anyway, as often as she could. She brought him infusions and soups, but nothing seemed to help, and in less than a week he died. Louisa had understood when May Belle was heartbroken and distraught, and had told her kitchen helper Minnie to take over some of her duties in the kitchen. Sally could not stop her tears sometimes when she was dusting the furniture, which aroused Sidney's irritation and curiosity. Louisa told him it was "female trouble". Then May Belle came down with typhoid, and soon her two young sons did too. Louisa and Sally nursed the three of them, making and feeding the infusions and soups May Belle had taught Sally to make. They carried clean bedclothes and blankets upstairs to the servants' sleeping quarters in the attic, and brought down the soiled ones for Melanie to wash. Louisa had even brought in Dr. Squire for advice and medicine. She paid him well out of her housekeeping allowance to overcome his distaste for treating Negroes and to keep silent. In spite of May Belle's thinly disguised disgust for Dr. Squire, she started to recover with his medicine, and so did the boys. May Belle told Louisa she would not forget how Louisa had helped them. And she had not. When news of the coming emancipation was out and the field hands and house servants had left, May Belle had stayed on with Sally for the spring and summer.

Louisa came back again to thinking how May Belle had taught them how to survive. With Joseph, they had learned how to plow and prepare the soil, grow food. With May Belle, how to harvest and prepare it. How to salt or smoke meat when they trapped a rabbit. How to preserve or pickle vegetables and fruits. How to dry corn, peas, and beans. And when they had made it from spring to fall, May Belle knew they could do it. She and Sally just disappeared early one morning in

September. Louisa still wondered where they were now and whether May Belle had found her sons.

Louisa found herself missing May Belle. She was lonely sometimes, even with her daughters and grandchildren there. It had been nice to have somebody her own age to work with. She had sort of wished May Belle would be her friend. Why had May Belle always kept a wall up? But how in the world could she miss a slave? And how ungrateful of May Belle to run away after she was so good to her! Sometimes from deep down her jealousy of May Belle would rise, and she would find herself wondering if May Belle's face and body looked less haggard than her own. Or she would notice with irritation that Sally looked even more like a pretty female version of Sidney as a young woman than she had as a child.

As soon as the war started, Mary and Ellen and her two children had come back home to live with Louisa. Laura was born here, and May Belle was the midwife. She had never delivered a baby before and Louisa could see that she was trying to hide her fear. May Belle said she remembered watching her mother, who had delivered most of the babies on the plantation. And she and Ellen had done it. Louisa still remembered the elation on their faces and Ellen's joy in looking at her baby girl.

When Joseph became bedridden, he refused to be moved from the stable room he had lived in for years, even though it would have been a lot easier to care for him in the storeroom off the kitchen house. What a stubborn old coot he was. One morning when Mary went to give him his breakfast he told her he did not need it that day because he was going to see the Lord. So she sat there with him. After a while Joseph sat up, looking joyfully at something Mary could not see. Then he fell back and was gone, dead as a stone. Mary told Louisa she was sure he must have seen Jesus. Louisa was sad to lose Joseph. He was a kind old man, even though he was just a slave. His courtly manner was the last of the way things used to be.

With May Belle and Sally gone, they had somehow managed. It had not been easy. There had been lots of failures, but the victories were real. Growing healthy corn and vegetables. Cooking and preserving. For some meals there was just not enough, and they got very tired of black eyed peas, but it got easier with time. Louisa and Mary were proud of their accomplishments. Ellen did not want to say so to Mary, but she was ashamed to be "laboring like a darkie" , as she put it to Louisa one day.

Lately Louisa had found herself wondering about their slaves, and all the slaves all over Pittsylvania County, all over Virginia, all over the South. Where did they go? She had heard they went up North, and many even joined the Union forces. Well, good riddance to them. But she had also heard that some of them were living in the mountains and the hollows, not too far away. What if they came back and tried to take the farm? How would she and the girls defend themselves? Once Sidney came back they would be safer, since Grant had let the Confederate soldiers keep their sidearms. But even so they could be easily outnumbered and overtaken. Louisa's chest felt tight and her heart pounded whenever she thought of it. She remembered hearing the old folks tell about the Nat Turner rebellion not too far away, and others that gave her chills.

She pushed down her fear and her mind raced on. How would they get back to producing a large tobacco crop with no field hands? She, Sidney, and the girls could not begin to do what forty-six field hands had done, even if a lot of them had been lazy as sin. What would become of her family? She rubbed her calloused hands together and sighed.

They were all thin and tough now. No more smooth fair skinned ladies. No more lovely full-skirted gowns. They had cut up the fabric of those ample skirts to fashion the simple shifts they worked and lived in. What would Sidney Turner think of a wife who liked being in charge and two grown daughters who were strong and capable? Would he be proud of them for holding on to Oak Hill? Would he be surprised that they had learned to grow enough food to sustain themselves? Would his face show disgust at how they looked? He had loved his "three beauties", as he called them. What would he say about the war? He must be devastated, exhausted. Would he talk with her, or swallow his sadness with whiskey? What would it be like between the two of them in bed? Louisa picked up the burned-down candle and carried it inside. She had better get some sleep so she could hitch up the horse and plow the second field in the morning.

Sidney

Late April 1865

Sidney walked slowly down the road, his pistol tucked into his belt. Even without ammunition it still felt crucial. He was tired to his bones. One step dragged behind to follow the next…and the next. He scanned the uphill slope of the dirt road ahead. At the bend he could finally see Oak Hill. In two of the fields he passed, he noticed young corn plants growing. He stepped up his pace and approached the house.

On the veranda two little boys were playing "battle" with guns made out of sticks. As Sidney drew near, they "shot" him, yelling for him to "withdraw". Too exhausted for such games, he yelled, "Stop that right now!" Wide eyed, the boys ran inside to their mother. When Ellen came to the door, she saw her father climbing the stairs to the veranda, gripping the railing to pull himself up. He was filthy, both hair and beard overgrown. His uniform was stained and ragged. She hardly recognized him, but drew closer, knowing he was her father. Sidney held her awkwardly, and when she stepped back he apologized, "I am sorry to be so dirty, Ellen"

"Sit Papa."

As he collapsed into the rocking chair, Ellen went to the side edge of the veranda, knowing the boys would be hiding underneath. "Henry, come sit by your grandfather while I get him some food. Wally, you run get your grandmother. She's plantin' in the third field."

Henry came reluctantly up the steps and sat in a chair near his grandfather, looking down at the floor. "So you're Henry," Sidney said. "I'll wager you don't remember me."

"No sir, I was only a baby, one year old."

"So you are five now?"

"Yes, and Wally is six."

"Yes, sir," corrected Sidney.

"Yes, sir," Henry repeated.

"You have not had much chance to practice your manners, young man, with no one around."

"No sir."

Ellen appeared, carrying a tray with two pieces of cornbread, some raspberry jam, and a cup of tea. Sidney grabbed a piece of cornbread and stuffed it into his mouth. He reached for the tea, took a gulp and spat it on the floor. "What is that stuff?"

"It's sassafras tea Papa. There is no real tea, so we've gotten used to it. We also have mint tea, if you would like to try it."

"Just get me some water, Ellen."

Sidney watched as Ellen walked away. When he turned around he saw Louisa walking toward the house with Wally. Louisa looked even more changed than Ellen. She was thin, her face and arms were browned by the sun and it looked as if there were lines around her eyes. She was wearing a strange looking garment similar to Ellen's that bore little resemblance to a dress. But it was her walk that stunned him. Her stride was long and firm, not the soft small steps he fondly remembered.

Louisa climbed the stairs quickly. Sidney pulled her into his arms. They held each other for a long time before they kissed. And then they did. Finally. When Sidney pulled away he apologized for being filthy.

"You need not be sorry for that Sidney. We've seen a lot worse things than dirt."

"Where is Mary?" Sidney asked.

"She's plantin' corn in the fourth field," replied Louisa. "Do you want me to send Wally for her or wait a bit?"

Sidney decided to wait. After some leftover stew, more cornbread, and some cider he fell into bed. He slept for three days, waking only to eat, drink, and use the chamber pot. For a few hours the first night, Louisa tried sleeping with him, but his odor drove her away. She went across the hall and slept in John's room, weeping again as she felt her son's absence there. She left both doors open so she could hear Sidney if he needed her in the night, but he was sleeping the sleep of the totally depleted and did not.

When Sidney woke up on the fourth morning he called for Louisa. Ellen came. "Mama is out plantin'. She's always out in the fields."

"Well send one of the boys to get her. I need her."

"Would you like a bath first?"

"Do I smell that bad? I can't even smell myself anymore."

Ellen brought the big tin tub upstairs, then heated water and carried it up for her father's bath. "Would you like to eat after your bath? I can fix you some eggs and cornbread."

"Yes Ellen, but no tea."

"How about raspberry tea?"

"Why did you not say that before?"

"I just dried it for you yesterday."

After his bath Sidney slowly put on the pre-war undergarments, trousers, and shirt that Louisa had put out for him. He combed and trimmed his beard and tied his hair back. He missed having his man Fred, who had done such a good job shaving him and cutting his hair and beard. Louisa would have to cut them now. He went down to the dining room, where Ellen had his breakfast ready on the table. The little girl with her had to be Laura. "You must be four now," Sidney said cheerfully. Laura burst out crying and cringed behind her mother.

"She's frightened of you Papa. We have almost no neighbors any more, so she only sees us. She'll get used to you." She took Laura with her out to the kitchen. So Sidney ate alone, listening to the soft sounds of Ellen preparing their dinner and Laura at play with her doll.

Then he stood up, stretched, and walked outside. He stood at the top of the veranda steps, surveying the farm. The stable looked shabbier than he remembered it. So did the barn. He descended the stairs quickly, crossed the yard and went to the stable. A sturdy post stood near the entrance, with an iron ring hanging from it. "A whippin' post," Sidney muttered. "I knew I couldn't trust that bastard." He turned away to walk by the stalls, looking into and smelling each one. Just one stall was being used these days. For that workhorse Joseph had saved. Louisa had written him about that. So either she or Mary must be plowing with him now. They called him Prince because he rescued them. Sidney could just not get used to Louisa and the girls working like that. They were used to having servants, and by God he would get them servants again. It was just not right for his wife and daughters to work like they had been doing.

Sidney walked along the other side of the stable, looking in at the stalls where he had kept his thoroughbreds. He had sold all but his own before he left for the war, leaving only the workhorses behind. He had given Louisa most of the money from the sale of the thoroughbreds and kept the rest for his expenses. The money was long gone, along with his horse, which had been shot out from under him at the Battle of Fredericksburg. Remembering his horse, he stood looking at the empty stalls. Then memories of Louisa and the girls riding the others and laughing together washed over him and left him feeling bereft.

Outside he heard the clucking of hens. He went out and watched them in their pen. They looked at him with no curiosity at all. Deciding to find Louisa and Mary, Sidney headed to the fields. In a few yards he looked up to see the two of them walking down the path, towards him. He was surprised to see that Mary had the same way of walking that Louisa did. They both strode toward him with long firm steps, so deep in conversation they did not notice him. But in a moment Mary looked up and saw him. She hiked up her shift and ran to him, throwing herself into his arms. When Louisa caught up to them, her eyes filled and she and Sidney embraced.

As they walked towards the house they saw Ellen standing on the veranda with Laura. "Laura is scared of me," Sidney said. "Is she a fearful child?"

"No more than any child who suddenly sees a strange man in her house," Mary replied quickly.

Louisa and Mary went to the pump to wash up. Ellen was busy serving dinner. Sidney sat at the head of the dining room table, enjoying the delicious smells. Laura scampered through the room and out to the veranda, where she called Wally and Henry. In a few minutes the three children came in, muttered "Good day, sir," and sat down at the table. Sidney could not think of anything to say, and prayed for Louisa and his daughters to come in from the kitchen. They listened to the clock ticking on the mantle.

"How many Yankees did you kill?" Henry burst out.

Sidney looked down and swallowed hard. He studied the table.

"Mama said not to ask him about things like that," admonished Wally.

"Like what?" asked Mary, carrying in a plate of steaming cornbread. Ellen followed right behind her with a roast chicken, then Louisa carried a tray with gravy, black-eyed peas and collard greens.

Henry's question went unanswered. Sidney carved the chicken, which was nowhere near big enough for seven people, but he made it go around.

He knew it was a rare treat to eat a chicken, and was moved that they were doing it to celebrate his return. He looked down the table at his tired wife and daughters. He looked at his shabby grandchildren. And he looked at the meager serving of chicken on each of their plates. He was ashamed.

After dinner Sidney and Louisa went into the study. Louisa had been using his desk and had left her records of their corn and cornmeal production, long lists and numbers in her neat handwriting. Sidney sat in his desk chair, while Louisa cleared off a side chair and pulled it closer to him.

"How are you, husband?"

"Better after the rest and food. The walk down through Virginia to get back here was endless."

"We heard the Yankees destroyed everything."

"Well, a good many of the farms along the way were completely destroyed. Houses burned to the ground, fields torn up in battle…"

"It must have been awful…all those battles…"

Sidney held his head in his hands. "So many dead. In some battles almost everyone around me got killed. I can't talk about it, Louisa. I want to put all that hell behind me."

"I understand, Sidney," Louisa reassured him. "I'm so very grateful that the war is over and you're home. But will we be able to talk about John some time?"

"I don't know, Louisa. It's just too hard now."

In the days to follow Louisa showed Sidney how they had managed while he was away. Her letters had not made it clear to him, focused as they were on Mary, Ellen, and the three children. He was amazed at how they had learned to grow, cook and preserve food. Their corn production impressed him, from the plowing and planting to taking the kernels to be milled. And having enough cornmeal both to eat and trade for chickens. He could see Louisa's pride as she showed him the careful records she had kept, and later when she showed him the pantry and cornfields. And he understood that pride.

But still, it made him ashamed. Louisa, Ellen and Mary were raised to be ladies. They should not have to be doing these things, working so hard. How could he change that, now that he was home? They had no slaves any more. How could he give back to his wife and daughters the life they had known before the war?

As painful as the changes were to him, Sidney was glad to be back. It was good to stand on the veranda of his Oak Hill and walk his fields. He thought back to his father, Sidney Turner, giving him the plantation, teaching him the tobacco business, and the pride he had taken in his son's well run estate. He barely remembered his mother, who had died in childbirth, along with the brother he never saw. And he remembered Bess, dark and warm, who had been his comfort and almost-Mama. Looking back, he understood his father's loneliness and need for Bess. "He needed her for me, and for himself too. Of course I see why Bess didn't want me near her daughter May Belle. I just couldn't help myself. Well, all of that is past, with Father in the grave, Bess gone to Glory, and God knows where May Belle is. And here I am, in a fine mess."

Sidney felt alone with his shame over his wife and daughters working. Louisa was up early and worked all day, just as she had before he got back. Mary did the same. It was spring planting season and the two of them were determined to finish getting the corn planted in four fields this year. The vegetable garden had grown quite large in his absence, and even though it was already planted, it needed constant weeding and watering. Ellen was also busy, cooking, doing laundry, and looking after the children.

What should he do now? Louisa seemed to assume he was busy recovering. What did that mean? He would never recover from all he had seen, from all he had done. He could not stop seeing the blood and hearing the screams. His dreams were terrible.

There was no money. Sidney could not imagine going on living as they were living. He did not want to be a small corn farmer, raising barely enough to live on, even if Louisa and Mary were proud of what they had accomplished. Most of his land had been lying fallow, so the soil would be rich again, after being depleted by tobacco. He was ready to raise tobacco again, sell it and make a nice profit. But how could he raise the money to buy seed and put in a tobacco crop? His biggest asset had been his slaves. He resented their desertion. After all, he had been a good master. It was George McCann who had been cruel to them, God damn him. Maybe he could sell some land to raise money for tobacco. He certainly had more land than he could work now. But who could buy his land? None of his remaining neighbors would have the money. It seemed that everyone was poor now.

Sidney's thinking went around and around as he walked his property. Their situation seemed hopeless. Louisa must have noticed that he seemed depressed at meals, but she was probably too exhausted from fieldwork to talk much with him in the evenings. Once, when they were lying in bed talking, Sidney brought up the possibility of selling some land. He looked over to see her response and she was sound asleep, softly snoring. He studied the face he loved, browned and lined by the sun. Her once perfect white hands lay calloused and brown on the sheet, with dirt under the fingernails. Yes, he still loved her. But he was angry that she did not understand that they could not go on this way. He was home, the man of the family. He would make the decisions now. He would tell her.

The next day after dinner he pulled her into the study and told her he needed to talk with her that afternoon. Louisa explained that she could not afford to miss an afternoon this late in the planting season. "Can it wait?"

"To hell with the corn," he replied. "We are not corn farmers."

"Corn is what got us through the war," Louisa replied evenly.

"Well, it's no answer for the future. We need to sell some land to raise the money to put in a good tobacco crop."

"But Sidney, no one has the money to buy our land. And is there even a good market for tobacco now?"

"There is always a market for tobacco. Folks just cannot do without it. And lying fallow these past years has given the land a chance to recover. The soil must be rich now.

"That may be. But everything is different now, Sidney. Who would work the tobacco fields? You and Mary and I could not begin to work enough land for a profitable crop."

"That is my problem now Louisa. I am back, and you do not have to worry about those things any more."

"But I want to, Sidney. I learned a lot while you were gone. We managed to get by pretty well for four years. Does that not count for something?"

"Yes, it does Louisa. But it is a poor life we have here now. I want a better life for us. And I want you back, Louisa."

"I'm right here Sidney"

"No you are not. You are always workin'. I want you to have time for me. And time for your reading and sewing. And your grand-children."

"Dear Sidney," she sighed. "I believe the easy days are over now. Everyone who is not dead is poor since the war. We all have to work, and that is not so bad. I love you and want to please you, but I can't go back to bein' a lady of leisure."

Sidney's face flushed red. "What has become of you Louisa?" He jerked the study door open, went out and slammed it behind him. He went to the stable, hitched the horse to the wagon, and rode off, noticing that Louisa was returning to her corn field.

When Sidney returned it was well past midnight. He smelled of whiskey and tobacco. Louisa seemed to be asleep when he came into their bedroom. His steps were quiet and sure; he wasn't drunk. He slowly took off his clothes and slipped in bed beside her. Gently he turned her over as she woke up and he pulled up her nightgown. He felt her resentment about their argument dissolve as he softly stroked her body. She moaned in pleasure as he kissed her all over. And they made love.

Afterward Sidney rolled over and fell asleep. The next morning he slept late and was disappointed to find Louisa gone when he awoke.

As soon as he ate the breakfast Ellen prepared for him, he headed for the fourth field, where Louisa was planting corn.

"I think I have found a buyer for a sizable piece of our land," he told her.

"Who?"

"The Stantons have a wealthy Yankee cousin who is looking to buy land down here. So John Stanton is sellin' him a large piece of his that adjoins our land. If the cousin also buys a piece of ours adjacent to John's, he'll have a decent amount of property."

"And you plan to use the money to put in tobacco."

"Of course Louisa. This is tobacco land."

"And who will plow, plant, harvest, and cure it, Sidney?"

"I told you not to worry about that. John Stanton says there are plenty of free Negroes around who do not know anything but field work and need to work to survive.

"But how do you pay them without any money?"

"You get them to work a piece of your land and pay them a share of what they raise."

"Where do they live?"

"You let them build themselves a shack on your land. You even provide seed and tools and deduct the cost from their share."

Sidney picked up Louisa and kissed her. "So what do you think of that, Miz Louisa?

"Well, it's not a certainty that the Stanton's cousin will buy our land," she said. "It sounds like there are a lot of things we don't know about this plan."

"If only you would be happy for us Louisa! Here I have figured out how we can live much better than this, and all you do is question me. That is not the Louisa I remember."

Louisa looked at him hard. "Sidney, I have had to learn to ask questions to find out how things work. I didn't know much of anything before, except how to order the house servants around."

"What are you talkin' about? You were always real smart about literature and history and art."

"But I didn't know how to cook a meal or grow food or preserve it. Without Joseph and May Belle we would have starved, or come mighty near to it."

"I know they helped you a few months. But they abandoned you. Well, Joseph could not help dying. But May Belle and Sally should have kept on helping. We were good to them. And they just ran off and left you."

"I have come to understand why they left, Sidney." She looked down at the row of corn kernels. "But I have still been puzzling about them. Neither one ever let on what she was thinkin'."

"What does that matter? Anyway, Ellen says even before they ran off, you were all working like darkies."

Louisa stepped closer. "We did what we needed to, Sidney. We kept ourselves and the three children alive and healthy. And we stayed here and kept Oak Hill for the family."

"You did that, Louisa. I understand, and for that I am deeply grateful," He embraced her and said quietly, "I should have said that before."

"Thank you for tellin' me that Sidney."

I saw so many farms abandoned and ruined, Louisa. Where did those families go?"

Louisa shook her head. "No one knows. Some fled to relatives in other counties, or North Carolina or Tennessee. Some died." She squatted down and started on the next row. "Meanwhile we need to grow corn."

Sidney watched for a moment. Then he walked slowly back to the house and sat in his study, figuring.

Mary
Spring 1867

Mary was twenty-two now and full of energy. She was pretty like her mother, with dark curly hair, and used to love dressing up for dances. But two years had passed since the war ended, and the time before the war seemed a lifetime away. She'd had enough time to do some thinking and had been reading some of the abolitionist pamphlets she found at the grist mill. The war and its aftermath had left her in turmoil about life, with pressing questions about slavery and the newly free Negroes. For generations people like her family had depended on the labor of enslaved Africans to run the farms in Virginia and all over the South. It had worked in some ways. The South had produced tobacco and cotton for the whole country and even England. And everyone had said the Africans were better off here than in Africa. At least with good masters like her father. But Mary was beginning to question that. And what if their masters were cruel like George McCann or careless like Walter? Mary remembered how Walter broke up a large family when he sold the children off to pay some debts. And she was haunted by the memory of the time in '62 when three strong field hands ran away at once. McCann sent slave catchers after them with their blood hounds. When they were gone for nearly a week, Mary thought they had escaped. But one hot morning the slave catchers returned in their wagon. They dumped out Jake, whose left ear they had cut off, and Simon, whose right ear they had cut off. Then they dumped out Simon's brother Silas, and he was lying there on the ground, dead. Mary could not get the picture out of her mind. Nor could she ignore her awareness of how evil it was. She thanked God when the beastly McCann left, but it did not stop her nightmares or the questions that were starting to nag her.

Like her mother, Mary was grateful that May Belle and Sally had stayed on for a growing season after the others left and taught them what they needed to know so they could survive. Mary had watched with curiosity Louisa's futile efforts to be friends with May Belle. She had seen her mother's mixed feelings, as she swallowed her jealousy and let herself depend on May Belle for help. Sensing that she did not want to discuss May Belle, Mary never brought her up with Louisa. Mary and Ellen had somehow always known that Sally was the daughter of their father and May Belle. Mary thought it was ridiculous that her mother never once acknowledged it to them, even when the tension between Sally, Ellen and her became unbearable and they stopped playing together.

"Was that not absurd, pretendin' not to notice?" Mary mused to Ellen one afternoon as they sat sewing.

"Not at all," Ellen returned. "Sally was and is a disgraceful shame."

In that moment Mary remembered what she had forgotten. At some point Ellen had begun pinching Sally, secretly and hard. Sally would pretend not to notice, but there would be welts and bruises on her arms the next day.

Ellen went on, "What I don't understand, is why Mama kept Sally around. Why did she not make Papa sell her? I know May Belle was indispensable to them, but Sally was only a child."

"Papa was firmly against breakin' up families. I don't think he ever did. I hope not," Mary said. But then she began to wonder.

Mary and Ellen had grown apart in the last year or so, especially regarding the freed slaves. But Ellen still wanted her sister to be her children's tutor. Never having been an enthusiastic student herself, Ellen had realized it was right for them, when Mary had suggested teaching the children before. Mary had always loved books and had already spent many winter evenings during the war teaching the children to read. But there was never enough time.

After their father had been home almost four months, Ellen approached her.

"Now that the corn harvest is over, will you have time to be the children's teacher?"

"Yes, absolutely. We can start as soon as I pull together some materials."

Wally was six, Henry five and Laura only four. Mary gathered some books, looked until she found the old slates and McGuffey primers she, John and Ellen had used, and even found some blank copy books in the bottom of a cabinet in the library.

At first Mary found it difficult to be their teacher and not their doting "Auntie", which made it hard to get them to settle down and work. She tried to remember how Mr. Williams had commanded their attention, but could not. One day she told them she was not "Auntie" for lessons. "I'm 'Miz Mary' for lessons. And you will pay attention. Is that understood?"

"Yes Miz Mary," they mumbled, and after that things went more smoothly. Wally and Henry made rapid progress in reading. Henry clearly loved it. Laura surprised them all one day by reading "The Tortoise and the Hare" aloud before they even realized she could read beyond her simple primer.

Now Mary had been teaching the children for almost two years and she enjoyed every session. The children were getting interested in history, so Mary would read parts of the history tomes in their library and "tell" them to the children in simpler language. She was also seeking out poetry to share with them. She liked basing mathematics lessons on tobacco figures.

There were quite a few books in their library. Most of them had come from her Grandfather Charles. He had died in '62 and left them specifically to Louisa in his will. He had even arranged for his manservant Jonah to bring them to her before he died, because he was afraid everything would be destroyed at any moment. It was. Three weeks after Charles died of heart trouble, the Yankees came for their horses and someone set the place ablaze. Grandmother Lou fled to her daughter-in-law, where she discovered her son James had been killed at the Second Battle of Manassas. Lou died a few days later and everyone said it was because her heart was broken. Louisa had been grief stricken too, losing both parents and her brother. She had spent some evenings in the library reading parts of the books she had shared with her father. But she really had no time to grieve them any more than she had grieved for John.

There were also books from the children's father, Walter Singleton, in the library. "I reckon he never even opened any of these," thought Mary as she examined them. "He had no curiosity that I could see. Just pretended to know everything." Walter's children were curious, however.

At six, seven and eight now, they were trying to understand their world.

"Miss Mary, why did all our field hands run away?" Henry asked one day.

"Well, in September of '62 word got out that President Lincoln was going to free the slaves all over the South. As soon as they heard that, a lot of slaves ran off."

"Were they bad to run off?" Laura asked.

"If you were a slave, would you run off if you had the chance?" Mary asked.

Laura looked thoughtful. Then she nodded her head.

"Where did they go?" Wally asked.

"Some of them signed up with the Yankees and fought in the Union Army."

"Against us?" asked Wally

"Why not," Henry said slowly. "We were the ones that made them be slaves. Miss Mary, do you think those men sharecroppin' our land might have fought against our father?"

"I don't know. War is a hard thing," said Mary.

The next day Ellen and Mary were sitting and sewing after dinner.

Ellen cleared her throat. "I realize it is a great deal to ask of you to be the children's tutor Mary. I know you are doing a good job, because I see how well they are readin'. Better every week, even Laura." She crossed and recrossed her legs, bent her head closer to her sewing.

"Is there something wrong?" Mary asked.

"I do not want you to discuss the war or slavery or sharecroppin' with them."

"Why not Ellen?"

"You have some wrong ideas, foolish ideas."

"Is it foolish to question whether it is right to own other people?"

"But Mary, they were not and are not people like us. They were African savages, trained by us to do useful work and given the gift of Christianity."

"How can you say that when you knew May Belle and Sally? Were they savages?"

"Well, May Belle was an exception, smart as she was. And Sally was half white, Papa's daughter, I still hate to admit. So of course she was bright."

Mary pressed her lips together and looked hard at her sister.

"Ellen, it will be hard not to answer the children's questions. They are such good ones, it doesn't seem right to ignore them."

"Well, I would prefer for you to tell them to ask me in the future," Ellen said firmly. "I am their mother."

Mary winced.

Lately Mary had been thinking about their lives there on the plantation. Before her father had returned, her contribution had been vital. Growing the garden and the corn with her mother was demanding work, plowing, planting, harvesting, preserving. And getting the corn to the grist mill. It was necessary and satisfying work though. Her mother thought so too. Her father kept saying they would have servants in the house again soon, which pleased Ellen. She did not find her work cooking and housekeeping satisfying at all. Mary could tell she was resentful. And ever since she became their tutor, Mary had the best part of the children's day.

Sidney had found plenty of sharecroppers to move onto his land and work the tobacco. They used the wood from the old quarters to build cabins for their families. Mary and Louisa had helped them with seeds and plants for their vegetable gardens. Some had left, but new families came. Times were hard.

That Sunday Mary and Ellen took the children and went to church. Ellen seemed irritated and embarrassed to be riding in their old wagon, pulled by tired old Prince, with Mary driving. "Listen here children," Ellen said, "Things used to be so different. I wish you could ride with me in our lovely old carriage. It was shiny and black with the most comfortable green velvet seat cushions —a beauty."

"What happened to it?" asked Laura.

"The Yankee soldiers who stole our horses must have seen it, because a few days later two Union soldiers came back and one of them hitched his horse to our carriage and they rode off."

"Why did nobody stop them? Asked Henry.

Mary looked over her shoulder. "Do you remember George McCann, our overseer? He was supposed to scare off any Yankees with his gun. But he was so scared himself that he cowered up in the hayloft and did nothing." The children giggled.

After the service Mary noticed a small table in the back with a few pamphlets about Freedmen's schools. She picked one up and tucked it away in her sleeve. When she saw Mrs. Stanton, she went outside to greet her. How is your father's tobacco doing?" asked Mrs. Stanton.

"Fairly well, I think. Tell me Miz Stanton, what do you know about the Freedmen's Schools?"

"Well, I've heard tell of them, but I do declare Mary, it is a fool's errand to try to educate the darkies. They are just not smart enough."

"Maybe folks will find out something different, now that they can go to school," Mary ventured.

"The whole idea is absurd Mary. Who would do the field work if they did manage to learn? I have no interest in those schools whatsoever. Thank goodness we don't have any near here!"

But Mary had a great deal of interest in the Freedmen's schools. She had watched the sharecroppers negotiating with her father over the deductions from their shares for seeds and tools. She realized how little they could understand of these negotiations and saw how easily they could be cheated because they could not reckon with numbers and read. She observed that Sidney drove a hard bargain with them, but at least he seemed honest about it. What about folks who had to deal with landlords who were not? She thought also of the children who came with their fathers. Their eyes were bright and curious and their bodies very thin. As soon as they were barely old enough they joined their parents working in the fields. Before that they played and napped at the edge of the field. What would it be like to teach children like these to read and figure? Mary could not stop thinking about it.

The next time she and her mother were working in the garden she brought it up. Louisa had heard about the Freedmen's schools from someone at the grist mill. "I just don't know Mary. It certainly would change things if Negroes got educated. They would not want to do field work or house work any more. And then what would we do?"

"Maybe we would have to pay them, fairly."

"Hmm. We certainly can not pay them in money now. Do you really think they want an education?"

"I don't know whether they all do, but I think lots do, like May Belle and Sally."

"Well of course, but they are different. I wonder where they are and what they are doing."

"I hope they are up North and safe."

"Look at these beautiful greens Mary. Your father will enjoy them for dinner. Please don't worry him with this talk about educating the Negroes. He has enough on his mind as it is. We are still not making a profit, you know. We are not even making ends meet."

That night Mary could not sleep. She climbed out of bed and looked out her window at the farm. Moonlight shone on field after field of young tobacco plants glistening with dew. "I don't want to live my life out on a tobacco plantation struggling to regain its former glory," she thought. "I don't want to live on any plantation. I want to teach in one of those Freedmen's schools." She went to her bureau and pulled out the pamphlet she had picked up in church. Quickly she wrote to the address given, inquiring about a teacher's position. When she finished, she climbed back into bed and slept.

Mary woke up excited. Her lessons with the children seemed long that day, even though they were doing Aesop's Fables, which they all loved. The children were making up a play based on The Lion and the Mouse. Laura insisted on playing the mouse, Wally was the lion, and Henry the narrator. The boys thought that Laura was giving the mouse entirely too many lines, but Mary was inclined to go along with her and make the boys do so also. As they were ending for the day, Mary mentioned that Aesop was a slave in ancient Greece. The children's eyes widened, but no one said anything. "They are minding their mother, as they should…and yet…" Mary mused.

After dinner Mary decided to take the last of last year's corn to the grist mill. It really did not need to go now, but it gave her the excuse she needed to go to the mill, where she could drop her letter in the box and hope it would be picked up before too long. When Ellen saw her getting ready to go she asked, "What is the purpose of takin' the last of the corn now? We have plenty of meal."

"Oh, I just thought it would be a good time. I am caught up in the garden, and with only one field of corn now, Mama and I have already got it planted."

"Well, you could help me with the housework you know. I'm tired of workin' like a slave. Mama has started helping me with the cooking now, and that makes a difference."

"Ellen, I see how much you do. Would it help if I take over the laundry?"

"Do you even know how to do it? I'll have to show you how."

"How about if you show me tomorrow, and then it's my duty."

"That would help some," said Ellen slowly, still puzzled.

"I'll see you late this afternoon Ellen. I want to get on my way there and back home before dark."

Mary left quickly. Ellen looked after her, as the wagon disappeared up the dirt road. Sidney appeared beside her on the veranda.

When Mary looked behind her she saw that they were deep in conversation, and suspected they were wondering about her eagerness to go to the grist mill.

Mary arrived home just in time for supper. She fed and watered Prince, then joined the family at the table. She looked flushed. No one mentioned her afternoon errand, but after supper Sidney asked her to come into his study. "I know you Mary," he began, looking into her face. What are you excited about?"

"Well, maybe nothin' will come of it, but I have written to inquire about a teacher's position in one of the Freedmen's schools. They are teachin' freed slaves, children and adults, all over Virginia."

"Whoa there young lady. I've heard about those schools. What makes you think I would ever let you do such a thing?"

"Papa, I am twenty-two years old," said Mary, standing up. "I was waitin' to tell you about it when I got a reply from my inquiry."

Sidney jumped up with fists clenched. "Tell me?" he hollered. "As long as you are under my roof you are still my child. And if I say no, that means no."

"Papa please. Just talk with me about this."

"What gave you this ridiculous idea to start with?"

"Watching our sharecroppers negotiating with you about their shares. I realized how easily they could be cheated because they can't read or write or figure."

"But I don't cheat them, so they have nothin' to protect themselves from. Don't you know that? I look out for my sharecroppers."

"But not everyone is honest with theirs. And besides Papa, to really be free, people have to be independent. And for that they need learnin'."

"And with thousands and thousands of ignorant Negroes all over Virginia, you think you can help the situation?"

"I hope so, for the folks I'll teach."

"Mary, it is just not our problem what becomes of freed slaves. Why do you think about such things? You just need a husband and children of your own."

Mary paused and stepped back. "I've been reading and thinking a lot Papa," she said quietly, but her eyes were flashing. "The world is changin'. Good night."

Louisa

Spring 1867

Sidney bounded up the stairs and burst into their bedroom, where Louisa was sitting and reading by candle light. She was almost to the end of Frederick Douglass's autobiography, which Mary had urged her to read. She quickly put it down in her lap, so that the title was out of sight. "Did you know about Mary's crazy plan?" he demanded.

"What plan, Sidney?"

"She wants to go teach in one of those Freedmen's schools."

"Well, I knew she was thinking about it, but I did not think of it as an actual plan."

"How could you not tell me?"

"You have so much on your mind right now, it didn't seem like the right time to bring it up."

"But if you had told me I could have stopped it before she mailed off a letter of inquiry. She is ready to go, Louisa! Why did you not just tell her it was an impossibility?"

"I really didn't talk with her much about it, Sidney. I truly did not realize how serious she was."

"Well I too am serious, Louisa. And I forbid it."

"Sidney, she is not a child. If this is what she wants, it is her decision."

"What she needs is a man to marry and children of her own."

"There are mighty few men around since so many died in the war. And I'm not so sure that is what she wants at the moment anyway."

"What, is she unnatural somehow? That is what all women want."

"Mary has always thought for herself. We noticed it when she was just a child, you must remember.

"I know she's smart and a thinker. She gets that from you. But that does not mean that she should go off and teach in a so-called Freedmen's school."

"Maybe what it means is that Mary is going to figure out for herself what she will do in her life."

"I am finished with this kind of talk Louisa."

Sidney went back down stairs and poured himself a whisky.

Louisa put Frederick Douglass in her desk drawer for tomorrow. Reading Douglass made her understand Mary's desire to get involved in teaching. Then she undressed, put on her nightgown, and sat at her dressing table to brush her hair. Mary was lucky to have such an adventure coming up. But Louisa was also afraid for her. Her dreams that night were troubled.

Several weeks later Mary returned from a ride to the mill waving a letter from the Chimborazo School in Richmond, offering her a job. She ran up the steps two at a time and hugged her mother with glee. Louisa hugged back and they laughed.

Ellen

Spring and Summer 1867

Ellen awoke just before dawn. For a few minutes she lay and listened to the rooster crow. Every day was the same as the one before. She got up, washed with the cold water left in the basin from the night before, and slipped downstairs while everyone slept. She opened some windows in the dining room and went out to the kitchen house. She lit the fire there, cooked and served breakfast, ate with the family, and then cleaned up the kitchen. The children had their lessons with Mary all morning, which left Ellen free to do the endless house cleaning. When Mary left at the end of summer, Mama would take over their tutoring. That would be just as well, since Mary's ideas were getting odder and more foolish by the day. Even so she would miss her sister's company, as well as her help with the laundry. When she thought about it, she was sorry that she and Mary were not close like they used to be.

Mama had been helping with cooking dinner, but would not be able to when she took over the teaching. Thank goodness Mama had said she would help with supper. Even though it was the simple meal, it would help.

And then came the evenings. Ellen used to love reading and singing with the children. But now it often felt like a burden when she was tired. Or it seemed like they would rather read by themselves. After the children went to sleep, Ellen felt empty. Mary was always curled up with a book in the library. Sometimes Mama sat and chatted with her, but Ellen sensed that her father would rather have Louisa to himself.

Then Ellen would go to bed. Alone. Again. And it would all be the same the next day. Unless she got into an argument with Mary.

One afternoon after she finished cleaning up from dinner, she passed by Mary's doorway and looked in. Mary was cutting fabric out of the skirt on one of the last of her lovely dresses from before the war.

"What are you doing?" asked Ellen. "Surely you are not plannin' on making any more of those hideous shifts you made us wear."

"No, but I think I can make some dresses with much narrower skirts. Suitable for teaching."

"You are going to be a sight to see in Richmond. I heard from Edith Stanton that the fine families are reestablishing themselves there. That means they dress."

"As long as they do not close down the Chimborazo School, I do not care one whit what the 'fine families' do or wear."

"You are so strange Mary. I still cannot fathom why you want to go up there and teach Negroes. You can stay right here and teach Wally, Henry, and Laura, who deserve a good teacher."

"Mama will be a wonderful teacher for them. You know that. And she loves them like I do."

"But the Negroes, why do they deserve an education? They should stay in their places and do field work and housework. That is what they are trained for. Comfortable with."

"But what about those that want something different, something more? Have you heard of Frederick Douglass?"

"Of course Mary. He learned to read and write and has not stopped making trouble since."

"I read his book Ellen. It really made me think. I wish you would read it."

"The very idea of reading a book written by a runaway slave makes me ill. I just can not understand you any more. Maybe it's a good thing you are leavin'." Ellen's eyes filled with tears as she left, slamming the door behind her. Mary watched her leave, tears in her own eyes.

All the next week Ellen observed Mary's growing excitement. She had seemed elated ever since receiving the letter from the Chimborazo School. Immediately she began figuring out how to get to Richmond, studying train schedules for railroad connections from Danville. She packed a few suitably altered dresses and a few books and belongings in two small carpet bags, so that she could carry them herself. Henry and Wally teased her about being a "carpet bagger" like the Yankees and she just laughed.

The children spent as much time as they could with Mary. Almost every afternoon they walked with her through the woods to the creek, where they would splash and play in the water. It was clear that they would miss her. Ellen was jealous of their open mutual affection, and watched how they talked with her so easily. Ellen had to admit, Mary had kept her word about not talking any more with them about slavery and freedom. Ellen knew the children were dying of curiosity about why Mary was going to teach in Richmond. She knew her own answer had not satisfied them. But so be it. They were her children.

Ellen wished she had something as exciting in her life as this teaching job was to Mary. Thinking of spending her days this way for the rest of her life filled her with gloom.

Louisa decided to take Mary in the wagon to Danville to catch the train to Richmond at the end of August. She wanted to settle in and get ready for her new job. Sidney was too angry to help in any way with her scheme, which he considered ridiculous. Wally begged to go to keep his Grandmama company on the return trip, and since Ellen knew how eager he was to see the train, she decided to let him go. "You are getting to be a young man now," she told him, and Wally stood straight and eight year's tall.

Ellen, Sidney, Henry, and Laura watched quietly for a long time as the wagon disappeared into the distance. Rousing himself, Sidney headed for the stable and saddled his horse to ride the fields and check on the tobacco and the workers.

"Come children," said Ellen. "Aunt Mary left you your lessons for today. It is time to see what they are."

"Aw Mama," said Laura. "It will never be fun any more without Aunt Mary."

"It's not fair," said Henry. Why would she go teach Negro children she doesn't even know, when we need her to teach us?

"What did she tell you about that, Henry?"

"She said to ask you Mama. But you did not tell us either. You just said she was making a mistake because she is mixed up."

At this point they reached the library, where they found that Mary had left each of the children a letter. Mary wrote to Henry that she would miss his curiosity to understand things and then think about them. She wrote to Laura how much she liked the way she would stand up for herself. She asked them to write to her often and said she would write back. There was also a letter for Wally. And she left them each a reading and writing assignment for that day. Ellen realized that her sister had avoided mathematics and had chosen assignments that she was comfortable with, and was grateful.

Louisa and Wally arrived home just before dark, exhausted. They told the family they had pushed the horse to go fast because of what they had learned in Danville. Louisa said that folks at the train station were full of stories about the Ku Klux Klan, who were supposedly protecting white people. "They said black men have been attacking white women," she reported. "So the Klan catches the accused attacker and hangs him. Sometimes they burn big crosses to scare the Negroes into behaving."

"I've heard all about it, Louisa", Sidney replied. " I am so relieved that both of you are back home and safe. Wally, go take care of this poor tired horse." Sidney and Louisa went inside and sat at the dining room table, where Ellen served a late supper.

"The folks in Danville said it was no longer safe for a woman to be driving without a man along, particularly after dark", said Louisa. "But I have to say we did not run into any men, black or white, who seemed threatening. A Negro man did get us some water, same as a white man did."

"Well, most darkies here in Pittsylvania country might still remember how to behave, but I have heard tell of some terrible stories." said Ellen.

"A lady told me they don't know exactly who the Klan members are," said Louisa. They wear white masks and robes so you can't tell. That seems a little silly."

"You say that because you have been sheltered Louisa. You do not realize how dangerous these freed Negroes can be," said Sidney, and Ellen nodded

Wally joined them at the table. "Well it certainly scares me," said Ellen, "hearing there are Negro men wandering around the countryside, just lookin' for an unprotected white woman to attack."

"But Mama," said Wally, "Grandmama and I saw a lot of Negro men workin' in the fields today and not one of them tried to attack her. Isn't that right,Grandmama?

Louisa nodded.

"Thank God. But you just never know these days," Ellen went on.

"Maybe it was because I was along. I am almost a man."

"So you are Wally, so you are." And she put an arm around him.

In the days that followed the family began to adjust to Mary's absence. But Ellen was surprised at how much she missed her, and not just because Mary had started doing the laundry. Ellen was thinking that, except for the first year of her marriage to Walter, she had been with her sister every day of her life. When she had been in deep misery after Henry was born and needed Mary, she had come to stay with them and help, even though it meant giving up her lessons and time with their brother. They had been so close then. When had Mary begun to change? Ellen had not changed. Or had she? When did she stop singing and laughing with the children? It had been a gradual thing.

She was so often exhausted from housework and taking care of everyone. Mary and Mama had been working hard too, doing backbreaking field work, but they did not seem exhausted by it. They almost seemed to like it. They might not mind hard work, but Ellen did, and she was angry she had to do it. What made it even more unbearable was that she was alone.

Mary might not need a husband, but she did. And nobody even realized it. It seemed she was supposed to go to her grave unmarried, just because Walter had died in the war. Ellen wished he had died in battle instead of from typhoid, but the truth was that she was relieved that he had died.

He had given her three children she loved, and she would never speak badly about him to them. But it had not been long after the wedding that she saw that Mary was right. Walter was pompous. And he did have too much pride to learn from others. So he managed his estate poorly, gambled and drank, and regularly ended up having to sell off slaves to cover his debts. When he died she had to sell the few that were left, as well as the house to cover the rest of the debts she had discovered. She was angry and disappointed, having assumed she would come into some wealth. Instead she had ended up working like a darkie, back in the same house she grew up in.

Near the end of June their neighbor, old John Stanton, had a heart attack and died. The funeral would be held at the Episcopal church up in Chatham. The folks would come back to the Stantons for a collation. Ellen found Edith Stanton overwhelmed when she rode over to give her condolences, so she offered to prepare the food. They would need a lot. In addition to one or two neighbors, John and Edith's children, brothers, sisters and cousins from Lynchburg, Halifax, and Mecklenburg County would come. Ellen was aware that funerals were a rare opportunity to meet people, since there had been almost no social life since the war. There was simply nothing left for celebrations at the few plantations in the county that had started to become productive again. And "productive" was an exaggeration.

Ellen surveyed her remaining dresses. They looked far too frivolous for a funeral. The deep blue one would do though, if she cut some of the fabric out of the skirt and used it to raise the neckline. She hated to do that since she was proud of her bosoms, but she could take in the bodice so it would be tight enough to reveal their shape. She would ask Mama to pull her smooth blond hair into an elegant chignon and hope for the best.

Ellen washed and ironed the best of the children's clothes and sighed. They would have to do. The day before the funeral she was still baking, while she heated and carried water for baths. When evening came and it was finally her turn for a bath, she fell asleep in the lovely warm water. Louisa came in to see what was taking her so long and found her. "Oh you poor girl Ellen. You are exhausted. Quick, get out, dry off and go to bed. I will get the children to bed."

The next morning the church was as full as Ellen had ever seen it. Ellen looked beautiful and the children looked respectable. She looked around at the crowd. "Slim pickin's," she thought, then bowed her head to look somber. At the collation after the service she was so busy serving her little buttered rolls filled with thin slivers of country ham that she did not notice the tall man with silver hair at his temples who was watching her from the side of the drawing room.

He made his way through the guests and when he reached Ellen he said, "Good day Miz Singleton. I'm Samuel Roberts, Edith's cousin. May I have one of your rolls? I can tell they are delicious by the way everyone is devouring them."

"Why of course Mr. Roberts. I hope you like them. I need to refill the platter. It was a pleasure to meet you."

When Ellen returned from the kitchen with a full platter, she glanced around the room. No Mr. Roberts. He must have left. She served her rolls and conversed briefly with young John Stanton and his wife.

She looked up to see Mr. Roberts just a few feet away, smiling at her. "There you are Miz Singleton. May I have another of your delicious rolls?"

"Why of course Mr. Roberts. Where are you from?"

"Lynchburg. I have a small dry goods business there. It's not much but it supplies fabrics folks need and provides me a livin'."

"I can not imagine what it is like to live in the city. I've lived here in the country my whole life."

"Well, the city has some advantages. But I do like it out here. I plan to visit Edith in the near future to help her with some decisions. Perhaps I could call on you, if it is not inconvenient?"

"I will have to see Mr. Roberts. I have three children to take care of."

"Oh, I did not know, Miz Singleton."

In the week following the funeral Ellen wondered if she would ever hear from Mr. Roberts. He had not shown any interest when she mentioned her children. And she had her own reservations about him. He seemed much older than she was. But that could be an advantage also, she thought, because maybe he was beyond the age to insist on having children of his own. Ellen was certain she did not want more children. But it was necessary that any man she would marry would like her three and be kind to them. The chance for Wally, Henry and Laura to have a good father was important to Ellen. Walter had been a disappointment in that way too.

About two weeks later, when Ellen and Wally rode to the grist mill, there was a letter for Ellen from Samuel Roberts. He said he would be coming to see his cousin Edith Stanton in two weeks and would like to call on her if she would permit it . Ellen found herself delighted and wrote back an encouraging note.

When she told her father about the pending visit, he was concerned. "Ellen dear, I saw you speaking to Roberts at the funeral. You are a beautiful woman. Why would you be interested in a man who must be fifteen years older than you? Do you want to be his nursemaid in a few years?"

Louisa was listening. "Sidney, look around. There are almost no young men left. So many died in the war. If Ellen finds this Samuel Roberts to be kind, intelligent and practical, I think it is good."

Ellen knew they were jumping ahead too much, but she could not stop doing the same thing herself.

The morning of Samuel Roberts' arrival Ellen could hardly swallow her cornbread. "Children," she said swallowing hard, "we are goin' to have a visitor for tea."

"Who is it?" asked Henry.

"He's Miz Stanton's cousin from Lynchburg. When he arrives you are to wash your hands and come into the drawing room to meet him. Then just be polite and we will have a nice tea."

"But why is he comin' here?" pursued Laura.

"Enough questions," said Ellen. "There will be sweet biscuits. Time for your lessons with Grandma."

Teatime arrived and with it, Samuel Roberts. Ellen introduced him to Louisa and Sidney. They sat in the drawing room while she went to fetch the tea tray. Samuel wanted to know about Sidney's sharecropping arrangements and then they moved on to the tobacco business, which they both knew well. They hardly noticed when the children came in. Louisa introduced them to Mr. Roberts, who then went back to his conversation with Sidney. Louisa scowled. First at the two men, and then at the children. They had chosen the moment just before to have a water fight at the pump, and looked thoroughly wet and muddy.

"Go quickly children, and wash again. And dry yourselves well before you come back," Louisa said. Just as they disappeared, Ellen returned with the tea. The children came back, much cleaner though still a bit wet. Ellen introduced them to Mr. Roberts. This time he noticed and smiled at each one.

When Ellen passed the sweet biscuits Wally exclaimed, "Thank the Lord you came Mr. Roberts! We haven't had these since Christmas."

"I am honored," said Mr. Roberts, and smiled at Ellen, who felt the blood rush to her cheeks.

After tea Ellen and Mr. Roberts sat on the veranda and talked. Looking out over the rolling fields, he sighed. "I used to be a country boy myself, Miz Singleton. Grew up on a tobacco plantation east of here, in Halifax County."

"Why did you not return there after the war?" Ellen asked.

"While my brothers and I were off fightin' in the war, the Yankees burned the farm, and both of our parents died in the fire."

"A tragedy, Mr. Roberts"

"Yes, certainly to us. When we came back and saw what had happened, we were devastated. To lose both Mother and Father that way. And like most folks, their capital had been their land and the slaves to work it. Without the slaves the land was worthless, unless you had the capital to rebuild the whole farm and set up for sharecropping. We did not. We had nothing."

"It must have been very hard," Ellen said.

"Yes. So we sold the land for the little we could get and went to Lynchburg."

Ellen was moved by his story. She began to see that her lot had not been as terrible as she portrayed it to herself. She was fascinated that Samuel Roberts did not seem to be as bitter as she had become. When he asked to call again, she found herself eager to know him better. Shortly after he arrived the next time, he asked to call her Ellen and said for her to call him Sam. They walked beside the fields. Sam wanted to know how they had gotten along during the war, with only three women to run things and three children to take care of. Ellen told him how May Belle had taught them to grow food and cook and preserve it and old Joseph had taught them to plow and Mary and her mother had raised corn. Sam was amazed and impressed.

"You are some extraordinary women, that is certain. How you did that and took care of your children too, you must be the most extraordinary of all."

Ellen felt like crying with gratitude, but she did not. "Thank you Sam," she said. "Where were you in the war?"

"All over Virginia. The worst for me was at Sharpsburg. My youngest brother was there with me. He was right beside me as we were crawling up the hill, and somehow I thought I would be able to protect him. There was a barrage of bullets and he was hit in the head. He only lived a few seconds after that. I couldn't save him."

"That must have been terrible," said Ellen, moved by the tears in his eyes.

She told him about losing her brother John in that very same battle and they walked in silence.

"This is no way to court a lady, with all this sadness. I am afraid you will no longer want my company if we go on like this."

"Is that what we are doin' Sam, courtin'?"

"Why yes Ellen, is it not clear?"

Ellen was happier than she had been in years. Sam's visits were the high point of her life. The children got used to him after a few more visits, and he seemed to be becoming genuinely interested in them. Sidney had changed his mind about the age difference between Ellen and Sam when he found out that Sam was forty. There were still sixteen years between them, but in Sidney's mind Sam's congeniality made up for that. He was pleased to have a prospective son-in-law he enjoyed, and encouraged Ellen. Louisa listened and watched, glad to see her daughter happy.

When Sam asked Sidney for Ellen's hand in marriage, Sidney was delighted. When Sam asked Ellen to marry him she said yes and began to cry. They embraced for several moments while Ellen's tears soaked his shirt. And then they kissed.

The small wedding would take place in the Episcopal church in Chatham where they had met. Then Ellen and the children would move to Lynchburg and live with Sam. Sam and Ellen decided that there was no reason to wait. They wanted the children to start in their new schools in September when school started. Laura was excited about living in the city, but the boys were not so sure. All of the children were worried about leaving their grandparents.

They had always been close to their grandmother, but recently the boys had also been spending time with their grandfather. He had bought some horses at auction and was teaching them to ride.

"You have been there loving and caring for them as long as they can remember," Ellen told Louisa. "What will they do without you?"

"I will miss them every day, and you too," said Louisa. "But it will be good for you to have your own life now Ellen. And they will all be able to go to real schools in Lynchburg."

"I know Mama. Sam has already looked into the schools. So much to get used to. Besides running a new household and taking care of the children, I must learn to be a good wife."

"But you know about that from before, with Walter."

"No, I was not a good wife then. And Walter was not a good husband. Things were never right with us after we married. He drank so much we could rarely even have a real conversation. I felt sick when I was pregnant and miserable afterward, so I did not want to be around him anyway."

"Well Ellen, now you have a second chance. I hope with all my heart that you will be happy this time. And I hope the children will have a good father."

Mary
Fall 1867

Mary stood in front of her classroom in the long low barracks of the Chimborazo School and swallowed. Looking at the fifty-three expectant faces before her, she thought, "What in the world was I thinking? Whatever made me think I know how to teach these children anything?" She swallowed again and said slightly tremulously, "Good morning children. I am Miz Turner."

"Good morning Miz Turner," some of them replied.

"Let's try that again, louder this time." Most of them replied.

The children ranged from six to eleven. The older ones would come later. There was a large slate board in the front of the room that she could write on, but nothing for the children to write on yet. They were sitting crowded together on benches. It was only eight o'clock in the morning and already it was hot. Mary explained that they were going to learn to read and write and figure. Quite a few nodded. She said they would start with the alphabet, and the letters each had a sound. Writing the letters on the board, she pronounced them slowly.

A few of the girls in front were already familiar with the letters and repeated them with her. "That's wonderful girls. Please stand and say the letters as we all recite. I will point to them on the blackboard." When most of the children seemed to be saying the letters, Mary asked for volunteers. The girls up front were eager to say them, as well as one or two others. "Very good, children," said Mary. Next she tried to teach them the "ABC Song" she had learned from a teacher who had come down to Richmond from Boston. At first they would not sing and Mary felt foolish singing it over and over by herself. But then the girls in the front joined in softly. One by one the children joined in the singing. Mary tried not to worry about those who did not. After all, it was the first day for all of them.

The children seemed restless, so Mary suggested a standing up game. Coming closer, she counted them, telling each child to remember the number she said. Then she called out numbers in order and the children had to sit when they heard theirs. Then she called out numbers out of order, and they were to stand when they heard theirs. This produced some confusion and a great deal of laughter. The class was starting to relax a bit. "Maybe I can figure out how to do this," thought Mary.

The rest of the lesson went by swiftly, as they started working with the numbers from one to ten. Mary knew they needed to have something more than their fingers to count and figure with for it to make sense to them. So she asked them to bring pebbles or acorns the next day. "How many, Teacher?" asked one of the girls. "Ten would be perfect," said Mary, and smiled at her helper. Then Mary read them a favorite story, "The Lion and the Mouse". She read dramatically, enjoying herself. "Our time is up for today, children," she said after the story. "I will see y'all tomorrow." She dismissed them with a smile and they left quickly, pushing the benches out of the way.

The next class came in while Mary was straightening the benches. They stood along the wall and watched her. "Y'all could help, you know," said Mary with a smile. Several boys stepped up and finished lining up the benches. "Thank you boys," said Mary, and some girls giggled. "Why is that funny?" wondered Mary. She walked quickly to the front of the room and introduced herself. This time the pupils ranged from twelve to eighteen, but their lesson was the same. Some of them had been exposed to letters and numbers, but only superficially. The very idea that letters stood for sounds and that together they make words was still new for most of them. "The prohibition against teaching slaves to read was faithfully followed by way too many slaveholders," Mary thought angrily. She looked at her pupils and said, "We have a lot of work to do, so that you can all learn to read and write. But I believe you can if you want to." They looked at her hopefully.

They recited the alphabet and worked on the sounds of the letters, but the Alphabet Song did not appeal to them at all. They simply would not sing it. So Mary moved on quickly to the stand-up-sit-down number game. That worked. Then they worked on counting one to ten, first their fingers, then their classmates. For some it was easy, for some still impossible. They listened attentively to the story and seemed pleased to discover that the author had been a Greek slave. Reminding them to bring pebbles or something else to count, Mary dismissed her second class, asking them as they left to keep the benches lined up straight.

Mary took a deep breath. She was still nervous but not as much as earlier. She felt the perspiration running down her neck as she straightened her shoulders and stood tall. She greeted her next class, another group of young ones. The lesson went rather well, she thought, even the Alphabet Song.

After one more class of young ones came the dinner break. Mary was hungry, so she made her way along the few blocks to Mrs. Wilson's boarding house as quickly as she could, avoiding puddles, broken bricks and horse droppings. The hot streets were busy, loud and dirty, filled with horses, wagons and laborers, black and white, at work rebuilding Richmond. Finally she saw Mrs. Wilson's house ahead. Her sturdy brick house had escaped the fire of 1865, set by the Confederates so that the Union would have only worthless rubble when they took over the city. Just one outer wall of her house was blackened with soot. Mrs. Wilson had three bedrooms to rent and a large dining room table. That was all she had in the world, but it was enough to earn her a living.

Mary was late and sat down apologetically at the table to join her fellow boarders for dinner. There was Priscilla Atkins, her Quaker roommate from Philadelphia, who smiled at her with relief. And there were four burley men who were overseeing construction projects in the city. Presiding at the head of the table was Mrs. Wilson, who gave Mary a chilly nod and then returned her attention to the men. " I declare," she said. "We would be in such a dreadful state if it were not for you men rebuilding our beloved city."

"It's good of you to say that, Ma'am," said the oldest looking man, speaking with his mouth full. "It's a rare thing to be thanked for our efforts, ain't it fellas?" They nodded and grunted their assent, not missing a bite as they shoveled their soup.

"Do them darky children thank you ladies for teachin' them?" he went on, and the men laughed.

Mrs. Wilson nodded at the young Negro woman in the doorway to remove the soup bowls and answered for them. "Now that's a thankless task if there ever was one—teaching Negroes. I do not understand at all why you girls are trying."

Priscilla, who was used to explaining such things, replied, "How can a person be free and independent in this world if they can't read and figure?"

"Well, here comes dinner," said Mrs. Wilson as her helper carried in ham and vegetables. The rest of the meal passed with little conversation, though Mrs. Wilson tried to encourage it with small talk.

As soon as dinner was over Mary and Priscilla walked back to the Chimborazo school. "I am so grateful you are staying at Mrs. Wilson's," Priscilla told Mary. "I can not abide that woman. The way she flatters those men makes me ill. And her attitude towards the Freedmen's schools makes me furious."

"I thought Quakers were peaceful," said Mary.

"We do try to be, but I'm afraid I'm not a very good Quaker sometimes," said Priscilla.

"I'm very glad you are at Miz Wilson's too," said Mary. "And also at the school." Mary told her how nervous she was about teaching, since her only experience had been teaching her niece and two nephews. She was worried that she wouldn't be able to help her pupils live up to their expectations. She wanted so much not to let them down.

Priscilla nodded in understanding. "I know how you feel, Mary. This is my fourth year teaching, and at the beginning of every year I still get nervous and wonder if I'll be able to teach the children anything. But then I get to know them and work with them and good things start happening. It will be the same for you, I believe."

"What a relief it is to hear that. It gives me hope. Thank you Priscilla."

The afternoon classes went by quickly, even in the afternoon heat. In the evening there were two classes of adults. "These folks are even more tired than I am," Mary realized, "working all day doing physical labor." Walking home to their boarding house, Mary asked Priscilla many questions about teaching. Priscilla was happy to be able to share her experience. She readily admitted she was no expert and felt at a loss when she could not help some pupils learn.

"I think these children and their parents must be like us," said Mary, thinking of Ellen and her children. "Some have a hard time with numbers and some with words, and for some it all comes easily."

The following days at the Chimborazo school were easier, but it would be months before Mary completely stopped feeling like an imposter. The smiles of her pupils and their eagerness to learn kept her going, along with Priscilla's encouragement. One of the daily difficulties they faced was the lack of writing materials for the pupils. They now had narrow tables in front of their benches, but no copy books to write in. One afternoon Priscilla came into Mary's classroom with the news that there were copy books at the office of the Freedmen's Bureau. The next day during dinner break they walked over there. Mary was overwhelmed as they walked to see how much of Richmond had been burned in the fire of '65. There was block after block of rubble and wreckage, with random scorched brick walls still standing. Mary and Priscilla dodged horses, wagons, mud and debris, arriving sweaty and dirty at the office.

Mary's heart leapt when she recognized the secretary. It was Sally. Mary ran to her and started to embrace her, but Sally shrank back. "Hello Mary," she said calmly. "I heard you were over at Chimborazo."

"Sally, I'm so happy to see you safe and well! How is your mother?"

"Mamma is dead,"

"Dead? No!"

"Yes."

"How?"

"I don't want to talk about it now Mary."

Mary was stunned. May Belle dead? Tears welled in her eyes and rolled down her cheeks. Priscilla came forward. "I heard there are copy books," she said to Sally.

"Yes," said Sally, "but not enough for all the pupils at Chimborazo. They will have to share."

Mary wiped her face and said, "Sally, this is Priscilla Atkins. Priscilla, Sally Turner."

"It's Sally Freeman," Sally corrected.

"Oh, you're married," Mary said.

"No," replied Sally, and went into the store room, beckoning them to follow. "You can't carry all these. Please send some young men with wheelbarrows this afternoon."

After thanking her they left and Mary broke down. She told Priscilla through tears that Sally was her half sister, they had the same father. And Sally's mother May Belle had saved them. They walked in silence until Mary was calmer. "How could she be dead?" she repeated as they walked.

"It must be hard to find out that she died, especially when you didn't expect it," said Priscilla. "I'm so sorry." They walked around a massive pile of bricks. "Does your father treat Sally as his daughter?"

"No," said Mary, "far from it."

"And I can guess how he was with her mother," Priscilla continued. "I've heard about these things."

Mary looked down as they walked in silence again. Then she stopped and looked into Priscilla's eyes. "Have you always been an abolitionist?"

"Yes. Haven't you?"

"No. I never was until recently. My thinkin' has changed gradually over the last few years, as I began to realize what slavery meant and what it has done."

"I cannot imagine owning other human beings. I know some Quakers did. But my family didn't. I don't say this to hurt you Mary. It seems like you care about Sally and her mother. But I also think I understand the way she responded to you just now."

"You do? Well I want to. But I can't today."

When classes were over for the day and supper was over, Mary headed upstairs while Priscilla was conversing with Mrs. Wilson. She sat down at the small desk and wrote to her mother, telling her about her meeting with Sally. She knew Louisa would be grieved to hear of May Belle's death, but also knew she would want to know. As she wrote, the tears came again, with memories. She remembered May Belle bringing them warm sweet biscuits when she, John, Ellen, and Sally were little and so close. She remembered her scolding them for playing in the mud. She could hear her in the kitchen house, singing in her rich warm voice. And hear her laughing when she and Ellen attempted to give black eyed peas more taste by adding sassafras. By the time Priscilla came into the room, Mary was in bed, face turned to the wall. Priscilla picked up her sewing and went quietly downstairs.

Weeks went by. Mary poured herself into her teaching and began to know her pupils. As they knew her better and felt more relaxed, some of them began to fool around and talk among themselves during class. She kept those pupils after class and spoke earnestly to them, but then the next class would arrive. She thought the source of the problem was teaching them all at the same pace. The ones who caught on quickly were bored. And the ones who didn't were lost. She needed primers so they could work at their own pace. Mary went to the Head of School, who made a request to the Freedmen's Bureau for primers for the whole school. Amazingly, the Chimborazo School soon received a shipment of primers. All of the teachers were elated, even though the primers were a used hodgepodge of different editions and levels, sent down from white schools in the North. They still gave the pupils useful material to work with. And that made a difference.

Mary was very grateful. She decided to go to the Freedmen's office to thank them in person, and also in hopes of seeing Sally again. She told Priscilla she wanted to go alone this time. Again she made her way through the bustling dirty streets during her midday break. When she arrived, Sally was sitting behind the desk as she had hoped. "Hello Mary," Sally said coolly.

"I came to thank you all for the primers Sally. They will make a great difference for our children."

"I wish we could have sent them new ones in sets of ten, graded according to different levels, like the white schools get. Imagine Mary, what it would be like to give Negro children what they really need."

"You must be a teacher, Sally."

"Yes, I started teaching during the war," said Sally.

"Can we talk sometime Sally?

Sally looked sad and sighed. "I have a dinnertime pause now. We can sit behind the building."

They went outside and sat on the bench against the wall, warm in the October sun.

"I wrote to Mama about May Belle. I know she'll be heartbroken."

"Your Mama," said Sally, and sighed. "She never could understand." She noticed Mary's surprise and continued. "She said she loved us, but she kept us enslaved. She saved my Mama and brothers from typhoid, but still kept us enslaved. She taught Mama and me to read and figure, but didn't free us. She let Mama and me run away, but did not give us freedom papers. What kind of love is that?"

"It's confused and confusing, to everyone, including her." Mary looked down, and then looked into Sally's face as she said, "We were brought up to accept slavery. Now I've learned that we were wrong. Slavery was evil."

"You didn't know that? When did you realize slavery was evil?

Mary was shaken. "It wasn't until those three boys ran off and were brought back by the slave catchers, that I finally started to see. It was the shock of seeing their suffering."

"They were not boys. They were young men, my friends."

"So much I don't know."

"That is the truth."

They sat, just looking at each other. Mary nodded and then said, "Sally, please tell me what happened to May Belle."

Sally took a deep breath and looked into the distance. "When we left you in '62 we went down to Forsyth County in North Carolina because Mama had heard that my brothers were down there. It took a while, but eventually we found them, workin' on a tobacco farm. The owner, Mr. Perry, was glad to bring Mama and me on to work too. A few days later we found out from another field hand that Perry was planning to sell us all South. You know folks were still buyin" and sellin' slaves all during the war." Mary nodded.

"He was gonna sell us down to Mississippi. Do you know about Mississippi, Mary?" Mary nodded and Sally went on.

"Those people are still workin' their people until they drop dead. Anyway, Mama went to Mr. Perry to beg for our lives. He told her my brothers and I could go free with papers if she would stay behind with him. She knew what that meant. But she came to us and convinced us to get those freedom papers and go. She promised she would get away and find us."

Sally stopped and took a heavy, sad breath. " We knew how dangerous it was for her, but we also knew that, to her, our freedom meant more than her life." Sally struggled as her tears spilled over.

She went on in a hollow voice, "So we left. The boys went up and joined the Union Army near Petersburg and I eventually got a teachin' job in a Freedmen's school back in Pittsylvania County."

Mary put her face in her hands, "How did you find out about your mama's death?" she asked softly.

"Before I got the teachin' job I was doin' housework for one of the tobacco barons in Danville. He bought tobacco from Perry's neighbor. I heard the neighbor tell him that Perry had killed his Negro mistress when she tried to escape." Sally sat, breathing hard.

"Horrible…terrible…I'm so sorry Sally," Mary whispered.

They sat, both breathing hard. There were no words for a moment.

"It was too late to get Mama's body by then," Sally said. "And of course nothing happened to Perry as a result of his crime. When I reported Mama's murder to the sheriff in Danville, he said he would be sure to let the sheriff down in Forsyth County know. And then all the men in the office laughed."

Sally and Mary sat in silence for a while.

"I need to get back to work now," said Sally, standing up and wiping her eyes.

"And I do as well," said Mary. "Thank you for tellin' me the truth, Sally. I'm so sorry you lost your Mama. She stood and reached for Sally, who stepped away.

"Goodbye Mary."

"Goodbye Sally."

Mary walked back to the school, feeling overwhelmed by all she had heard. She had been becoming more aware of how hard the lives of slaves had been, but had never felt it in as visceral a way as she did now. She thought back to her childhood, growing up on Oak Hill plantation with enslaved field hands and house servants. It had seemed normal and pleasant. She had never questioned it. Her childhood was easy and fun, riding her horse, playing with her sister, brother and Sally, dressing up and pretending. As she got older, she was working with her tutor, reading, going to parties and dances. As a child and "young lady", she never thought about the system of slavery that made her comfortable life possible. She was ashamed now that she had never questioned it. That it had taken seeing those three young men brought home by the slave catchers to shock her into questioning. Then, when she read Frederick Douglass's book her awareness grew and she saw the direct connection between education and freedom. That was why she was teaching. It pained her that Ellen and her father were still thinking the way they had before the war. Her mother was a question mark though. She knew Louisa was reading and questioning, but not where it would lead. Mary was delighted to find out from Sally that Louisa had taught her and May Belle to read. What a good surprise that was. It had to have been before the war, when Mary was going to so many social events she wouldn't have noticed.

Louisa
Fall 1867

Louisa awoke as the liquid pink of dawn poured into the bedroom. She went to the window and watched the sunlight sparkling on dew-covered grass. In the hills the oaks had turned orangey brown, and here and there red maples glistened.

Sidney was still asleep, snoring regularly. Suddenly chilled, Louisa dressed quietly, wrapped a shawl around her shoulders and slipped down the stairs. "How still the house is," she thought as she did every morning. "I miss those children more every day." Louisa had been telling herself that she would get used to all of them being gone, but it had not happened. After all, Mary and Ellen had lived here all their lives, except for Ellen's two years at Walter's. And Wally and Henry had lived here since the war started. Laura was even born here.

Louisa lit the fire in the dining room fireplace and then in the one out in the kitchen. Sidney had Jim, one of his sharecroppers, keep a good supply of fire wood cut. Louisa was grateful and liked to see him when he came. He was always humming and had a smooth deep voice. It was unfortunate that it had caused an argument though. Louisa had asked Sidney how much he was paying Jim. Sidney had said that he was not paying him, that Jim just did it for them because they were his employers, as he should. Louisa said that was just the point—they were employers, not masters now and therefore should pay for any service they received. Sidney got furious and told Louisa she did not know the first thing about handling Negroes. "Give them an inch and they will take a mile. If you start treating them like they are white, they will rob us blind."

The tea kettle boiled and Louisa filled the pot. Then she carried it and a piece of yesterday's cornbread into the dining room. It had been a bad argument, but in the end Sidney decided to pay Jim and the wood kept coming. Sidney told her she had made him feel like a criminal. Louisa poured herself a cup of tea, inhaling the aroma of sassafras with a sigh. She bit into the cornbread and sipped her tea. It was hard to talk with Sidney about Negroes. They could talk about Ellen and Sam in Lynchburg with the children. They could talk about young John Stanton and his new wife and baby up the road. And of course they could talk about tobacco, but Louisa's mind would wander. She kept remembering that they had never really talked about the death of their own son. When Louisa mentioned John, Sidney would say he didn't want to talk about him. So they had never shared their grief. And now this situation with Mary. They didn't seem to be able to discuss it at all. When Louisa told him how much she missed Mary, he became enraged.

"How could she forget us to go teach God knows how many strange Negroes? What is wrong with her?" he had asked.

Louisa had looked at him sadly.

"You can be sad all you want, Louisa. I never want to see her again, as long as she is doin' that. "

And then Sidney had poured himself a whiskey. And then another and another. It was pointless talking to him anyway when he was drinking. And so often now he was drinking.

Louisa felt lonely when Sidney drank heavily. He seemed like someone she did not know. She longed for the companionship and love they used to have. But just as deeply, she longed for something useful and interesting to do. She was making clothes for Ellen's children, who outgrew them with astonishing speed. She had forgotten how fast her three had grown. She had also been reading her way through the treasures she had not yet gotten to in their library, like the Bronte sisters. That was truly a pleasure, but she looked for more.

Sidney was happy to see her skin lighter, as the brown from the sun had faded. And her hands and arms were softer again, in spite of her gardening and housework. Sidney had even employed Caroline, one of the sharecropper's wives, to do the laundry, because he wanted to lessen Louisa's work and keep her hands soft. A wan smile crossed Louisa's face as she finished her tea. "He really means well," she thought.

That afternoon the Stanton's stable boy knocked on the door. He had a letter for Louisa from Mary. The first one she had received since school had started. The letter was disappointingly short, but it became immediately clear why. Mary had written to tell her that she had met Sally at the office of the Freedmen's Bureau and learned that May Belle had died. Louisa sat down, stunned. There was no explanation. Just pain. She knew Mary was in pain too. Louisa sat rocking back and forth on the sofa while her mind raced to terrible scenes of rape and murder. She was still sitting there holding the letter when Sidney walked in.

"What happened Louisa? You're white as a sheet."

"Read this," she said and handed him the letter.

Sidney's face fell when he read it. "How dare Sally tell Mary that May Belle is dead without telling her the circumstances! What are we to think?"

"I expect it was not the time for Sally to talk about it", said Louisa.

"As good as we were to them, she owes it to us!" yelled Sidney.

"That is something I'm starting to understand, Sidney. They really did not owe us anything. They stayed on to help us that spring and summer of '62 because May Belle felt she owed me for helping her and her boys get well when they had typhoid. But I only did that because it was right. Isn't that what the Bible tells us, to help others?"

"I do not think it is referring to others who are your property," he said.

Louisa winced and went on, "Even if you do think they owed us something, they more than repaid any debt by teachin' me and the girls to survive. Think of all the women and children in Virginia who suffered and starved during the war because they didn't know the most basic things to do to keep themselves alive."

"I can't understand you any more Louisa," Sidney said, and went to the sideboard to pour himself a whiskey. He stood with his back to her as she said, "Well I wish you would try to understand, Sidney. The truth is we owe them." She left the room.

Weeks went by. Neither Louisa or Sidney mentioned May Belle. Sidney was absorbed in his tobacco business. Louisa sought sunny windows to work in and began making an intricate quilt out of the remnants left when she and the girls cut down their dresses. Finally another letter from Mary arrived. Louisa read Mary's account of May Belle's terrible murder and felt sick. She read it again and shuddered. Sidney was in Chatham for the day. She returned to her quilt but could not concentrate. When Sidney arrived home for supper she was quiet, not wanting to bring up the letter. But later, when he became concerned that she was not well and put his arms around her gently, she told him.

Sidney was aghast. His face darkened. "Who murdered her?"

"A man named Perry," answered Louisa. "He had a small tobacco farm down in Forsyth County."

"May he rot in Hell." He clenched his fists. "How could May Belle ever have agreed to stay with him?"

"It must have made sense at the time, Sidney. Because her children's freedom was the most important thing to her. It meant that Sally and her two boys could go free with papers. To her, that was more important than her life."

"I could imagine you sacrificing your life for your children, Louisa, but not a Negro woman."

"Even May Belle?" Louisa couldn't resist asking.

"Of course, not even May Belle."

"Well it certainly does get me wondering Sidney. Maybe there is not as much difference between Black folks and white folks as we thought." She left the room quickly before he could reply.

A week later, very early one morning, Louisa was startled out of sleep by a soft but insistent knocking on the front door. Leaving Sidney snoring, she grabbed her dressing gown and ran downstairs. She opened the door to find a young girl, one of the sharecroppers' children. "Please come Miz Louisa. Mama in a bad way and the baby be comin'." Louisa wrapped a shawl around herself and stuck her feet in some boots. She followed the child beyond the near fields to a cabin nestled up against the woods. She learned her name was Jewel. She entered with her, intending to tell the expectant mother that she was sorry but she had never midwifed a birth in her life. Rachel was groaning with the pain of a contraction, while her husband Tom was mopping her brow and holding her hand.

When the contraction ended Rachel said, "Please help us Miz Louisa. My cousin May Belle said you was right beside her helpin' when she birthed your daughter's baby girl. We had two babies die since Jewel here was born."

"I'll do the best I can Rachel," said Louisa, surprising herself.

But Rachel was lost in the next contraction and did not notice. Louisa asked Tom to boil more water and then tried to help Rachel get into a more comfortable position. Rachel told her she had been in labor since yesterday at dusk. No wonder she was exhausted. Louisa wondered if the baby were turned around, so that it could not slide out headfirst. She knew that, with cows, you could turn the calf around. She thought you could do the same with people. So apologizing to Rachel, she reached in and felt. Indeed the feet were at the opening of the birth canal. She explained the situation to Rachel and Tom. They looked at each other and Tom said, "I done that before with a calf. I can do that." Carefully he reached in and felt the baby. Rachel cried out in pain and yelled "Hurry up Tom!" Slowly and deliberately he turned the baby. Then he sat on the floor in relief. Almost immediately after that, their baby girl came sliding into Louisa's hands. She cut the cord and handed her to Rachel. Tom wiped the infant with the clean boiled water. The placenta followed soon after and Rachel began to smile through her exhaustion. Then Louisa lifted Jewel onto the bed and looked at the little family, all beaming.

"Thank you Miz Louisa," said Rachel.

"Well actually Tom did it," said Louisa.

"But I didn't know to try til you came," said Tom, "so I thank ya too."

"I'm so glad I could be of use," said Louisa, and left.

When she told Sidney about it later, he seemed confused. He would not have denied such assistance to his horses, but the idea of his wife serving as midwife to a Negro, a former slave, was unsettling. "I thought they all birthed their own babies, or at least helped each other if help were necessary. I remember women givin' birth right in the field."

"Well if there is a problem like with this baby, and no help is close by, any woman would be in a bad way and might lose the baby and die too."

Louisa felt proud that she had had the courage to help Rachel with this birth. And she liked the feeling of usefulness it left her with.

Sitting in the library reading that afternoon, she found herself thinking about Jewel and imagining what it would be like to teach the children of the Turner sharecroppers. There were no Freedmen's Schools in the county that were near enough for them to attend. She could use Joseph's old room in the stable for a classroom. Another letter had arrived from Mary that morning, describing her pupils and classes in Richmond. Mary sounded excited and happy, knowing that she was doing work that mattered. Louisa shook herself out of her daydream and returned to her reading.

A few days later Jim arrived with her firewood shortly after Sidney had ridden off on his horse to meet with one of his buyers in Danville. Jim's three sons were with him.

"How old are your sons?" Louisa asked Jim.

"Six, seven and eight, Ma'am," he replied. "Joshua's oldest, then Luke, then David."

Louisa turned to the boys and asked, "Would you boys like to learn to read and write and figure?"

"No Ma'am," replied the youngest immediately. "Yes Ma'am," replied the oldest brother Joshua, quite firmly.

Jim looked worried. "I don' know Miz Louisa. Might be trouble on me and on you too."

"There are no longer any laws against you learnin'," said Louisa.

"What about Mr. Sidney? What would he say?"

"There's no need for him to know Jim."

Jim looked thoughtful. "I sure would like for them to get some learnin'. And they could teach me some. Thank ya Miz Louisa. Lemme think on it."

Two days later Jim and the three boys brought more firewood. They were smiling. "Mama say we better say yes to learnin' or she gonna whup us," said Joshua.

"Their Mama know a good thing when she hear it," said Jim. "When can they start?"

"Tomorrow. As soon as you see Mr. Sidney ride away, meet me at the stable. We'll meet every morning that he rides away, to the fields or anywhere else."

Jim looked worried again. "I don't much like sneakin' behind Mr. Sidney's back."

"I don't either. But that's just how it is right now. I hope it will change."

Louisa smiled at the boys. "I'll see you tomorrow boys. Just wait way in back of the bushes until you see Mr. Sidney ride away."

Louisa was excited. She got a broom and went straight to Joseph's old room, where she pulled down all the cobwebs. She swept the floor clean and arranged four wooden crates for seats. Then she went into the library and found the box of materials she had used with Henry, Wally and Laura. She gathered story books that they had loved and brought everything out into the stable room. What could she use for a table? Suddenly she thought of the serving table out in the kitchen house that was no longer necessary with just the two of them at home. The children would have to help her with that tomorrow, since it was too heavy for her to manage alone.

Sidney noticed Louisa's buoyant mood at dinner and again when he returned for supper. He had brought a letter from Ellen, which he read aloud. They laughed at her exaggerated description of her problems learning to cook on a wood stove, the first time they had laughed together for a while. And that night they made love with passion they had missed for some time.

The next morning, after Sidney rode away, Louisa went to the stable room. Joshua, Luke and David came a few minutes later.

"Good morning boys!"

Good morning Miz Louisa." Louisa asked them to help her and they all carried the table from the kitchen house.

When they got back to the stable, Jewel was standing by the door.

"Mama says to ask you, can you teach me too?"

"Yes Jewel, but no more after you right now." She wasn't clear about why she had to stop at four pupils. Was it because she was afraid she couldn't manage more than four? Mary had fifty in some of her classes in Richmond. Or was it because the more people who were involved, the more likely that Sidney would find out? Louisa put her worry out of her mind and concentrated on her pupils. As she had with her own children, she read them fables to start off. It felt especially important with these children, who had been prevented from having books and being read to. They seemed to like the stories very much. They didn't ask many questions yet, but Louisa sensed that would happen as they felt less shy. Then she started working with them on the sounds of the alphabet, using the alphabet cards and pictures she had made for her children. They worked on counting next, using fingers and then pebbles. Two hours flew by and she ended the lesson, telling them how well they were doing.

As soon as the children left Louisa organized herself for the next day's lesson and headed for the kitchen. She wanted to make sure she kept Sidney's dinners acceptable, so that he would not feel neglected. Then when she told him about her pupils, he would realize she had time for being a teacher as well as a wife.

Months passed. On very cold days, they moved into the library to work. Jewel loved it there, but the boys said they liked the stable room better. Louisa was happier now, enjoying teaching, helping her four pupils learn and watching them grow in skill and confidence. They were bright and eager to learn. Joshua and Luke competed with each other, racing to see who could get the most sums correct in an allotted time. Jewel and David joked and teased each other over the sentences they composed about farm animals. She encouraged them to draw, which they enjoyed. When she showed them a map and told them a little Virginia history, Joshua began to ask questions. The others did too, questions which made Louisa think all day. On the rare days that Sidney did not take his horse to ride the fields, check the drying sheds, or go to somewhere in the county, the children were disappointed and so was Louisa. She still had not brought herself to tell him about her pupils. She felt guilty about keeping her teaching from him. But she could not bear the thought of having to end it if he vehemently objected. So she pushed her guilty feelings away and concentrated on her pupils.

In spite of her deception, Louisa felt warmer toward Sidney now that she was doing something useful. She read some of the Freedmen's literature that sometimes appeared at the grist mill and began to understand more about the effects of the system of slavery. She wished she could talk about these things with Sidney, but didn't know how to begin. For the time being, Sidney was more content too, pleased that the price of tobacco was rising. With his profit he was able to buy a fine horse for Louisa. She was grateful and named her Sadie. Once again they enjoyed long rides through the surrounding hills and valleys.

One night they were lying in bed talking after making love, when they heard horses galloping down their road, toward the house. They ran to the window and stood with their bodies pressed together, hiding behind the curtain. "Don't move Louisa," whispered Sidney. A dozen horses came to a halt and lined up in front of the house, facing it. The riders were dressed in white robes and tall pointed hats. Each one carried a lit torch. In the flickering light they saw one of the riders throw something onto the veranda. Then they all galloped away. Sidney ran down to see what was on the veranda. It was a corn cob with a note tied around it. The note said: "See to your wife. This is your only warning."

Sidney ran back upstairs and handed the note to Louisa. "What does it mean?" he asked. So Louisa told him about her four pupils.

"What are you thinking of? How could you do this behind my back?" he yelled.

"I don't like sneaking either"

"Do you realize that the Klan has been burnin' out white folks who are soft on Negroes, all over Virginia, all over the South?"

"I've heard. And they are even more vicious to Negroes."

"Why Louisa, why would you do this?"

"The children need to learn, Sidney. Otherwise they have no choice but sharecroppin' and housework all their lives. How is that freedom?"

"We need them to be sharecroppers! Do you not see that?"

"Do Negroes not need doctors and teachers and carpenters?"

"Oh Louisa, you still do not understand. Tell those children tomorrow—it is over! And we still might get burned out by the Klan. And you brought this on us!"

Louisa was heartbroken. When she explained to Joshua, Luke, David and Jewel why their lessons were over, their faces fell. Then fear replaced disappointment as they realized the Klan might come after their families too. "Are they gonna burn our house?" asked Joshua. "

And lynch our Papas? asked Jewel. They knew there would be no warning for them.

It was devastating to think of. She had put her pupils in more jeopardy than she had put Sidney and her. Why hadn't she thought of that? And how had someone in the Klan found out about their lessons? It was terribly upsetting.

"I hope their warning to me will be the end of it," Louisa said to the children. "I'm so sorry we have to stop workin' together. And I'm just as sorry that you have to worry about the Klan." They all looked at her and nodded.

"You have done so well in your learning. I want you to know, I'm very proud of you."

She gave them each a story book and asked them to read to each other and other children they knew. Then she told them how much she had enjoyed working with such bright and eager pupils. "Thank you Miz Louisa, for teachin' us," said Joshua. "And thank you for the books," said Jewel. The others thanked her too and they walked slowly away. When they were gone Louisa sat at the empty table and cried, for the children, for herself.

Ellen

September 1867

Sam had hired a carriage to take his new family with him from Chatham to Lynchburg after the wedding. Ellen was pleased with the comfort of riding in a carriage again and the children found it exciting. When they reached the "hill city", as it was known, they were quiet, fascinated by the new sights and sounds. So many people, walking, or in carriages and wagons. White folks and Negroes. Large stone churches with tall steeples. Gas street lamps. Many stores and street after street of houses. Finally the carriage came to a stop on Federal Street. Samuel's house was a small white clapboard two story, set fairly close to the street in a treeless and slightly muddy yard. There was no porch, Ellen noticed right away. Leaving the driver to unload their belongings, they climbed the wooden steps and entered the house. Sam seemed proud to show Ellen and the children around. In the front of the house was a sparsely furnished parlor and a dining room. In the back was the kitchen. "No kitchen house," thought Ellen, so it will be boiling hot." As soon as she entered the kitchen she saw it—a large cast iron cook stove. She had heard about them from young Amy Stanton. They were supposed to be a great advance over the fireplace, but she hadn't the first idea how to cook on one. She just stared. "Don't worry Ellen," Sam said smiling. "I'll show you a little about it tonight. Then tomorrow we can cook simple things together. On Monday Ada comes and she can show you everything about it."

"Who is Ada?" asked Ellen.

"She's the Negro woman I just hired. She'll come Monday and Thursday mornings and help with cooking and cleaning, whatever you need."

"Thank you Sam. What a nice surprise."

"I wish I could afford to have her more. If business picks up I hope I can." Next Sam showed them the gas lights. " I have them on the wall in every room," he said. They were all impressed and wanted to see how they worked.

The children ran upstairs to find their rooms. The largest room was clearly for Sam and Ellen. One smaller bedroom had two beds and the other one had one bed. Laura put her doll on that bed. Sam had been using the room as an office, and there were still stacks of papers on the bureau. Sam had moved his desk into the master bedroom and came now to get the papers. He knocked on the door jam. "Come in Mr. Sam," Laura giggled. "It appears that your doll is taking a nap," he said. "I'm glad she's made herself at home."

"Yes, she's fine," Laura said, and smiled.

Sam showed them the water pump and the privy out back, which was cruder than the one at Oak Hill. Ellen and Laura each decided privately to stay with their chamber pots. Wally and Henry were ready to explore the area and asked to take a walk down the street. Ellen seemed worried about it, but Sam said it was safe, so they did. Meanwhile Sam showed Ellen where to put wood in the stove and they made real tea. When the boys returned they drank it with ham rolls and sweet biscuits left over from the wedding refreshments. Wally and Henry were excited, having seen a number of dogs, cats, chickens and children on their walk. Ellen felt exhausted and relieved. That night she and Sam made love carefully, both of them shy about their bodies. Afterward they held each other, feeling warm and happy.

The next day was Sunday. Sam asked Ellen to come to the nearby Baptist church, even though she was Episcopalian. "The reason I am an Episcopalian is because that was the closest church to us at Oak Hill", she said. I expect the Baptist church is just as nice. The children and I will all come." The children looked unenthusiastic, which Ellen ignored. As soon as they all got dressed, they walked several blocks to the church. On the way, Sam pointed out some of the main streets and where they led. "One of the good things about living in a city is that everything is close by, so you can walk to most places," he said. They arrived just as the service was starting. Many of the hymns were different and the sermon seemed somewhat fiery, but it all seemed fine to Ellen. As soon as the service was over, Sam proudly introduced his new family to the congregants sitting nearby. "Are your children going to go to school?" asked a tall woman named Mrs. Hamilton.

"Yes, I am going to enroll them tomorrow," Ellen replied.

"Which schools?"

"John Cary's School for Boys and Mrs. Botsford's School for Girls", Ellen said.

"Well, it's good you don't have to send them to public schools like they do up North."

"What is wrong with public schools?" asked Ellen.

"Public schools are open to any white children at all, even poor white trash. You would not want your children mixin' with them. The Reconstruction advocates are promoting public schools here in Lynchburg, but so far a group of us has stood up against them successfully. The Freedmen's Bureau runs schools for the Negroes, you know."

"I know. Well, I really must find Sam and the children, Miz Hamilton," Ellen said, and she did.

When they arrived back home Sam fed wood into the stove and pulled bowls and pans out of the cabinets while Ellen and the children watched. He cooked eggs, ham and hotcakes. The children laughed over breakfast for dinner and Ellen was amazed. "This is about the limit of what I can cook," said Sam while they were eating. "It will be wonderful if you learn to do real meals like you did in the fireplace, Ellen dear. Meats, vegetables…"

"I'm glad Ada will be here tomorrow," Ellen said. "Cooking on a wood stove is very different from cooking in a fireplace."

"I didn't know a man could cook," said Wally and giggled.

"Well Wally, in France the very finest cooks are men," said Sam. "They are called chefs, and some become famous."

"Are you famous in Lynchburg because you cook, Mr. Sam?" Laura asked.

"No, not at all Laura. I learned to cook a little because I had to eat. There was no one to cook for me."

"Why didn't you have a colored woman cook for you?" asked Henry.

"Well, to tell the truth I could not afford it until now. Ada will come two mornings a week because that is what I can afford."

"Enough questions for Mr. Sam now," said Ellen. "Mama is sending Jim up in the wagon with our things this afternoon. I'll need your help to put everything away."

Ellen was trying to be hopeful and not hurt Sam's feelings, but she found his house disappointing. He had furnished it minimally with used oak pieces, some of which were battered and worn. The wood floors were clean and waxed, but they were bare, and so were the windows. He had rigged up butcher paper on rollers to provide privacy in the bedrooms, but that wouldn't last long. She would have to make curtains soon. It all felt barren and cold to Ellen. The children did not seem to see anything wrong though. To them this seemed like an adventure, Ellen realized, and was glad.

The next day Ellen and Sam enrolled the boys in John Cary's Boys' School and Laura in Mrs. Botsford's Girls' School. Sam had already paid their tuition, so they were expected. Ellen was nervous and so were the children, but they all acted calm. Then Sam walked on to his store and Ellen walked back to the house, worried now about meeting Ada. Ada was standing at the back door, a slender woman with smooth dark skin, her plentiful black hair pulled back into a bun. "You must be Ada," said Ellen. "And you is Miz Ellen," she replied. "Mr. Sam said you need to learn to cook."

"I know how to cook in a fire place," Ellen said defensively.

"Well a wood stove be different. But it be a whole lot easier once you get the hang of it," said Ada.

They went into the kitchen. "What you want to cook for dinner today Miz Ellen?"

Ellen had not thought that far yet.

"How 'bout we fry up some chicken?" Ada suggested.

She looked in the cupboard until she found a large cast iron frying pan. "That's what this pan is for. Let's go to market."

So they walked down to the Market Hall and bought two plump live chickens, oil, collards and rice, paying with the money Sam had given Ellen.

"You need to get you some chickens in your yard," Ada said on the way back. "That way, no matter how scarce the money is, you always got eggs for the children."

"Yes, I already found that out," said Ellen.

"Truly?" said Ada, surprised.

Ellen nodded.

When they reached home Ada reached for one of the chickens and quickly broke her neck. Ellen did the same and they both gutted and plucked their hens. Then Ada cut them into pieces and instructed while she fried them and cooked the rice and collards. "You make it look easy Ada," said Ellen. When Sam and the children arrived for dinner they exclaimed over the delicious smells. Ellen asked Laura to help her set the table and then Ada carried in the meal. Ada stood at the dining room doorway and smiled as they began to eat.

"Wait for grace," said Ellen.

"Lord make us thankful, for these and all our blessings…", Wally said the familiar blessing.

"So children, how was school this morning?" Sam asked.

"It was alright I guess, Sir," said Wally.

Henry spoke up. "In my class they are learnin' things we did a long time ago with Aunt Mary."

"Most of the boys in your school have probably not had a lot of schoolin', with the war and the expense. And not everybody has an Aunt Mary. See how it is after a little time passes," said Sam.

"What is your teacher's name, Laura?" asked Ellen.

"Miz Johnson and she said I did not read the Fox and the Grapes all by myself. She said not to tell lies in her class," sobbed Laura.

"Oh dear," said Ellen, handing her a handkerchief and patting her hand. "I never thought Aunt Mary teachin' you all so well would cause problems. I have a mind to walk back to school with you and talk to your teachers." "Please Mama, no. None of the other mamas will be there," said Wally.

"Well, we'll wait a bit and see how things go. It's almost time to go back now. You boys be sure to walk Laura all the way to her school and then go back to yours. And do not forget her after school."

"We would never forget her Mama," said Henry.

"Don't worry, Mama," said Wally.

The next day after the children left for school and Sam for the store, Ellen sat down on the lumpy horsehair sofa in the parlor. The empty house felt hollow and hard and she felt the same way inside. Shaking off the feeling, she pumped and heated water and washed the breakfast dishes. Then she went upstairs and made the bed in the master bedroom, after checking to see that the children had made theirs. In the small mirror above the bureau that was now hers, she stared at her face for a long time. She looked older than her twenty-four years, she thought. How long it had been since her maid Lulu had curled her blond hair. She swept it up into a simple bun. "Sam thinks I'm beautiful," she thought, and looked back into the mirror. Then she looked at Sam's Sunday shirt, neatly folded on his bureau. She smiled when she thought of him. He was very good to her. She wanted to be just as good to him.

Walking to the market to shop for pork and vegetables and preparing dinner with much struggle took the rest of the morning. After dinner, when the front door shut and the family returned to work and school, the hollow feeling returned. And with it worry. This time about Sunday. On Sunday they were invited to Olivia's for dinner. Olivia was Sam's older sister. Her husband Adam had done extremely well in the tobacco business, and they had moved to Lynchburg even before the war. They even had lucrative business connections in England. Unfortunately Adam had been badly wounded in the war and had a wooden leg. Sam's other brother, Mathew, would also be there with his beautiful young wife Emily, their daughter Emmy, and son Micajah. Ellen wanted to make a good impression on her new in-laws, but she was afraid she had forgotten how to act in such a social situation. Of course she had met them all at the wedding, but there was so much going on then that she had paid little attention. It had been all she could do to look after the children and smile at Sam. That evening when Ellen told Sam of her worries, he reassured her that they would like her. "Will they not see me as countrified?" she asked.

"They grew up on a tobacco farm too, remember. We all remember and miss that life, especially Mathew and me."

"I forget you miss it, Sam. You did so well to leave it behind when you had to, and start a business. You must be proud."

"Well, I'm glad I have the store, but I wish it were more profitable, so that we could make this house more like what you are used to."

Ellen looked down. Did he know how disappointed she was?

"You grew up in such a beautiful home. If business picks up we'll make some improvements here. Would you like that?"

Ellen looked up and smiled. "Yes, I would. And meanwhile I have an idea Sam. Do you know what a braided rug is?"

"No, I do not."

"It's a rug made of coils of cloth. Edith Stanton taught me how to make them. All I need is rags, old clothes, useless pieces of fabric."

"How about remnants from my store that are too small to sell?"

"Perfect," said Ellen, and began the next day by cutting up some of the children's outgrown clothes. Then Sam brought home a large bag of remnants and Ellen felt encouraged. It was good to have a project.

The next day after breakfast she walked downtown with Sam to see his fabric store. She exclaimed over the floor-to-ceiling shelves holding rolls of fabric on every wall. Sam explained that most of it was cotton, grown in the deep South, shipped north to the textile mills to be transformed into various types of cloth, and then shipped south again. There were some woolen fabrics, also from the north. Occasionally Sam could get some silk or brocade, but that sold immediately. Sam introduced Ellen to his clerk Mr. Hudson, who was eager to open the double doors at the front of the store and get started. "Your husband has a fine business here, Miz Roberts." "So I see," said Ellen, and left to go to market.

Cooking on the wood stove was a daily challenge. One day she scorched the potatoes, and the next the green beans. The pork roast was black on the outside and raw in the center. And she could never get everything ready at the same time. Every time she had to cook she felt like weeping. When Ada came back on Thursday morning Ellen greeted her with great relief. "You probably don't believe I was a pretty good cook in our kitchen house with a fireplace and side oven. I'm just a failure with this stove."

"It just take some gettin' used to, Miz Ellen," Ada said.

They walked to the market and bought ingredients for a stew to use the pork roast that was raw in the middle, combined with vegetables and herbs that made a delicious broth. Ellen asked Ada about the stove as they worked. The family liked the stew and Ellen was grateful for Ada. Sam had explained to her that part of Ada's pay was having "totin' privileges" so Ellen was glad there were some good leftovers for her to take home.

Sunday came far too quickly. Right after church the family walked across town to the home of Olivia, Adam and their daughters. Their wide stately house was set back on a tree lined street. Olivia stood on the graceful veranda to welcome them. "Hello Sam dear," she said, kissing his cheek. "So lovely that you are here my dear," she said, clasping Ellen's hand in her cool one. "And Laura, lovely. Now which of you is Wally and which is Henry?" she asked in mock alarm.

They entered the drawing room with its richly colored Persian carpets and polished mahogany furniture. Sam's brother Matthew was deep in conversation with Adam, so Emily came to greet them with Emmy and Micajah. "We are so glad you are here," said Emily, and introduced her children. The children stood awkwardly by, while Ellen and Emily conversed. Seeing the children's awkwardness, Sam suggested they go out on the veranda. Olivia's daughters Susanna and Amanda came to the door, looked in and then joined the others on the porch.

Dinner was elegant, with two uniformed servants waiting on the table. The cook was clearly well trained, since one delicious dish followed another. Ellen was reminded of the lovely dinners in the gracious surroundings of Oak Hill when she was younger. They had plenty of house servants then and Louisa and Sidney had presided over many dinners like this. Being here made her long for those times. Would life ever be so lovely again? She brought her attention to the conversation. Olivia was talking about schools. She and Adam still had a tutor for their girls and planned to continue. Susanna was fourteen and Amanda twelve. "You know, you can't be too careful these days," Olivia said. Some teachers might still have abolitionist notions, and try to influence your children."

"Well, we would not want that, would we children?" said Matthew with a twinkle. Ellen looked at Sam, who seemed to share his brother's amusement over their sister's pontificating. The meal passed agreeably and ended with peach tarts.

The children retreated to the veranda, and the three men to the drawing room, while the women moved to the window seat under the bay window in the dining room. "Ellen, I hope you will come over often with the children," Emily said warmly. "They are almost the same age, and cousins, so I hope they will be great friends." "Thank you. I do too," said Ellen, wishing she could exude such sincere warmth.

"Sam tells me your children are unusually smart," Olivia broke in. "They must have had an excellent tutor."

"They did," replied Ellen, hoping she would not ask for more detail.

"Well who was it? Maybe I could get him up here for my girls."

"It was my sister Mary. But she has a teaching job now, in Richmond."

"Really? I know there are some very good schools in Richmond. Thank goodness the fine old families are getting things back to normal in the city, like it was before the war. So which school does Mary teach in?"

"I've forgotten the name," Ellen lied.

"Well, when you can remember, please let me know. Susanna and Amanda need a better tutor. Perhaps I could lure her away. Now Ellen," she continued without a second's pause, "we really must tell you about Lynchburg, mustn't we Emily." Emily nodded and opened her mouth to say something, but Olivia charged ahead. "Lynchburg is the only city in Virginia that the Yankees did not overcome in the war. That is how well defended we were. Isn't that right Emily?" Emily nodded. "Some of the finest families of Virginia live here, the aristocracy. Of course you will need to know who the right people are. I will introduce you." Ellen looked at Olivia and Emily and tried to smile. Then she felt a wave of relief as Sam's arm encircled her shoulders. "Olivia, don't fill Ellen's dance card yet. I just got her here."

Sam brought her to speak briefly with Mathew and Adam and then it was time to go home.

When they walked into Sam's house, it seemed more barren than ever to Ellen. But Sam seemed pleased about their visit and how much everyone seemed to enjoy it. "Even the children had a good time. Is that right Henry?"

"Yes Sir, the food was great."

"Wally kept staring at Amanda," said Laura.

"At least I didn't stare at Uncle Adam's wooden leg," said Wally.

"Enough!" Ellen said crossly. They all looked at her in surprise.

The next day Ellen walked to school with Laura to see her teacher before class. The teacher had sent home a letter on Friday saying that Laura was misplaced and asking to speak with her mother. Ellen was berating herself for not going to Miss Johnson the day after she had accused Laura of lying about reading The Fox and the Grapes. She just could not seem to get herself to do things lately. So she was determined to deal with this decisively. Laura led her to the classroom.

"Hello Miss Johnson," Ellen said. "I'd like to have Laura moved to the second grade. And I would like her to start today."

"That is exactly why I wanted to speak with you, Miz Roberts. Laura should definitely move up. She is quite a good reader for her age. She says it's because her Aunt Mary is the best teacher in the world."

"She is an excellent teacher. She's at a school in Richmond now."

"Oh yes, I know all about it, Miz Roberts. Laura told us. She's at the Chimborazo school, one of those absurd Freedmen's schools, where they teach Negroes to be uppity and forget their places. Why would your sister want to teach in a place like that?"

"I truly do not understand it." Ellen looked down and saw that Laura's face was defiant.

" Well your daughter thinks her Aunt Mary is doin' something important."

"We really have not talked about it," Ellen said softly.

"Now you be a good girl, Laura and do not pay any attention to that Freedmen's nonsense," said Miss Johnson.

Ellen took Laura to the second grade teacher, introduced her, and left.

On the walk back home Ellen thought how angry she was at Mary for putting her in embarrassing situations two days in a row. And she was jealous that Laura looked up to Mary so much. The letter they had gotten didn't clarify why she was there at all. Ellen really could not grasp why Mary wanted to teach Negroes, why she thought it was important. She missed Mary though. She was lonely and wished she would visit. She could take the train from Richmond to Lynchburg so easily.

Entering the empty house brought on that hollow feeling again. She walked from room to room, listening to the clack of her shoes on the bare wood floors. Then she sat in the parlor and pulled out the braided rug she was working on. Maybe if she made a small one for the foyer the children and Sam would wipe their feet on it, and there would be less mud in the house.

Sidney
Spring – Fall 1868

The trees were budding out and the soil was warming. Sidney was eager for Oak Hill's tobacco planting to progress. Last fall he had harvested his first barely successful crop of bright leaf since the war. He had seen to it that his sharecroppers had dried it to just the right golden shade. And it had brought a decent price in Danville. It made him wish he could raise more. Of course for that he would need more land, but that was not possible yet.

A loud rooster and fresh breeze blowing in the window woke him up before Louisa. He dressed quickly and went out to the stable. While feeding the horses, he decided to hire Jim's nephew Elijah for a stable hand. The horses needed care and the stable needed regular cleaning. Sidney saddled his horse and rode out to where his men were cultivating the little tobacco seedlings. "They're looking mighty fine," said Sidney. "Can we plant any more?"

"These here will fill up the fields, Sir," Jim replied. "Won't be long before we have to thin 'em."

"You just keep 'em healthy Jim, and send Elijah to see me," said Sidney and rode away.

Sidney had still not gotten over Louisa's betrayal last year when she was teaching those "cropper" children. Her going behind his back had hurt him deeply. And realizing that she thought completely differently about so many things made her seem like a stranger to him. She did not understand about Negroes at all. Was she becoming as foolish as Mary? Not only were things strained between him and Louisa, his anxiety about another visit from the Klan was always in the back of his mind. Whenever he went to the warehouses in Danville there was talk of Klan activities. Sidney thought the Klan was too violent, but he did understand their desire to protect the way of life of white folks. He just wanted to steer clear of them and let them do their business.

Lately he had been enjoying smoking his pipe and drinking whiskey with young John Stanton. John reminded him of the son he and Louisa had lost, and not just because of his name. Like their John, he was a no nonsense sort, interested in tobacco and horses, not in worrying about the rights of the Negroes. Whether he was with John or by himself, Louisa was distant when he drank, which irritated him and kept him at it longer. When he finally came to bed on those nights, Louisa would be so sound asleep that he couldn't rouse her. Not what he wanted. She was his wife, after all.

Spring became summer and the tobacco was thriving. Sidney rode by field after field filled with rows of healthy green plants. There had been just the right amount of rain and the field hands were busy getting rid of the weeds and hornworms. Anticipating a lucrative harvest, Sidney was proud. As they finished dinner, he told Louisa how well they were doing and suggested they go for a ride. "I don't want to work this afternoon and I want you to come with me."

"That will be nice. Just let me put the food away and I'll be ready," Louisa said.

"Just leave it. I don't want to wait."

"It will just take a few minutes, Sidney," said Louisa as she cleared the table.

"Put the dishes down Louisa. Now."

Louisa did, and her face looked tense as they walked out to the stable, saddled their horses, and rode away in silence. It was a sunny afternoon, but the breeze cooled it off and kept the insects away. Louisa was watching the distant sky when Sidney rode up beside her.

"Talk to me," he said. "Even when we are together it seems like you are somewhere else. Where are you?"

"There is so much to think about since the war. Everything is different."

"No it is not! Can't you see how hard I am workin' to make our lives like they were before? We've got acres and acres of tobacco again, and field hands to work it, even if they are sharecroppers now. And you could have all the help you wanted in the house, just like before. I can pay for it now. You have just refused it."

"I have what I need."

"No, you need kitchen help and I am going to see to it that you have it. I want you to spend your time like a lady, and with me."

"I don't remember what I did as a lady Sidney."

"We used to entertain our neighbors, for one thing. And go to parties and musical evenings. Don't you remember the lavish dinners, and the dances, and your teas with the ladies?"

"No one does those things since the war. So many people died or lost their property. And the ones who are left are strugglin' to get back on their feet."

"Well, let's go visit some people who are not strugglin'—young John and Amy Stanton."

When they arrived John Stanton seemed surprised and pleased to see them. He called his stable hand to take care of the horses and led his guests up the wide stairs to sit on the veranda. Amy joined them, holding little Johnny by the hand. She was obviously pregnant. A young Negro woman appeared and served refreshments. She was tearful and seemed to be trying hard to control it.

"That's enough Libby," said Amy. "You may take Johnny upstairs for his nap now."

As Libby disappeared with Johnny, Amy commented on how annoying she was. "She's been cryin' for three days now."

"What is she cryin' about?" asked Louisa.

"I really don't care," said Amy. "She is supposed to do her job. I think she said that her mother died."

"She seems so young. That must be awful for her," said Louisa.

"I don't know. I don't think they feel things like we do."

"I do," said Louisa, and looked at all three. Amy looked puzzled and the two men looked down.

Sidney suggested that he and John had tobacco business to discuss, so they moved to the other end of the veranda.

"Amy will be glad to be able to talk about the baby with Louisa," John said. "We think it will be born about three months from now."

"That is good to hear John. I hope you get another fine boy!"

"That is my hope as well."

He called for Libby to bring more whiskey. When she didn't come, he fetched the decanter himself. He poured more whiskey in both glasses. He offered Sidney a cigar, and they both lit up. Sidney swirled his whisky and then drank. "How is your crop this summer?"

"I am expecting an excellent crop. And you?"

"Best yet. It was very fortunate that we could raise capital to start over by selling land to your Mama's Yankee cousin. But now that tobacco is getting a good price, I want to plant more. What about you John?"

"I've been thinking the same way"

"How's your cousin doing with that land?"

"I really don't know. Never met him. I don't believe he even lives there. I have ridden over and the fields were still fallow. Couldn't see whether he built a house behind the trees."

"Do you think he might want to sell the land back to us?"

"There is only one way to find out," said John. "I'll ask him. Mother will know how to get in touch with him. We're goin' to Danville to see her next week."

On the ride home Sidney talked enthusiastically about the possibility of buying his land back. Louisa rode quietly, looking off into the trees. "Don't you hear me Louisa?," he asked.

"Yes Sidney, I hope you can do it."

He rode up beside her. "Why did you have to ask about the girl weeping? That is none of our business."

"How could we just ignore it? It felt cruel."

"And asking about it gave you an opportunity to teach Amy your notions about Negroes."

"We all have a lot to learn, Sidney. The things we thought about Negroes just weren't true."

"What makes you so sure?"

"Well for one thing, once they got started, those four sharecropper children I was teaching took to learning exactly like our children and grandchildren."

"How dare you bring them up! You know what a disappointment your little escapade was to me."

They rode the rest of the way home in silence.

In a few weeks the lower leaves of tobacco were ready to be stripped off the plants and dried. The sharecroppers strung them on poles and kept the drying cabin fires going just right. As more leaves ripened they were stripped and dried too. Everybody was exhausted, keeping up the pace.

One Sunday morning Sidney sent his new stable hand Elijah with an invitation for John and Amy Stanton. When he returned with a note of acceptance, Sidney went to find Louisa in the library.

"We're having company Louisa. John and Amy are coming this afternoon."

"Well that's fine Sidney, but I don't have anything to serve them."

"Why not Louisa?"

"I didn't expect company."

"This is why we need a cook. I like to be prepared to have company, like we used to be."

"Well today we'll serve whiskey for you and John and tea for Amy and me. It's too hot to eat anyway."

"Please see if you can come up with a little something."

Louisa went to the pantry and cut the morning's cornbread into thin slices, which she spread with her raspberry jam. She arranged them on a blue and white porcelain plate and decided it looked quite presentable.

In the afternoon John and Amy arrived in their shiny new carriage. Amy climbed awkwardly up the stairs to the veranda, clinging to John's arm.

"I can't ride a horse any more with the baby on the way, so John bought me a carriage. Was that not the sweetest thing?"

"It is a beauty," said Sidney, admiring it. He and John went down the stairs so he could inspect it. "This year's crop will pay for this carriage and a lot more," said John. They lit their pipes.

"It certainly is a good crop. And the demand is high, with so many planters ruined in the war. Just wish I had more to sell," said Sidney.

"I haven't heard from Mother's cousin. Mother says he still lives up in Boston and gave me his address. She thinks he may have bought the land as an investment for the future."

"We'll just have to wait and see."

They went up to join the ladies on the veranda. The whiskey decanter stood ready and Sidney poured. Louisa excused herself to get the tea.

"Where is your maid?" Amy asked Sidney.

"Louisa insists that she does not need a cook or a maid, with just the two of us," Sidney said.

"How odd," said Amy. " I wouldn't know anything at all about cooking or takin' care of the house either."

Louisa returned carrying a tray with tea and cornbread. She poured a cup of tea and handed it to Amy. Amy sugared and stirred her tea and then took a sip. She choked and spit into her napkin.

"Excuse me! What kind of tea is this?"

"It's sassafras. I dry the leaves myself and find it quite refreshin'," Louisa said.

"But why would you make your own tea Louisa? Sidney can afford to buy you tea, can't you Sidney," teased John.

"I learned how during the war when we had no tea, and I grew to like it. I make raspberry and mint tea too, but I'm out of them now."

"May I please have a glass of water?" Amy asked. Sidney poured her water from the cut glass pitcher. She sipped daintily, smiled and sighed.

"Oh John, isn't it lovely to be visiting on a Sunday afternoon?" She smoothed her silk skirt.

"It certainly is, Dearest."

"It reminds me of our life before the war. Do y'all remember the merry times we used to have? The dancing, the music, the lovely dinners?" Amy asked, gesturing gracefully with one hand.

"I remember it well, Amy. It was a very pleasant life," said Sidney.

"Oh, I wish our children could grow up in a world the way it was before the war," Amy continued. "I don't like the way the world has changed."

"Well nobody does," said Sidney. "That is why we do the best we can to make it the way it was before."

"I don't want to go back. I don't want the world to be like it was before," said Louisa quietly.

"That's enough Louisa" Sidney said as quietly, looking intensely at her. "Have some cornbread with my wife's raspberry jam." He passed the plate to Amy. Everyone helped themselves and the conversation turned to children.

After Amy and John left, Sidney turned to Louisa and said, "Why? Why could you not just let my comment go? What good does it do to air our disagreement? I am mortified Louisa."

"I'm sorry you are mortified, but I can not pretend to agree that we should go back to life as it was before the war. To slavery and all it meant."

"Have you forgotten that everything several generations of your family and my family had came from tobacco raised by slaves? How can you suddenly reject that world when it gave you so much?"

Sidney asked. "This is our legacy—Oak Hill, the fine furnishings, the horses and fields. The library you love so much, our education."

"How did we train ourselves not to see that it all came from denying generations of human beings their freedom?" asked Louisa.

"I refuse to talk about this any longer," said Sidney and poured himself another whiskey. Louisa carried the tray with the tea things inside and did not return. Sidney sat on the veranda, smoking his pipe and wondering what had become of the wife he knew.

Things remained tense with Louisa. Sidney was glad when the tobacco was dried and ready to go to the warehouse in Danville. He had wagon load after wagon load to deliver and rode along beside the wagons to make sure they got there safely. Once there, he had to negotiate the tricky business of price with the buyers or sell it at auction. Either way it was exciting and Sidney enjoyed it. He felt at home talking with the planters and buyers and stayed longer than he needed to. He arrived back at Oak Hill very late, long after Louisa had gone to bed. He left the letter he had picked up at the reopened post office in Danville on the dining room table for Louisa to see in the morning. It was addressed to both of them and the handwriting was Mary's, but he hadn't opened it.

Sidney woke up late. Louisa was in the storeroom checking supplies of various beans she had dried that summer. She reached into her apron for Mary's letter and handed it to him. As Sidney read, his face fell. Mary wrote that Ellen seemed overwhelmed. Mary had just been to visit them in Lynchburg for a week and had to return to Richmond for school. She was worried about Ellen. Even though it had been over a year, she was still having a hard time cooking on the wood stove. Sam had hired Ada to come another day, which he couldn't really afford. Ellen was lonely. Her only friend was her sister-in-law Emily, but Ellen usually made excuses for why they couldn't get together. She was obsessed with the bare floors in the house and spent most of her time braiding rugs instead of paying attention to her family. Sam was kind and patient, thank God, and the children loved him. Mary ended with a plea for Louisa to go up there for a visit.

"I want to go as soon as I can," said Louisa. "I'm worried about her, and the children too."

"What's happened to Ellen?" Sidney asked. "She has just what she wanted. A good husband, three healthy children, and a home. What is wrong with her?"

"I don't know what's happening now. I'm wondering. Do you remember how miserable she was after Henry was born? How she didn't even feel like gettin' out of bed to take care of Wally and Henry?"

"Yes," said Sidney, wrinkling his brow. " That was when Mary went over to Walter's and stayed with them, to help. Then the war started and Walter and I left."

"Maybe Ellen's melancholia from then has come back."

"Melancholia sounds like nonsense to me. Ellen is my normal daughter. She has everything a normal woman needs. Maybe it's hard for her to get used to living a life that is less luxurious than at Oak Hill before the war, but it is time she did. It sounds like she needs you and I'm glad you will go"

"Thank you Sidney. I know how busy you are now with the tobacco. I can go with your next wagon train to Danville and take the train to Lynchburg."

"Good. We're taking another load at the end of the week. It will be a help not to have to take you to Lynchburg."

"And I am looking forward to my first train trip."

"You are a remarkable woman, Louisa."

Louisa looked back to the dried beans. Sidney put his arms around her.

She turned to him and they held each other. Louisa looked up and suggested that she ask Jim's sister Lucy to cook and do housework while she was away. Sidney agreed and they held each other longer.

Mary
1868 – 1869

"You know why I like teaching?" Mary asked when Priscilla came into her classroom at midday break. "These children come to us and we teach them to read and write and figure, and when they walk out of here, there is no telling what they are going to do."

"But that's only true if they keep on getting a chance," Priscilla reminded her. "Most of the white folks here in Richmond hate Reconstruction and are just waiting until it is over to put the Negroes back in their places."

"I know," said Mary. "But they won't be able to get nearly all of them back in their places."

"I don't think they will either," agreed Priscilla.

Mary's second year at the Chimborazo school was going well and she felt that she was learning how to reach her pupils more effectively. So she was surprised when the mother of a pupil named Billy stormed into her classroom one day after school. "I know who you be, Miz Turner," she announced. "You a Turner from the Oak Hill plantation. Your papa held my cousins Silas and Jake."

When Mary heard "Silas and Jake" her heart lurched , as she remembered.

"Your papa had a evil overseer name of McCann. When your papa was off at war my cousins run off and that devil sent slave catchers after them. They killed Silas and cut a ear off Jake and Simon too." Billy's mother was quivering with anger.

Mary felt sick as she pictured the scene in the stable again. "There is nothing I can say that would make that alright. I'm sorry."

"Not like Silas's mama is sorry. She miss Silas every day. And Jake ain't never been right since then."

"That is awful," Mary said softly.

"Well, I just came by to tell you why I'm takin' Billy outa your class and puttin' him with Miz Atkins. I don't want him in your class since I found out who you is."

Mary felt completely deflated when she left. She sat down and stared at the primers on the benches. Deciding to wait and organize them in the morning, she walked slowly back to Mrs. Wilson's.

That night when they were in bed, she told Priscilla about her visit from Billy's mother.

"You didn't send the slave catchers after those men," Priscilla said. " You didn't have their ears cut off or have Silas killed. It was that awful overseer."

"Yes, but my father hired him and gave him the chance to treat the slaves as he did. And we all lived with that."

"Well," said Priscilla, "it seems to me that your teaching here might be a way you're trying to make up for that."

"But nothin' will ever change how wrong it all was, Priscilla. I know that nothin' can make up for it."

There was a long silence. "We'd better go to sleep now."

Priscilla went right to sleep, but as tired as Mary was, sleep would not come. She kept thinking about what Billy's mother had said. Then the scene she had witnessed from the hayloft returned to her mind. Finally her mind went to her mother's last letter, full of troubling news. Louisa had said that she and Sidney had been arguing a lot. Their main point of contention was the Negroes. Sidney was for going back as much as possible to life as it was before the war, while Louisa was questioning almost everything she had formerly thought about slavery. They still loved each other though, so Louisa felt they had not given up.

Louisa went on to report that she had been to stay with Ellen, Sam and the children in Lynchburg again. It was wonderful to see the children. She had missed them dreadfully. The boys were fine and seemed to really enjoy school and their friends. Laura was doing very well in school, but Louisa was concerned that she was affected by Ellen's melancholy. She seemed quieter than usual and a little wistful. Ellen was doing her best to act cheerful, but she admitted to Louisa that she could not stop longing for the old days at Oak Hill before the war. Louisa said she felt sad for Sam, who seemed to keep everything going. He clearly loved Ellen and the children. He seemed to be a natural father, thank God.

Mary thought it sounded pretty much the same as the last time she was there, except for Laura. But Laura worried her. Deciding to visit soon, she finally went to sleep.

As soon as Mary could get permission to miss two days, she bought a ticket on the train from Richmond to Lynchburg. Miss Martha Simms from the Freedmen's office would take her classes that Thursday and Friday. There was no time for a letter to let Ellen know she was coming, so she just hoped it would suit. Mary boarded at dawn. She still got a thrill out of riding on a train, and did not mind the soot and noise as she watched the soft colors of the springtime world slide by.

When the train screeched to a halt in Lynchburg she was surprised to be there already. Carrying her carpet bag, she walked to Sam and Ellen's house. She knocked on the front door but there was no answer. Wondering where Ada was, Mary walked around to the back yard. There she found Ellen, sitting on the back steps, staring at the new chicken house. Ellen looked up at Mary and said, "Mama told you to come. That's why you are here." Her face was blank, her voice toneless.

"I wanted to come. I wanted to see how you are."

"Well now you see. I spend my time sittin' and frettin'."

"Where is Ada? I thought she came on Thursdays."

"Her Mama died and they're burying her today."

"I'm sorry to hear that Ellen. Is it a big family?"

"Of course it's a big family. They're Negroes. They aim to outnumber and overpower us whites you know."

"No, I don't know. But I didn't come here to argue, Ellen. How would it be if we made a quick trip to market so we can get some dinner together before Sam and the children get home?"

Once at market Ellen could not decide what to buy, so Mary picked up some okra, carrots, and onions for soup. Then she got collards and sweet potatoes to go with the ham Ellen said she had. On the walk home Ellen said she was having trouble making the least little decision lately. "It takes me an hour to decide which dress to wear sometimes, and I don't have that many." "Maybe that's a good thing," Mary joked. But Ellen's indecisiveness troubled her.

When the children came home for dinner they were delighted to find their Aunt Mary there. As they hugged her enthusiastically, she realized how much she missed them. Then Sam arrived, tired but glad to see her. She and Ellen got dinner on the table and there was much talk from the boys about what they had heard at recess. It seems that two of the Yankee soldiers stationed in town had gotten into a fight with some Negroes, while folks just watched and yelled at all of them.

"Why are the Yankee soldiers still here, Mr. Sam?" asked Henry.

"You know they have been stationed all over the South since the war," said Sam. "They are supposed to make sure we follow Federal regulations and keep the peace. But it doesn't seem to work very well. Soldiers are just human beings, whatever side they are on. Some do good things and some do bad things."

After the children left to return to school, Mary asked Sam more about the situation with Reconstruction in Lynchburg. "It is very hard, Mary. I won't deny it. Commerce in general is struggling, currency is still a problem, even tobacco is unstable, though some growers with sharecroppers are starting to do well. People are worried and afraid. And to make it worse, the Klan is terrifying Negroes who are workin' hard and doin' well. They lynched a fella just last week."

"I think the situation is just as bad in Richmond," Mary said. "The efforts to rebuild the city are all for the white folks. There is no acknowledgement that over a third of the people are Negroes whose houses and streets need rebuilding too.

"This is gettin' over my head Mary. I'm just a storekeeper you know." And Sam went back to work. Mary was disappointed, because she suspected that he had more opinions she might share. But Sam was not going to upset Ellen, that was clear.

Ellen was quiet when Mary joined her to help clean up the kitchen. When they finished, Ellen said she was exhausted and needed to take a nap.

"Would it be alright if I walked over to Emily's and invited them over for Saturday?" Mary asked. I enjoyed her the last time I was here and the children seem to like each other."

"Yes, I suppose we ought to. I just haven't felt up to it."

"I can prepare a light supper so you won't have to fuss, Ellen."

"But what about the silver? The silver needs polishing."

"Maybe Laura and I can do that together," said Mary. "You take a nap and I'll be back by the time you wake up."

Mary walked the few blocks over to Emily's and found her sewing on her front porch. She accepted Mary's invitation for Saturday with obvious pleasure. "But I don't know about Mathew. He may have a meeting."

"A meeting?"

"A small group of business leaders has started meeting to protect us from the worst excesses of Reconstruction."

"What do you mean?"

"It's all very secret, so I don't know much."

Mary's heart sank. "Are they like the Klan?"

"Good heavens no, Mary. These men just want to make sure they get back their political power."

"Just for white men?"

"Of course, Mary. But no more about this. I'm so glad to have the chance to talk to you alone. About Ellen."

"Tell me what you think," Mary said. "I'm worried about her."

"Something is wrong but she won't talk about it with me. Half the time when we make plans to get together, she sends one of the boys to tell me she is feelin' ill and can't come. Then when we do get together she's vivacious at first and after a half hour or so she becomes anxious and doesn't seem to want to talk any more. Sometimes she seems quite cross with her children for no reason at all."

"I've seen the same thing," said Mary. "I'm hoping she'll talk to me about it this time."

When Mary arrived back at the house, she studied it, once more noticing the lack of a front porch. She thought how much Ellen would like one, how she had loved the veranda at Oak Hill. Maybe Sam and the boys would build one someday. But Mary knew that a porch would not make everything better for Ellen. Ellen was struggling with something much bigger. She was still asleep, so Mary began chopping the vegetables for soup. Just as she set the soup on the stove to cook, Wally, Henry and Laura returned from school. It was another chance to hug them, which Mary savored. "Go kiss your Mama awake and change your clothes," she ordered.

When Ellen came downstairs her hair was messy and she looked annoyed. "Why didn't you wake me up?" she asked Mary.

"I thought you must need to sleep, so I made the soup."

"Did you put onion in it? I can't abide onion any more."

"You can pick it out of your bowl," Mary said curtly, then regretted it.

Later, when Sam came home from work, Mary noticed how gently he held Ellen and how tenderly they kissed. "Whatever is wrong, it must not be between the two of them," she thought.

At supper Sam announced that he had had an important customer that afternoon, his sister Olivia. She was full of news. "Guess who just came through Lynchburg on the way home to retire in Tennessee?"

"I know." said Wally. "It was President Johnson. Jake Harrison at school, his parents were invited to the reception at Norvell House."

"Well so were your Aunt Olivia and Uncle Adam. She said it was a great honor, and only the finest people were there," Sam said, looking at Mary with a twinkle in his eye. " There was a sumptuous banquet and they toasted President Johnson as the champion of the Constitution and the friend of the South."

"What a travesty," Mary burst out. "Johnson opposed the Civil Rights Bill and the Freedmen's Bureau."

"Enough!" Ellen cut in. "Stop!"

There was silence, as they all ate their soup.

At bedtime for the children Mary went up to say goodnight. When she got to Laura's room, she had already made herself a pallet on the floor so that Mary could sleep in her bed. She was snuggling in her blanket with her doll. "I love it when you come, Aunt Mary," she said sitting up. "You can sleep in my bed whenever you want."

"Thank you Laura. I love being with you."

"Aunt Mary, what is wrong with Mama? Is she sick?"

"Why do you think she might be sick?"

"Well, she sleeps so much. When I am sick I sleep a lot too."

"I don't know what's wrong Laura. I wish I did. I am glad you asked me though. And we can talk about it again. But tonight Laura, how would it be if I read to you? I know you read to yourself, but I would like to if it's alright." As soon as Mary began reading, Henry and Wally knocked on the door. So Mary read from Robinson Crusoe to all three of them, "just like old times," said Henry.

The next morning Ellen suggested that she and Mary walk down to the James River before going to market. Since it was early spring, there were soft green buds on the trees. Ellen knew just where she wanted to go, and led Mary down a hill to a small clearing on the bank. "This is my place," she said, and stood gazing at the river and the railroad trestle that crossed it upstream. "Sometimes, if you look very carefully, you can see someone standin' on the trestle." Mary looked at the scene—the trees, the water, the trestle, and the sky. It looked like a painting. "I see why you like it here," she said quietly.

"No you don't, Mary," Ellen snapped.

"Then tell me," said Mary.

"I don't want to talk about it," said Ellen. "And I don't want to talk about what's wrong with me either. Can we just have a nice day together without dwelling on that?" Mary listened and they had a peaceful day going to market, cooking and braiding rugs.

That evening Ellen and Sam were sitting together in the parlor when Mary joined them after talking and reading with the children. "Those children are certainly growing up," she said.

"They talk to you more in one evening than they talk to me in a week," said Ellen.

"You're forgetting that it's been a while since they have seen her, Ellen," Sam said. "The children adore you."

The next afternoon when Emily and her children came, it was much as Emily had described. Ellen was welcoming at first, but then became irritated when she noticed that Mary had not cleaned the silver. "Nobody notices things like that," said Emily. "I just like seein' you." But Ellen was mortified and exhausted and went straight to bed when Emily's family left. The boys went out to play, but Laura stayed to help Mary clean up the supper things. "What has happened to my Mama, Aunt Mary?"

"She certainly seems unhappy," said Mary.

"Do we make her unhappy, Henry, Wally and me?"

"No, that is one thing I do know. You all are not her problem. She loves you."

The next morning was Sunday. Ellen announced that she did not feel up to going to church. So Sam and the children went and Mary decided to stay with Ellen, hoping to finally talk with her. They were still at the breakfast table.

"I'm worried about you," Mary started. "Mama, and Sam and the children are too. Please help me understand what is happening."

"I wish I could explain, Mary. You are always so clear about what you feel and determined about what is important to you. But I'm not that way." She looked down and paused. "Being here is overwhelming. I long for our pleasant easy life at Oak Hill before the war. And then I feel guilty because I ought to be grateful for Sam and our life here." Ellen paused again and then went on. "I feel hopeless about all the work it takes to run this house with only the help of Ada. I detest housework and resent having to work so hard. So many days I just sleep, alone in a thick fog."

Mary reached over to take her hand, but Ellen pulled it back.

"You have had to change your life and learn a lot, moving up here. It's no small thing Ellen, and you deserve credit. Have you talked with Sam about feeling overwhelmed?"

"Of course not. I don't want him to think I'm ungrateful."

"But he's your husband and loves you. He is worried."

"How can you give me marriage advice?"

"You are right. I can't." Mary stood up.

"And you are goin' back to Richmond today, to a life I can not fathom."

"I wish I could explain that teaching Negro children who were enslaved just a few years ago, is the best thing I have ever done."

"I don't think I will ever understand, Mary."

The children walked with Mary to catch the train, chatting as they went. Mary knew they wanted her to explain about their mother and she began,

"I know you're worried about your Mama. She feels overwhelmed sometimes. The move up here was a big change. But she loves you and Mr. Sam, and we can all hope she'll feel better soon."

"But why does she sleep so much?" asked Henry.

"I think it's part of feeling awful."

"What can we do to make her better?" asked Laura.

"Henry and I can chop wood without Mama having to ask us five times," said Wally.

"I can help in the kitchen more," said Laura.

"You are dears and those are very good ideas," said Mary. "I know how much you love your mother, and that is very important.

Mary boarded the train and waved to Laura, Henry and Wally as it pulled away. At first she could think only about Ellen, Sam and the children. She hoped she had helped the children understand that they weren't causing their mother's problems, even though she didn't know what was. She worried about Ellen not talking openly with Sam.

As the train approached Richmond, Mary's heart lifted. The faces of her pupils passed through her mind and she began thinking about tomorrow's lessons. Priscilla met her at the station and they started the walk back to Mrs. Wilson's.

"I need to tell you something right away Mary. It is so awful. I found this out from Martha Simms, the teacher who took over your classes last week. It turns out that she is a friend of your half-sister Sally. Sally has just left for Baltimore to teach in a school for Negro children started by the Quakers. Before she came here to Richmond, she was teaching in Pittsylvania County. She fell in love with another teacher there and they got married. The very night they moved into their own house, the Klan set fire to it and dragged her husband away. They lynched him. Of course Sally was devastated. That must be why she left and came here."

Mary was stunned. Tears came, and her nose ran. "It's so cruel, so horrible," she sobbed. They walked in silence the rest of the way.

Just before they went into Mrs Wilson's house, Priscilla said there was some important news about school. The Chimborazo School would be closing at the end of the school year. No one knew why yet. But students and teachers would have to move to other schools for the next year. Priscilla had already been looking out for opportunities. Mary was shocked. Finding out about Sally's husband and the school closing on top of her worries about Ellen was overwhelming.

Louisa
Spring – Summer 1870

Louisa couldn't believe it was her birthday again, much less that she was forty-eight. She felt young, and even though her curly hair was almost half gray, she looked young. Sidney had awakened her with gentle kisses and an armload of azaleas that smelled like rain. She dressed and went down to the dining room where Lucy served them breakfast. Lucy had stayed on as cook and housekeeper after Louisa had returned from Ellen's, because Sidney had insisted. But at least Louisa made sure she was fairly paid. Sidney hurried through his breakfast and waited for Louisa to finish hers. As soon as she swallowed her last bite of buttered cornbread, Sidney placed a small box before her. She opened it to find an exquisite braided gold necklace. "Why thank you Sidney," she said.

"Let me put it on you," He fastened it around her neck. "I know you don't wear much jewelry, even the pieces your mother gave you. But I hope you'll wear this." Sidney stood back to admire the gold around her slender neck.

"You look beautiful, Louisa."

"I'm glad you think so." She reached back to unclasp the necklace.

"Please don't. Wear it for me."

And so she did, even though it felt heavy against her neck. She wore it every day, until one day she forgot. And then she forgot another day. It seemed like too much fuss and bother for every day, so she decided to save it for special occasions.

Louisa had found herself getting restless lately. With Lucy doing housework and cooking, and Jim's other sister Caroline doing laundry, Louisa had endless free time. She continued to read avidly, but wished for someone with whom she could discuss the books. Recently she had met an expert quilter at church, who had invited Louisa to come to her home for instruction. As a result Louisa was working on some lovely and unusual quilts. Almost every month she would take the train to Lynchburg for a visit with Ellen and her family. To her great sadness, nothing seemed to change with Ellen, except that she seemed more despondent and irritable than ever. No one knew how to help her, and she refused to see a doctor.

Louisa had served as midwife for another child, since Rachel had told her sisters about the first time. Again it had been an emergency with no one else to help. And again, miraculously, the baby was born safely. But Louisa knew she did not know enough about birthing babies and had just been lucky.

Sidney was busy with his tobacco and looked forward to his trips to Danville to sell it at the bustling tobacco auction. The market fluctuated, so that sometimes he was buoyant and other times despairing. He took on two more sharecropper families so that he could cultivate every inch of his land. He still hoped to buy back the land he had sold to John Stanton's cousin, but nothing had developed on that front, and he didn't have the money yet anyway. Sidney's purchase of Louisa's fine thoroughbred had probably been premature financially, but they both truly enjoyed riding on Sundays.

Occasionally Sidney and Louisa visited John and Amy, who now had a baby girl in addition to Johnny. Sidney enjoyed John, but Louisa found Amy tiresome. So she was pleased when Sidney brought George and Eliza Willis to visit on their way home from Danville. Sidney had met them there negotiating over their tobacco. Louisa invited them to sit on the veranda and brought them cool water. She was intrigued that Eliza seemed to be as involved in the business as her husband.

"The tobacco business is interestin'," said Eliza. "A lot more interestin' than cards or needlework."

"How did you learn about it?" Louisa asked.

"I listened. George talks about it incessantly. Doesn't Mr. Turner?"

"No, not to me."

Eliza turned and looked back at the house. "Your home is lovely. Will you show me around a bit, Miz Turner?"

So Louisa invited her inside and showed her the drawing room and dining room. Eliza exclaimed over the rich colors and geometrical pattern of the large Persian carpet in the drawing room and admired the fine Federal table and the silver tea service on the sideboard in the dining room.

"Did you inherit all these things?

"When Louisa nodded, Eliza said, "Well, you sure are lucky. We have to buy our fine things. So it's a good thing there are folks now who have to sell them just to live."

Then she walked to the door of the library and looked in. "What a library! Who reads all these books?"

"Well, I love to read. And I tutored my three children and three grandchildren."

"Oh, I could certainly never do that."

The next time George and Eliza visited they had a request. Would Louisa tutor their three children? Alexa was twelve, Maxwell thirteen, and Robert fourteen. They could ride over on three days each week. And they would pay her well. They had had a series of tutors up until now, but were looking for one who was more scholarly, to prepare the boys for the University.

"I am no scholar and cannot teach Latin or Greek," Louisa said. But she was delighted at the idea of tutoring again. Teaching three older children would be interesting, using challenging books and dealing with inevitable differences due to age and talent. She was especially pleased that Alexa was included. She told Eliza she would talk about it with Sidney.

She wanted this conversation to go well, and not have tutoring become another bone of contention for them.

Sidney thought it a fine idea, except for Louisa getting paid.

"It would be nice for you. You like teaching. But we don't need their money. I take good care of you."

"But Sidney, they have been paying tutors for years."

"They were men."

"Paying a tutor makes it a business arrangement Sidney. I want both the parents and the children to take this seriously. Payment makes it serious."

"Now you are making some sense Louisa. That is probably true. But I will make sure they know we don't need the money."

The following week Alexa, Maxwell, and Robert rode over to meet her. It was an hour and a half ride from their home, and they arrived flushed and thirsty. Lucy served cool mint tea and sweet cakes on the veranda. After some initial conversation, Louisa wanted to find out what interested them and what books they had read. Then Robert asked to see the library. All three seemed stunned by its size and extent. Alexa picked up a volume of Shakespeare's sonnets, Maxwell found Frankenstein, and Robert started looking at maps. By the end of the visit, Louisa had a sense of where to begin with her new students and knew she would figure it out from there.

They agreed to begin in a few days. Louisa plunged into planning, once again marveling at the additions to the library that her father had left her, as well as those from Walter. First she selected The Decline and Fall of the Roman Empire. She remembered what a tome it was, but felt it gave some context for what came after. She would only assign parts of it, and they would have to take turns with the book. And of course she first had to read whatever she assigned so that she could discuss it with them. Louisa's father Charles had given her a copy of the Origin of the Species shortly after Darwin published it. He was excited about evolution and wanted to discuss it with her. But with the talk of war and then the start of war, she had missed reading it. When she found the copy of The Origin of the Species in her library, she sat down on the sofa and was immediately drawn in. Sydney came in from the stable and found her. "You've been reading for hours. That's enough. Come and have supper with me"

"Let me tell you what Darwin shows," said Louisa as they sat down.

"Who is Darwin?"

"He figured out how animals and people evolved over millions of years." Lucy served their meal.

"I don't know what you're talking about. And I don't see why we should talk about such things. I'm no scholar and I don't want you to be."

"Scholar or not, I still think the whole idea of evolution is amazing."

"I just don't understand you, Louisa. Aren't you interested in women's things any more? And where is your birthday necklace?" He looked at her with disappointment. "I noticed that Eliza wears gold jewelry. I want you to wear yours."

The next morning Louisa selected and reread the passages in Darwin she would use with her students. She was getting excited. She chose her beloved As You Like It for a Shakespeare to start with. They could take parts and read it aloud during class, which she hoped would be as much fun for them as it had been for her. Mathematics was easy to plan for, since she could use the old texts John and Mary had used. She felt a deep pang when she saw where John had written his name in the book. She would always miss her son.

The day came that Alexa, Matt, and Robert began coming for lessons. At first they were shy, but Louisa had always enjoyed young people, and she was able to put them at ease. When they seemed intimidated by the Rise and Fall of the Roman Empire, she assured them they would not have to read the entire volume, and explained why she thought it was important. They seemed to appreciate an explanation. Reading As You Like It was difficult at first. As Louisa explained a bit here and there, they laughed and enjoyed it.

"We had to read Julius Caesar by ourselves last year and I hated it," said Robert.

"I did too," agreed Max.

"I read it out loud and I took the different parts, so it wasn't boring. But I didn't understand much," Alexa said.

"Alexa loves to act," said Max.

Alexa blushed. Louisa put her hand on her shoulder. "Well, Shakespeare did intend that his plays be acted out."

The weeks passed quickly. Louisa was feeling more content, now that she was doing something useful again. Also, she was learning right along with her pupils, which was interesting and satisfying. But the letters from Ellen continued to be worrisome. Louisa was bewildered about how to help her, but the children seemed to feel that things were better when she was there. And Sam always made her feel welcome. So now she never let a month go by without taking the train from Danville early on Friday morning and returning on Monday evening. Sidney complained that she went too often, but did not want to accompany her. He was annoyed at Ellen for not being happy, and couldn't understand when Louisa tried to explain that it was more complicated than that.

From Mary came important news. She wrote that the Chimborazo School would become part of the Richmond Public School System next year. It would involve a turnover of the administration and some of the teachers would be replaced. Mary and Priscilla had decided to move to Philadelphia and teach in a Negro school there. They could stay with Priscilla's parents. Mary was really looking forward to the move.

Louisa sat on the veranda with Mary's letter. She was happy for Mary to be doing what she loved and glad for her to experience the excitement of Philadelphia. But she already missed her and now would miss her more. Sidney came out of the house, looking for Louisa. When he read Mary's letter he became furious and began pacing. He still could not understand why Mary wanted to teach Negroes in the first place, "Why don't you tell her to come back here and take over your tutoring? Your white pupils could use a professional teacher."

"For one thing Sidney, they are my pupils and I like teaching them. But Mary would not want to stop doin' what she is doin' anyway. She loves teaching there!"

"But why Negroes? Why not white children?" He stood in front of her.

"Because Negroes were never allowed to learn to read and write and figure before. They need education to live and work and take care of their families."

"My sharecroppers don't need to."

"We've talked about this over and over, Sidney. Lots of Negroes don't want to be sharecroppers. But they might want their own piece of land to farm. Remember, toward the end of the war, when that Union General Sherman proposed giving freed people forty acres and a mule along the southeast coast?"

Sidney looked at her with disgust and said nothing.

"Well, that hardly got started before President Johnson reversed it. So Negroes in the South are stuck sharecroppin' to live. Unless they get some education."

Sidney moved away and began pacing again." I don't want to hear any more about the damn Negroes. What is wrong with our family Louisa? One daughter is miserable and disagreeable and the other is crazy over Negroes. And you are too. What went wrong? Does Mary realize that thousands of Negroes fought for the Union when they ran away from their masters? One of them may have killed John!"

He threw the letter on the floor of the veranda and strode inside.

Louisa heard him pour himself a whiskey. She sat for a long time.

When she could concentrate again, she went back to reading Darwin. She was amazed at his studies showing how creatures could mutate over time. Now she understood why some Christians were upset by Darwin's work. It meant that God didn't create every living thing all at once in its final form. She was interested to see what her pupils would make of Darwin.

The following week they all read the pages she assigned in The Origin of the Species. Robert brought up the conflict between Darwin and the creation story in the Bible immediately. "That means the Bible is not literally true," he said. Alexa and Max had not thought of it, but understood when Robert explained. None of them seemed overly concerned. "Our grandmother would be horrified though," said Robert. "She believes that every word of the Bible is absolute truth."

Louisa was relieved not to have heard any objection from George or Eliza about assigning Darwin. She had begun to realize that they paid little attention to what their children were studying. They both seemed glad it was not their responsibility, and grateful that Louisa was taking care of it.

At the end of the spring school session in Richmond, Mary and Priscilla took the train to Philadelphia. Mary wrote that the city was astonishing.

"It is huge, hot, smelly, and crowded. Some of the Negroes wear elegant hats, dresses, and jackets, just like some of the white folks. But there are also an awful lot of poor Negroes and poor whites. Everywhere you see handsome red brick Georgian buildings built during the founding of the country. So much to take in!" Mary stopped there and said she would write again soon. Louisa put the letter on Sidney's desk after she read it. "I'll read it later," he said, and left it there. When Louisa checked later the letter was gone. It seemed that this time Sidney was not going to fly into a rage over Mary's choice.

A week later Louisa got another letter from Mary. In this one Mary told her about Sally's marriage and the terrible lynching of her husband. Mary said that it had shaken her badly and she was sad because she knew it would be a blow to Louisa. She didn't mention sharing the bad news with her father. When Louisa read about the gruesome death of Sally's husband, she was horrified. She moaned and began sobbing. Coming from the stable, Sidney found her sitting on the veranda, rubbing her eyes and nose with her handkerchief. "What is it, dear Louisa?" he asked, pulling her into his arms. When she told him his face went pale, but he did not speak. The two just sat beside each other in silence. Then Sidney asked, "Do you think you should have made her stay here all during the war? Then I could have protected her when I got back."

"No Sidney, that wouldn't make sense. And I couldn't have kept her here anyway, even if I had wanted to. She and May Belle were determined to leave. But what I should have done is give them their freedom papers so they could have gotten through Virginia and then to the North."

"They were still our property then Louisa!"

"Oh God, Sidney. Sally is your daughter!"

"That's enough, Louisa! Sidney went down the veranda steps and returned to the stable. Louisa watched him and sat, rocking.

The news about Sally and her husband weighed heavily on both of them, but they did not speak more of it then. Louisa was grateful to get back to her teaching and Sidney worked hard on his tobacco. One morning, as Alexa, Max, and Robert sat with Louisa in the library, Alexa asked, "Who is Frederick Douglass, Miz Louisa?"

"Everybody knows that," said Max. "He was a slave who learned to read and then escaped and went to the North."

"Does anybody know what he does and whether he is still important?" asked Louisa.

"I've heard folks say he's a terrible trouble maker," said Max.

"What do you know about him, Robert?" Louisa asked.

"I heard Papa say that he's dangerous and uppity," he said.

"Would you like to decide for yourselves about him," Louisa asked.

"How? Do you know him, Miz Louisa?" Alexa asked.

"No, but I have The Narrative of the Life of Frederick Douglass," said Louisa. "You can take turns reading it and when y'all finish, we'll see what you think."

"Can we do this instead of the Decline and Fall of the Roman Empire?" Alexa asked.

"For this week anyway," Louisa replied, and excused herself to get the book from the drawer in her bedroom. She didn't want to tell them to hide the Douglass book from their parents, but she hoped Eliza and George would not see it, at least not yet. She was enjoying teaching these children and did not want to jeopardize it. At the same time, it felt important to deal with real issues and encourage them to think for themselves.

The following week the Willises sent a note by way of Alexa. It was an invitation for Louisa and Sidney to come for dinner on Saturday. Louisa looked forward to getting to know Eliza better and to seeing a different household. It was a warm day and they rode their horses over, arriving hot and thirsty. Eliza and George greeted them hospitably. The children were riding and would join them later. "You must be parched after your long ride," said George, and filled cut glass tumblers full of cool water. Then he added a generous dollop of whiskey to Sidney's and his and passed them around. George toasted their visit and they all drank thirstily. As soon as George finished, he refilled his glass with both whiskey and water, drank deeply and then began refilling the others. This time Louisa noticed that he poured whiskey in Eliza's too. Sidney and George lit their pipes and plunged into a discussion of the prospects for a good tobacco harvest. Eliza was listening and nodding her head as she sipped her drink.

Then she turned to Louisa and said softly, "I know, ladies do not partake. But the truth is many do, secretly. George just lets me do it openly. His mother has a perfect fit over it!"

Louisa nodded and smiled, as she tried to imagine what Sidney and the girls would think if she took up drinking whiskey.

"Sometimes I like a pinch of snuff too. It seems like it's only fair that we get a taste of some of the tobacco we're surrounded with, don't you think so?"

"It does seem fair," said Louisa, hoping she wouldn't have to try it.

"So how are my children doin' in their studies?" Eliza asked.

"They are all three bright and are doing well," she began. She started to explain the individual strengths that each of them were showing, when she noticed that Eliza was not listening. She was listening to the men's talk of tobacco. When Louisa stopped speaking, Eliza looked back at her.

"I hope you don't think I am a terrible mother, Louisa, but I'm just not much interested in education. I didn't get much education myself, but I have learned about the tobacco business. I do find that interesting. So as long as the children are doing well in their studies with you, that is all I need to know." She looked over at George. "George is the same way. Neither one of us had a tutor when we were growin' up. My Grammaw taught me to read the Bible and George's Grampaw taught him to read and figure. So we don't know about the things the children study. Except mathematics, we do know figurin'. Are the children learnin' mathematics?"

"Oh yes," said Louisa, a bit stunned.

Alexa, Max, and Robert returned from their ride and a delicious chicken dinner was served in the dining room. The conversation was all about horses. After the meal, as they were leaving the dining room, Alexa whispered to Louisa that Maxwell would not let her have the autobiography they were sharing, even though he had finished and it was her turn. "Don't worry, Alexa," said Louisa. "We can talk about it on Monday." She could tell that Alexa was not satisfied, but did not want to go into it then.

On Monday morning when her pupils arrived, they all seemed upset. As soon as they sat down at the table in the library, Max said," I gave it to her Miz Louisa, just as soon as you left."

"Why didn't you want to give it to her?" asked Louisa.

"It's not fittin' readin' for a girl.

"I guess it was after all, 'cause I read it," said Alexa.

"That doesn't make it fittin', Alexa," Robert put in.

"What makes it not suitable, Max?" Louisa asked.

"Well to start with, he writes about masters who have children by their slaves", Max said softly.

"I hated that part too," said Robert.

"And the parts about whippin' the slaves," said Max.

"That did make me cry. There was so much whippin'. But that doesn't make it unsuitable for me. I need to know things," Alexa said.

"Do you think this narrative is true, Miz Louisa?" Robert asked.

"Yes, unfortunately. I'm sure it is. And ever since Douglass reached freedom himself, he has been working for real freedom for all Negroes. He writes and travels and gives speeches, even in England."

"Why is he still doing that, now that Negroes are free?"

"Good question, Robert. Think about the Negroes you know."

"We don't know any, except our sharecroppers," Max said.

"What are their lives like?" Louisa asked.

"I don't know. They just work in the field all the time for our father."

"Can they do anything else?" Louisa asked.

"No, I guess not," said Robert. "But they don't really need to."

"What if they want to be a doctor or a teacher or have a store?"

"We see what you mean, Miz Louisa. They need education to really be free," said Alexa.

"Well listen to you Miss Alexa, said Robert smiling, "you're becoming a regular abolitionist."

They discussed Frederick Douglass's Narrative until Louisa suggested they put it aside and come back to it the next time." I can see that y'all are doin' a lot of thinking and I'm impressed," she said.

They went on to mathematics and the rest of their lessons.

At the end of the session Louisa saw that Robert seemed preoccupied. He hardly noticed when Lucy brought them cool tea and sweet cakes on the veranda. As Louisa watched them ride away, it appeared that Max and Alexa were arguing, while Robert rode ahead by himself.

The next morning Alexa and Max were full of questions about some of the things Douglass had said in his autobiography.

"What about the lady who murdered her servant girl because the girl fell asleep while she was sittin' up all night with the lady's baby?" asked Alexa. "And the slave girl was only your age Robert," added Max.

"And the lady never even got punished," said Robert grimly.

"How could that be? It was murder," Alexa said.

"Slaves weren't protected by the law," said Robert. "They had no constitutional rights. None."

Louisa realized they were starting to come to grips with the evil and injustice of slavery, and was proud of them. But she was also afraid for them. While they continued to discuss what Douglas had said, Louisa was wondering how they would deal with this knowledge. What would they do with their new awareness? Shakespeare, mathematics and even Darwin seemed like safe and welcome havens that day.

When lessons were over Robert stayed in the library, looking for a book. He called to Max and Alexa as they were leaving, saying they should go on without him. He would follow soon.

"Miz Louisa," he said, "You know what Frederick Douglass said about slave holders fatherin' children with their slaves?"

"Yes Robert, I know," said Louisa, feeling a familiar pang.

"Well, my father did that. Mama and he don't know that I know."

"It must be hard, knowing by yourself.

"I found out shortly before Papa left for the war. I was only nine. I woke up one night and they were downstairs, yellin' at each other. Mama was yellin' something like, 'That baby looks exactly like you except he is light brown! Then she said, 'How could you do that again George?'

Papa yelled back some things I couldn't understand. And then he hollered, 'Don't you worry, Eliza. I will sell them both, Agnes and the baby.'

"I remember well because Agnes was our nanny. She took care of Alexa, Max and me and we loved her. All of a sudden she was gone. I don't think Alexa and Max remember, because they never talk about it."

"They might though," said Louisa, "and somehow know it's a secret."

"I wonder what happened to Agnes," Robert continued. "Was her baby son sold away from her like Douglass's mother was sold away from him?"

"We'll never know, but I think there were many situations like that. "Those are some of the terrible aspects of slavery that those of us who were slave- holders have to struggle with, Robert.

"I hate this, Miz Louisa. It would be so much easier to be like Mama and Papa and never think about anything but tobacco and horses."

"Well Robert, I respect your thinking and questioning. It takes courage."

"Thank you Miz Louisa. May I borrow this geography book?"

When Robert left, Louisa sat in the library, remembering. Sidney's fathering Sally still hurt. And Louisa's growing awareness of the extent of this crime against enslaved women made her feel increasingly angry. When she looked back on her life she could hardly believe how blind she had been to the many injustices that slavery had made possible. How could she not have seen?

That evening at supper Louisa was quiet, thinking about what she had learned from Robert about his father. Sidney looked at her and said she looked like she was carrying the weight of the world on her shoulders.

"Why can't you be like Eliza? he said. "She never worries about anything. She just likes to have a good time." He began eating his soup.

"Do you think I should take up drinking whiskey and pinch a bit of snuff?"

"Of course not, that would be vulgar, and you are a lady. But it would be wonderful if you knew tobacco like she does. She knows the whole process well, from transplanting the seedlings to thinning, topping, and priming, even curing. She's actually a help to George." They spooned their soup.

"I'm glad to hear that Sidney." She paused. "There's something troubling I found out today. George had a child by his children's nanny. When Eliza found out, he sold both the nanny and the baby, perhaps separately. It was very upsetting to Robert, so please keep this between us." They stopped eating.

"Of course it's between us. That's just ancient history Louisa! Why even bring it up?"

"Robert said it sounded like that happened more than once."

"What business is that of ours?"

"It made me wonder if you had children with anyone besides May Belle. Did you?"

"How dare you ask me that!" Sidney shoved his chair back, stood up, and went to the sideboard, where he poured himself a whiskey. He took it into his study and slammed the door.

Louisa ate a little more soup and then went into the library. She tried to read but was too upset to concentrate. What was happening between her and Sidney?

Mary

Fall – Winter 1870 – 1871

Philadelphia was fascinating. Mary had never seen so many people at once, all living so close together. And people who were so different from one another.

"In Virginia there are just white folks and Negroes," Mary wrote her mother. "But here there are also the Irish, who look like us but speak English in such a funny way it is sometimes hard to understand them. Then there are the Chinese, whom you cannot understand at all, and Poles and Germans, who look just like us, but of course speak their own languages. Going to the market on Saturday is exciting, because not only do the hawkers look and sound exotic, they sell such unusual food and household goods. I particularly admire the baked goods, and spend some time before I settle on what to buy for tea."

Mary went on to tell about the school where she was teaching sixth grade.

"It's fun to teach children who already know the basics of reading, writing, and figuring. They can read a good story, we can talk about it, and they can write about it, all in one lesson. But I'm disappointed that we don't have enough books and materials. I thought we would leave such shortages behind when we left the South. After all, Philadelphia has had public schools since 1834. But not very many Negro children attended school until much later and the Negro schools are not supported like the white schools are."

"Our school is in a poor neighborhood of small two-story row houses. Between every few houses are alleyways filled with garbage and animal manure. You can imagine the stench, Mama. There are alleyways like that all over the city because there is no place to put the stuff."

"With fifty in the class, my pupils are a handful. We are used to Southern Negroes, who have been taught to show deference to all white folks, and lower their gaze in respect. Or fear, I'm sad to say. Some of my students are like that, but most of them are different. It's not that they are rude at all. They seem to have more confidence. They look you in the eye and are often willing to ask questions or try something new, which I really like. That's the result of generations of freedom for Negroes here, Priscilla says. Many of her pupils are the same way. She says she can tell right away which children are from families who were recently enslaved. She says it will take generations for the toll that slavery took to wear off."

"Living with Priscilla's family is quite interesting and very pleasant. Her mother and father are quiet and serene. They are Quakers, as you know, and quite devout. Before the war, theirs was one of many safe houses for the Underground Railroad in Philadelphia. They worked with other Quakers, free Negroes and other abolitionists for years. When I asked them about it, they were completely humble. Mrs. Atkins said they were 'only doing what they should and could'. Priscilla and I went to Meeting with them last Sunday. Everyone sat in silence for a long time. Finally a man stood and spoke of his concern about the violence against immigrants that had occurred in the city recently. Later Mrs. Atkins explained to me that white nativists are against the immigrants because they think they will take their jobs. And it gets worse, Mama. The immigrants are against the Negroes because they think they will take their jobs. Mr. Atkins says that industries in Philadelphia are growing so fast that they actually need all the workers they can get, white, Negro, and immigrant. He's the manager of a textile company, and he says the whole industry is hiring now.

Well Mama, I need to go to bed now. I am sending dearest love to you and Papa.

Your devoted daughter,

Mary"

Priscilla was already asleep when Mary put out the gas lamp and climbed into bed. She was cold and couldn't get warm, even though she had a wool blanket and a quilt over her. That was something she hadn't mentioned in her letter– the cold. Even though everyone said she would, she could not get used to it. And it was only November. Her October pay had gone to buy a woolen cloak and gloves. Next she planned to buy a warm hat and long underwear. She would ride on one of the amazing horse drawn streetcars to that astonishing Wanamaker's department store, like she had done with Priscilla last month. They had walked through the store wide-eyed, admiring the beautiful readymade clothes and stylishly dressed sales clerks. Thinking about it, Mary fell asleep.

On Sunday Priscilla's older brother Ben brought his fiancée Susan Edwards for dinner. Mr. and Mrs. Atkins were in high spirits, in their own calm way. Dinner was simple, chicken and dumplings, served by Mary Lou, a middle-aged Irish woman Mrs. Atkins introduced as her helper. Mrs. Atkins was pleased to have her family together and was doing her best to make Susan feel welcome. "How are your classes at the Medical College?" she asked.

"I like it. It is exciting. And it is difficult," said Susan.

"I didn't know women could go to medical school," said Mary.

"There are not many places they can," said Ben. "Susan goes to the Medical College of Pennsylvania here in the city."

Mary could tell from his face that he was proud of her.

Ben wanted to hear about Richmond. "Priscilla, how can it be possible that so many of the people who were in power there before the war are still in power?"

"Mary and I wondered about that too," said Priscilla. "We think that those who didn't lose their wealth in the war are able to use it to hold onto their power. So they have the political and business positions to make decisions favoring white folks, especially the old families, including the ones who lost their wealth."

"It's so clear when you look at how the city is being rebuilt," Mary said. "Housing, streets, churches, and schools for white people are proceeding well, but the needs of Negroes are ignored."

"I thought Reconstruction was supposed to prevent that," Susan said.

"The white men in power are resisting Reconstruction with all their might," said Priscilla.

"The Negroes are resourceful though, and are building their own churches and forming benevolent societies to help those in need," Mary added. "And of course going to the Freedmen's schools."

After dinner Mary and Priscilla went for a walk along the Schuylkill River with Susan and Ben. Ben and Priscilla were clearly glad to see each other again. Priscilla asked about his newly established law practice and he wanted to hear all about her teaching in Richmond. He asked Mary how teaching in Philadelphia compared to teaching in Richmond. Susan was also curious about that. Mary wanted to hear more about Medical school, so there was a lot to talk about.

The next Sunday Ben and Susan came for dinner again. This time they brought Ben's law partner, Peter Stewart. Peter was tall and gangly, in contrast to Ben's compact, muscular stature. They were obviously good friends, in addition to being law partners. Priscilla had told her that they had gone together from grammar school all the way through school, to law school at the University of Pennsylvania. In between Peter had served in the Union Army during the last two years of the war and Ben, as a Quaker, had served in a Union hospital. Now they rented an office for their law practice and lived in the rooms above. They were starting off with contract law to pay the bills, but both were eager to get involved in defending the equal civil and legal rights guaranteed by the Fourteenth Amendment. Susan and Ben were waiting to marry as soon as he could afford to rent a row house.

Conversation was lively, centering on the Fifteenth Amendment, which had recently passed and held that no one could be denied the right to vote "on account of race, color, or previous condition of servitude." Priscilla and Susan were opposed to the amendment because it still did not give women the right to vote. "How much longer will we wait?" asked Susan.

Mary had been reading articles by Elizabeth Cady Stanton and Susan B Anthony and supported their work for women's suffrage. "Well, I wish the Fifteenth Amendment had included women too, but I think it was important to pass it anyway,' she said. "Negroes can't be left without the power of the vote any longer. Voting will mean they can put people in office who will work for Negroes. Women will get the vote anyway. It can't be much longer."

"I think you are right, Mary," said Mrs. Atkins. "Right now the most pressing need is for Negroes to vote."

"I think we need more women like you four–smart women who inform themselves and think," said Mr. Atkins. Peter and Ben nodded and smiled.

Later that afternoon Priscilla and Mary were sitting at a window in the front room to catch the weak afternoon sunlight so they could do their mending. "I don't understand how you can be complacent about women not having the vote, Mary. I've been reading suffragist literature all my life and I am tired of waiting."

"To tell the truth, Priscilla, I never heard of the suffragists until a few years ago, when I found out that Frederick Douglass was an advocate of women voting. It's not that I don't care about women voting. It's that what I've grown up with is the deplorable conditions for the Negroes. Changing that is what feels most pressing to me right now."

"I guess that's understandable. We have many Negroes here too, but at least some of them have been free and prospering for a long time."

"Priscilla, tell me about Peter."

"What do you want to know? He's like a brother to me, since I've known him so long."

"Do you like him?"

"Of course. How could I not?"

"I mean, do you like him like a sweetheart?"

"No, of course not. I told you, he's like another brother. Why do you ask? Are you smitten by him?"

"No, I don't know him well enough for that. But I do find him interesting."

"Well, I find that interesting."

The next Sunday Peter came for dinner with Ben and Susan again.

"I'm so glad you came, Peter," said Mrs Atkins. "We're having your favorite today."

"Beef and vegetable stew?" Peter asked hopefully.

"Be sure to leave some for me," Mr. Atkins teased.

As soon as they were all at the table, Ben brought up an issue he and Susan had been discussing. "Once Susan is practicing medicine, she will need her own office," Ben said.

"But I won't be able to own it because married women can't own property," continued Susan. "Ben will have to own my office, even though I will pay for it."

"It's absurd," Peter said.

"It's demeaning," said Susan.

"Like not lettin' married women teach," said Mary.

"I understand these dilemmas," said Mrs. Atkins. "I've been reading the Susan B Anthony piece you brought me Peter, and I agree that women should have equal rights. Tom thinks so too." Mr Atkins nodded. "But I'm old fashioned enough to think that women can have equal rights and still be best as wives and mothers."

"If that is what they want," Priscilla said softly.

Mr. Atkins changed the subject.

After dinner, when Susan and Ben were leaving, Peter lingered on the porch to speak with Mary.

"Would you give me the pleasure of your company for a walk along the Schuylkill next Saturday afternoon?"

"I'd like that very much, Peter."

"I like that about you Mary. You say what you mean straight away."

"I don't know how else to be."

"That's even better."

When Mary came back inside she heard Priscilla in conversation with her mother in the study.

"But what if I don't want to get married Mama?", she heard Priscilla say in a shrill voice.

Mary couldn't understand Mrs. Atkins' murmured reply.

"I don't want children, Mama." Priscilla's voice was firm.

Again an incomprehensible murmur.

Priscilla spoke again, with passion. "Mama, what I want is to teach for so many years that I'll become very good at it. I want to teach Negro children so they can learn and grow and be able to do whatever they aspire to. Someday I might even want to be the principal of a school, but I don't know about that yet. Can you understand me Mama?"

Feeling guilty about eavesdropping, Mary walked quietly back to the porch, as Mrs. Atkins' murmured reply went on. On the way, she pulled her cloak from its hook and shivered as she wrapped it around herself.

It was odd that she and Priscilla had not talked about marriage and children, she thought. Mainly they talked about their pupils, ideas for teaching them, and what worked and didn't work with them. They also talked about their families and Reconstruction. As for marriage and children, Mary had always thought she would marry and have children someday, but she was not in any rush. Recently, because of reading Stanton and Anthony, she had started feeling angry about the prohibition against married teachers.

The next day, Priscilla seemed even more enthusiastic than usual as they walked to school. "You're on fire this morning," Mary remarked.

"I guess I am. I had a conversation with Mama yesterday that made it absolutely clear that teaching is the most important thing in my life."

"I overheard some of that conversation," Mary admitted.

Priscilla looked at her with a puzzled expression.

"I'm sorry," Mary said.

"I appreciate your telling me. I guess I was talking pretty loud."

On Saturday morning Mary took the streetcar to Wanamakers. She was thrilled to be on such an outing by herself, and tried not to look around so eagerly that she would stand out. She disembarked at the stop she remembered from her trip with Priscilla, and then didn't know which way to go. So she followed some women who looked as though they knew where they were going, and ended up at Wanamakers. She bought the long underwear she wanted, and then realized she would have to wait for the hat, since it was too expensive. She spent a short while walking around admiring the stylish dresses and then left. Arriving home just before dinner, she donned her new purchase. Sitting at the table, she began to itch. Legs, arms, stomach, back. She tried to ignore it, but finally had to ask to be excused. She ran upstairs and tore off her new underwear, scratching herself vigorously. Priscilla came in and immediately understood the situation. "It's best not to wear long underwear inside," she said. "And always wash it first."

Mary was still scratching. "I'm goin' for a walk with Peter," she said. "And it's cold."

"Here, wear these this afternoon." Priscilla said, handing her some long underwear. "They're old and soft."

"Thank you Priscilla. You are always so kind."

Mary enjoyed her walk with Peter that afternoon. It was sunny and cold, but Priscilla's long underwear kept her warm. They talked easily about his law practice and her teaching. Peter was curious about her perceptions as a Southerner. "We hear so much about the animosity Southerners feel for Negroes, but you deliberately choose to teach them."

"Yes, because they were deprived of learning for two hundred fifty years, as you know, especially in the South. Now that they are free, they finally have a right to education that will prepare them to live and work as they want to. And it's our responsibility to see that they get it."

"I see that, Mary. But it sounds like a lot of people don't agree. I was just reading about recent attacks on Negroes in Virginia by the Ku Klux Klan. Lynching, burning houses. Why do they hate them so much?"

"I'm not an expert on that, Peter, but I have some ideas. Poor white folks have always considered themselves better than Negroes. If Negroes get educated and rise in society, they might be better off than poor whites."

"So with them, it's about pride and economic competition."

"For them, I think so. But the hatred is different for the former slaveholders and their families. People who held slaves know how terribly they treated them. They may fear retribution now that they are free."

"And they've heard of rebellions like Nat Turner's."

Mary nodded. "I think another reason former slave holders hate Negroes is that they feel guilty. They know they not only deprived them of their freedom, but they forced them into hard labor, forced women to bear their children, whipped them, and sold children away from their families. And worse."

"I've heard."

"Former slave holders usually don't admit their guilt. And they don't feel as guilty if Negroes stay in their "places", as sharecroppers and servants, particularly if they act cheerful. My father feels like that, so does my sister. They want life to be like it was before the war. For the Southern planters, it was a life of ease and pleasure, you know."

"Mary, I wish you would write about this in one of the gazettes. Most people around here have no idea that the whole issue is still so complicated."

"Well, it certainly isn't simple. I wish I could understand more.

When they arrived back at the house, Mrs. Atkins invited Peter for dinner the next day. After he had left, she asked Mary if he had told her about his family. " No," said Mary.

"Well, I had better not then," Mrs. Atkins said. "Just prepare yourself dear. It's sad."

"Mine is too," said Mary, realizing she was saying that for the first time.

Entering her room, she saw a letter on her bed that must have come that day in the mail. It was from Ellen.

Dearest Mary,

I wish I had good news to share. Well, the children are doing alright in school, which is one good thing. When we sit at table, Sam tries to engage them in cheerful conversation. But Mary, I fear I drag them all down into despondency with me. Yesterday afternoon I was worse than ever. I heard the boys in the kitchen talking with Ada. She said her husband fought in the war. Wally asked which side and she said the Union. That made me so furious, I couldn't stop myself. He fought against Sam and our own father and brother. Maybe even killed our brother! Who knows? Anyway, I ran in there, grabbed the butter paddle and smacked Ada. The boys looked horrified and Ada yelled "I quit!" and ran home. The boys cried and ran to tell Laura. They all stayed upstairs until Sam came home. I told him what happened. He sighed and put his arms around me. Then he went upstairs to comfort the children. They wouldn't come near or look at me all evening.

This morning it was the same, mainly silence except when Laura and Sam tried to make conversation.

How is it, when this is what I have always wanted, a kind husband and good children, that I spoil it? I hate this house, when I should be grateful for it. I hate the bare floor, the wood stove and the ugly oak furniture. I hate having to entertain Olivia in this shabby little house. No matter how much I clean the silver and Emily chatters like a magpie, it's an embarrassment. I hate seeing all the Negroes, walking around Lynchburg, free. I hate Lynchburg, with all these hills. I miss Oak Hill and the life we had there before the war. Papa raised us to be ladies and here I am doing housework and you're teaching Negroes. Nobody is supposed to say it any more, but life was much better when we had slavery. I know you do not agree, but I would wager a lot of people do. Sam says we have to change with the times. But we don't talk about that much because I get upset. I'm glad the children have him. He's much better at adapting than I am.

Sometimes I walk down to the James River to get away and just sit. The other day I watched some boys up on the trestle rail bridge that crosses the river. It is so peaceful there.

Stay well dear Sister,
Your loving sister Ellen

Mary read Ellen's troubling letter again. She thought back about how much of Ellen's life had been lost to melancholy. It seemed like an illness she had struggled with off and on for most of her life. And now it seemed worse than ever. Mary's heart ached for Wally, Laura, and Henry. And for Sam, who tried so hard to help. And for Ellen, who suffered.

Mary slept fitfully that night. The next morning she asked to go to the Quaker meeting with Priscilla's parents, thinking it might bring her some peace. But she worried about Ellen for most of the meeting. Walking home, she told Mrs. Atkins about Ellen.

Mrs. Atkins said, "You know, Ben's Susan might have read about melancholia in her books and could tell you what she knows. But in any case, I know it's very real and very hard. We've all known someone who suffers like your sister."

"But what can help it?" Mary asked.

"Some people take laudanum, but its main effect is to make them woozy."

"I know it doesn't work. Neither does whiskey. I think I will go down to Lynchburg during winter break. I know I can't solve the problem," but maybe being with the children will help."

"I expect that will be a great comfort to your sister, dear."

Peter, Ben and Susan arrived for Sunday dinner with pink cheeks and smelling like the cold outside. Conversation was lively, as usual. This Sunday Ben was telling of an article he read about the Fourteenth Amendment, that granted citizenship to Negroes and others born in the United States. It also granted equal protection under law. But the writer of the article was questioning whether a Negro would actually be able to get a fair trial, since Negroes were usually not allowed to testify in court, especially in the South. " Is the South ready to allow that? What do you think, Mary?" Ben asked.

"I don't know much about the judicial system, but I doubt it," Mary said. "None of the work of Reconstruction is at all complete. Lots of folks still just want to put things back like they were. I think the South needs a great deal more Federal support and pressure so that reforms can happen."

"Then President Grant is going the right way. Who wants more stew?" asked Mrs. Atkins, and the discussion went on.

After dinner Peter and Mary went for a walk. But first she went upstairs and put on her freshly washed long underwear.

"I like the way you express yourself so clearly on these issues, Mary", Peter said when she came down.

"Well, I like that you like it, Peter."

"Ben and I are learning everything we can about equal rights cases and the law. That's the kind of law we want to focus on."

"I know and I'm glad, Peter! Negroes need and deserve good lawyers, who will bring their cases to court and get them justice."

"It feels very important to Ben and me. Contracts and wills just pay the rent." He took her hand as they walked. "I'm looking forward to having more time with you during your winter break."

Mary looked up at him. "Well, actually, I'm goin' to Lynchburg to see my sister and her family. She's not doin' well and I'm worried."

Peter asked to know more, so Mary told him all about Ellen. He listened attentively, picking up her sadness. "What about the rest of your family?" he asked. She told him about Louisa and Sidney, and then about May Belle and Sally. Last she told him about John, killed in the war. He nodded slowly and looked at her sympathetically. "It sure isn't easy."

"Tell me about your family, Peter."

"I had a dear family, but they are gone."

"Gone?"

"They died. My father, my brother Abel and I all fought at Gettysburg. They were both killed. My mother was an angel. She volunteered as a nurse in the hospital during the war, and almost at the end, she caught tuberculosis. My sister Ann must have caught it from her, because they sickened and died within days of each other."

"Oh Peter," Mary murmured, and squeezed his hand.

"When the war ended I came home to an empty house that had been stripped nearly bare. There was so much poverty then and many had nothing. If it had not been for Ben and Mr. and Mrs. Atkins, I would have completely despaired. I wanted to die. But Ben kept coming around. He wanted us to study law, but I couldn't see the point in it, or anything really. Eventually he talked me into it. Mrs. Atkins kept inviting me for meals and Mr. Atkins helped me sell the house. Then they said it only made sense for me to live with them, since Ben was still at home and we were both studying law. I believe they saved my life. Whenever I got overcome with grief about my family, I had a home and people who cared. And think about it Mary, they are Quakers and don't believe in war. All three men in my family fought in the war. They were astonishingly kind to accept me into their family."

"I'm so glad they did Peter. And I'm so very sorry you lost your family." She put her arms around his waist and they embraced.

On the first day of winter break, Mary took the train to Lynchburg. When she arrived she looked around the station for the familiar faces of Sam and the children. After a while she sat down on a bench and waited, thinking there must have been some confusion about her arrival time. Her tapestry bags were heavier than usual, since she had brought each of the children and Sam a book for Christmas, as well as her warm clothes. When the next train arrived she was glad to see Sam's neighbor, Mr. Gooch, who offered her a ride when his groom came with his buggy. She climbed out in front of Sam's house. When she knocked at the door, no one answered at first. Then Laura opened the door, her face streaked with tears. "Aunt Mary," she sobbed, and fell into Mary's arms. Then Laura led her into the parlor. There was Ellen, lying on the sofa, dead. Mary cried out and held Laura. One side of Ellen's head was smashed and bloody, facing away from them, resting on a blood soaked pillow. The other side of her face was pale and unblemished. Sam, Wally, and Henry were kneeling beside the sofa, holding on to her arms and hands. Tears ran down their faces. The boys rushed to embrace Mary. She held them and they all cried. Sam looked up at Mary in anguish and said, "she jumped from the trestle bridge." Mary couldn't speak. With tears flowing, she nodded and knelt beside Sam and took Ellen's too cool hand. She remembered Ellen showing her the place she found so peaceful and prayed that she was finally at peace now. The children knelt beside Ellen again. After some minutes passed, Sam stood up, mopped his tears, and said he needed to go make arrangements.

"For us?" asked Wally in alarm.

"No, for your mother, to have a service and be buried. What do you mean, arrangements for you?"

"Well, can we still stay here with you, Mr. Sam?"

"Of course," said Sam. "Do you want to?"

"Yes," said Wally, and Henry looked up and nodded.

"I want to stay too, Mr. Sam, because you are so kind," said Laura.

"You are my family," Sam said.

Laura began to cry again. "Poor Mama," she sobbed.

"We will miss her," said Sam, his voice breaking.

He left the house quickly.

Mary and the children went into the kitchen. Mary built up the fire in the stove and put on the pot of bean soup that Ellen had made that morning. Wally stood watching. "Aunt Mary, two Negro boys saw Mama up on the bridge. When they saw her climb over the railing, they yelled at her to stop. But she didn't, so they ran and got their father. Together they went back and got Mama and brought her here."

"She was already dead, Aunt Mary," said Henry, and his tears kept coming.

"She must have hit her head and died right away," sobbed Laura. "Why would she do that? Why would she leave us and jump, Aunt Mary?"

"I don't have the answers," Mary said, and put her arms around the children. "I do know that she loved you very much. She was unhappy, but not about you all."

Sidney
December 1870

Sidney and Louisa found out about Ellen's death the next evening, when George Willis pounded on the front door. He had been in Lynchburg doing business with one of the large tobacco companies. While he was in town, he went to pick up a particular fabric that his wife knew Sam's store carried. He found a sign on the door: "Closed due to a death in the family." From a neighboring storekeeper, he found out what had happened with Ellen, and rode down to Oak Hill as fast as he could to tell them. Sidney and Louisa stood in the doorway listening, stunned, horrified. When George left, their tears came and they held each other for a long time. "Why, Why?" Sidney repeated.

Finally they sat on the hall sofa and Louisa put her head in her hands. It was silent, except for their sudden in-breaths and sniffling.

"I was afraid of this, you know," she said finally.

"I knew you worried about her, but I never thought it was this bad. What was wrong with her, Louisa?"

Louisa shook her head.

"We need to go now, before they bury her. I want to see her."

"It's too late to leave now. It's dark." He went to the dining room and poured himself a whiskey.

"I'll go upstairs and pack a few things. We can leave at first light and get the early train from Danville."

After a smokey train ride that seemed endless, Sidney and Louisa arrived in Lynchburg, in time for Ellen's funeral and burial.

They were disheveled and distraught, but relieved to be there. Having spoken with his neighboring storekeeper, Sam knew that they had been contacted. So he had scheduled the service as late as possible. Louisa and Sidney went straight to the Baptist church that Ellen had attended. The casket was in front of the altar, closed. Sidney opened it slowly. Ellen's head was turned so that the injured part was hidden. The visible part of her face looked still and unbearably pale. "Oh, my beautiful Ellen," Sidney choked.

Louisa knelt beside the casket and held Ellen's hands. "You just couldn't bear your sadness any longer," she sobbed. Sensing the presence of someone, she looked around and saw the minister standing behind her. "We need to close the casket now," he said coolly.

"One moment, Reverend," Sidney said. "This is my child." He leaned over and kissed Ellen's cheek. Louisa kissed her too. Then, weeping, she slowly closed the casket. The minister said nothing. They left the church quickly and walked to Sam's. They let themselves in quietly.

Sam was sitting in the parlor, dressed for the funeral. The children were upstairs, getting ready with Mary. Sam looked up at Louisa and Sidney. His eyes were red and he looked exhausted. "This seems like a terrible dream," he said. He stood up to shake hands and they both embraced him.

The Baptist church was nearly empty, and very cold inside. Sam's brother Mathew greeted them at the door. He had come with his wife Emily and their children Emmy and Micajah. Sam's brother-in-law Adam was there with Susanna and Amanda. But Olivia was not there. Their neighbors the Gooches were sitting alone in the middle of the church. Upstairs in the balcony Sidney saw Ada and her children. The minister conducted the service in an impersonal and perfunctory manner, that tacitly conveyed his disapproval of the way in which Ellen had died. Sam stood between Wally and Henry, arms around their shoulders. Mary stood between Laura and Louisa, holding their hands, and Sidney put his arm around Louisa. When the service ended, Sam,

Mathew, Adam and Sidney carried the casket to the graveyard. After the final prayers, as they lowered the casket into the earth, Sidney crumpled to the ground. "She was the only one who truly understood me," he thought. As they left, he noticed that Adam handed the minister an envelope. "The bastard must have expected a contribution to the church for allowing Ellen to be buried in hallowed ground. Good of Adam to take care of it," Sidney thought.

Emily and Mathew invited the family back to their house, which was a comfort. The men talked tobacco and spiked their tea with rum. While the women and children clustered around the refreshments, Sidney overheard Emily telling Mary that Olivia didn't come to the funeral because she did not want to condone taking one's own life.

"As if we're condoning it," said Emily. "How about comforting Sam and the children? How about comforting you and your parents?"

"We so appreciate your kindness, Emily," said Mary.

"I wish I could have done more to help her, Mary."

"I feel the same way."

"Emmy told me why Aunt Olivia didn't come to Mama's funeral," announced Laura when they got home.

"What does Aunt Olivia know about Mama anyway?" Wally asked. "Nothin'!" yelled Sidney. "Just stop talkin' about it, children."

Looking shocked, they went upstairs. Mary followed them.

"Sidney, Ellen is their mama. They have to talk about it." Louisa said quietly.

"Why does everybody have to know our business and have opinions about it? That minister nearly choked over sayin' the prayers for Ellen."

"I noticed," Louisa replied.

"Some people are very kind though," said Mary coming down the stairs.

"Look at the nice pot of chicken stew the Gooches next door brought. It's on the stove. And you know about Adam making a generous contribution to that dreadful minister, so that he would allow Ellen to be buried in his church yard."

That night Sidney and Louisa made a pallet and slept on the floor in the parlor. Neither one could sleep much. When Louisa finally did fall asleep, she woke Sidney up, calling out, "No! Stop!" in her dream. In the morning, they sadly bid goodbye to Sam, Mary and the children. They rode the train down to Danville, heavy with grief.

The house seemed empty when they returned, even though it had been some time since Ellen and the children had been there. They went into the dining room and found the simple supper Lucy had left for them. Louisa cut some bread, cheese and apples and they sat down at the table.

"Poor Sam," Sidney said. "He really had some terrible luck when he married Ellen."

"I don't think he looks at it that way, Sidney. Last night he told me how glad he was to have had her in his life."

"But what is he goin' to do with three children?"

"He said the children are a treasure he never thought he'd have."

"You mean he honestly doesn't feel burdened by them, now that Ellen is gone?"

'No, they are his comfort."

"I'm glad he feels that way. I don't think I would. Isn't he angry at Ellen for what she did?"

"I don't know. He may have some anger too."

"Well I would be angry. I am angry! How could she do that to us? To the children? To Sam?"

"I don't think she was doin' anything to any of us. She just couldn't stand being alive any more."

"So you're not angry with Ellen? Sidney asked.

"Maybe a little. But mainly I feel overwhelmingly sad. And I keep asking myself, what I could have done to help her. If only I could have done something."

"Don't blame yourself, Louisa." He lit his pipe, then stood and walked to the sideboard to pour himself a whiskey. "Let's not dwell on this any more now. It will be good to be back in our own bed after that pallet last night."

"Sidney, do you understand that when Mary goes back to Philadelphia at the end of her winter break next week, I'll need to go up to Lynchburg for a while?"

"How long?"

"It will depend on how the children are doin'. Wally's eleven, Henry's ten, and Laura's nine now. That's awfully young to cope with something like this. I've been thinkin' Sidney, how it could help the whole situation if we could pay for them to have some more help in the household. May I suggest that to Sam?"

"He's proud. I don't know that he would accept help."

"I hope he would because it would help the children. Maybe it would mean gettin' Ada's oldest girl to help out. I don't know without talking to Sam, but I hope I can help him figure out what they need and how to get it."

"Just help Sam figure it out and come back to me. And if he will accept some financial assistance, of course I can provide it."

"Thank you Sidney."

"Will you come back?"

"Yes dear, I'll come back."

He kissed her gently. Later in bed, he began to caress her, but in a moment they both fell asleep in each other's arms, spent.

Louisa
1871

A few days before she left for Lynchburg, Louisa and Sidney rode over to the Willises. Sidney thanked George for riding down to tell them about Ellen's death right away. Louisa told them about Ellen's funeral and they expressed heartfelt condolences. Then Louisa explained that she was going to help out with her grandchildren for a few weeks, and had brought books and writing assignments for Robert, Max and Alexa. "How did you ever think of that at such a hard time?" Eliza marveled. They visited briefly and as they were leaving Robert appeared. "I'm very sorry to hear about your daughter., Miz Louisa and Mr. Sidney. Thank you for coming. We appreciate your thinking of us."

Louisa took the train from Danville to Lynchburg on the day before Mary was to leave for Philadelphia. When she walked into the house, she was surprised to see a Christmas tree in the parlor. Mary smiled and embraced her mother warmly. "It helped to have something good to focus on sometimes, instead of Ellen's death. What do you think Mama?"

"It's beautiful dear. We haven't had a Christmas tree since before the war. I'd forgotten how much fun they can be."

"We were making little paper decorations for it for a week. And now they don't want to take it down, even though Christmas is over."

"Well, I'm glad I got to see it."

Louisa sat down on the sofa and patted the space beside her. "Please tell me everything I need to know before Sam and the children come home."

Mary described the days since Louisa had been there–the crying, the questions, the anger, the silence, the emptiness– and then always the questions. "Why did she do it? Did we do something wrong? Could we have stopped her? Why? Why?"

Mary said she listened to the children's questions and tried to reassure them that it was in no way their fault. The hardest question was "How could she leave us?"

Mary said it broke her heart when they asked that, because she couldn't understand it either. Neither could Sam.

Mary was full of admiration for Sam. Even though he was in pain himself, he listened to Laura, Henry, and Wally, explained what he could, and held them often. He helped with the Christmas tree, popped corn for the garlands, and played games with them. In the evenings he was very tired and let his sadness show more. Ellen's choice to take her own life was deeply painful. The only thing that made it bearable was the children.

Louisa was comforted to hear again how Sam felt about the children. "It does my heart good to hear that Mary. But with you in Philadelphia and me back at Oak Hill in a few weeks, how is Sam going to manage the store, the children, and the house?"

"I don't know, Mama. He already started bringin' in Ada for another day a while ago, because Ellen was overwhelmed. But he told me three days is all he can afford."

"Well I asked Sidney if we could contribute toward Sam's expenses, to make it easier for a while, and he said yes."

"I'm glad to hear that Mama. You know Ada has a daughter who is sixteen and is a good worker. Maybe she could help out."

"Why isn't she in school?" asked Louisa.

"She thinks she is too old, according to Ada," Mary said. "If you meet her, maybe you can change her mind, Mama."

When the children arrived home, they were happy to see their Grandmama, and show her the decorations they had made for the Christmas tree. "Aunt Emily made us help take their tree down today," said Henry. "I told them that Aunt Mary said we could keep ours up until Mr. Sam says it's time to take it down."

"Emmy and Micajah were jealous," said Laura. "Aunt Mary, I wish you didn't have to go back to Philadelphia."

"It would be fun if you and Grandmama both would stay here," said Wally.

Louisa and Mary looked at each other and laughed. "That would be fun," said Mary. "But I have fifty sixth graders waiting for me in Philadelphia."

While Mary and Louisa prepared supper, Mary told her about Peter Stewart. As she talked about him, Mary felt how eager she was to see him again. Louisa saw the happiness on Mary's face as she spoke and was glad. They were still talking about Peter when Sam arrived home. When they sat down at the table with Ellen's empty place at the foot, they all felt her loss anew. "How would it be if I sat in Mama's place for tonight?" Louisa asked, and moved to it. "That way I can serve the soup more easily."

After supper Laura requested that Mary read to them for an extra long time, since she was leaving in the morning.

"You know y'all read as well as I do now, but I do like reading to you," Mary said.

"And I understand why we like your reading," said Sam. "You read with such expression, you could go on stage."

"I may become an actress when I grow up," Laura announced.

Wally and Henry grimaced at each other until Louisa's glare penetrated. Everyone settled down and Mary launched into The Three Musketeers.

In the morning Louisa and the children walked to the train station with Mary and bid her goodbye. The next day school would be in session in both Lynchburg and Philadelphia. Returning to their house, the children fell silent. Louisa was relieved to find Ada there, preparing to do a large laundry. With the cauldron heating on the kitchen stove, she came to greet them. "I sure am sorry "bout Miz Ellen, Miz Louisa. I know you loved yo' mama, children. Like I tol' you before, she with God now."

"Thank you Ada," said Louisa. "It's a nice day," she said to the children. "So y'all can go outside, unless you want to help me pull the sheets off all the beds." Henry and Laura decided to help and then joined Wally outside. Louisa invited them all to go to market, but only Laura wanted to go. She was quiet on the way there, but on the walk back home she asked, "Grandmama, where do you think Mama is now? Is she with God, like Ada says?"

"Being with God seems peaceful. I like to imagine your mama completely at peace, so that feels right."

"It feels right to me too," said Laura.

That evening, while they were still at the supper table, Sam said to the children, "I know you heard that Aunt Olivia didn't come to Mama's funeral because she disapproved of the way she died. Some of the children at school might have heard their parents sayin' critical things about your Mama's death. They may repeat them to you. That will feel awful. I want you to try as hard as you can to ignore them and walk away. Do you think you can do that?" Sam asked each in turn.

Their eyes filled up and they nodded, "Yes, Sir."

Louisa suggested they have an extra long reading from the Three Musketeers, since it was the last day of winter break. "You're almost as good a reader as Aunt Mary," said Wally.

When the children were in bed Louisa and Sam sat in the parlor, talking about his store. "But what about you, Sam? How are you holding up?" Louisa asked him.

"The same way I see you doin' it, Louisa. Keeping goin'. Doing what needs to be done, paying attention to the people I love."

She looked at him for a minute and then nodded.

"Well now, I have something of a practical nature to bring up," she said. She told Sam that with Ellen gone, she thought he was going to need more help with the housework and children. She and Sidney would like to help with these additional expenses. "It would please us very much to be able to help." she ended.

"Your offer is extremely kind and I appreciate it, Louisa. But I really think we can manage. My business is picking up, as I said, and I have some new woolen fabrics coming down from Rhode Island that should be a success."

"I'm glad about your business, Sam, and we have nothing but respect for you." She paused and looked at him. "You have become the children's father, a good one. As their grandparents, if we could see that life is a little easier for you all, that would be a comfort to us."

Sam looked down, embarrassed.

"How about this," said Louisa. "I understand Ada has a sixteen year old daughter. How would you feel about her coming in the afternoons if she will, when the children come home after school and Ada usually goes home?"

"Well, I have been concerned about the time after school. Since the children are getting older, they don't need constant lookin' after, but they need someone who knows what they are doing. Emily offered to help out, but I don't want to ask her for every day."

"Then that's where we can help, Sam. Please let us do that."

"All I can say is thank you, Louisa, and thanks to Sidney."

"And now I won't worry when I go back home."

The next day Louisa asked Ada about her daughter Celia coming to be with the children in the afternoons after school. Ada smiled. "Celia good with children. She been takin' care of mine since she was six."

"How many children do you have, Ada?"

"Six that are alive. They eight, nine, ten, twelve, sixteen and seventeen. All in school except Celia and Harold. They workin'. Celia say she too old to be startin' school. They can all read and write except her. Ain't that somethin'!"

" I'm glad they're all doin' well, Ada. Please talk to Celia and see if she can help us out. Sam says she's a mighty good girl."

"I'll talk to Celia tonight. She workin' for some right mean folks now. She won't be sorry to give them notice."

At Sam's request, Louisa began the sad task of going through Ellen's things. In the back of Ellen's wardrobe, she was surprised to find one of her ball gowns, a shimmery pink silk with a very full skirt and a tight bodice. It still had the faint scent of sweat and the perfume she wore then, which flooded Louisa with memories of Ellen, beautiful belle of the ball, dancing and flirting with her partners. She folded it carefully and put it aside. She asked Ada if she knew folks who might want the rest of Ellen's clothes. Ada said she did and would take them. Louisa decided to save Ellen's jewelry for Laura, except for some gold rings Walter had given her. Those she would save for the boys to give their wives some day. Ellen's few books, her sewing basket, and all the silver and china from her wedding with Walter would stay right here, where they were using them. She thought how pleased Ellen had been when Walter's aunt and uncle had sent a dozen sterling silver water goblets as a wedding gift, and how angry she had been when two of them had soon disappeared. She had accused her laundress and sent her back to field work. She became obsessed with counting the silver after that, even after she moved to Lynchburg. She would walk around from the kitchen to the dining room to the parlor with eleven forks in her hand, looking for the twelfth, muttering that somebody must have stolen it. Louisa sighed. Sam used to joke that the formal silver tea service and serving pieces sitting on the battered oak sideboard in their dining room made it look like they had robbed a fancy hotel. Louisa smiled sadly as she remembered.

When the children burst in the door after school, it was clear that Laura had been crying. "Grandmama, Jane Turnbull said Mama is burnin' in Hell."

Henry broke in, "Jerry Hamel said the same thing to me! So I did what Mr. Sam said and ignored him. When I walked away he threw a stone at me."

"So then I punched him," said Wally.

Laura's chest was still heaving. Louisa put her arms around her. Laura looked up at her and said, " Jane says that the Bible says people who take their own lives go to Hell and if the Bible says so that makes it true."

"Well I'll tell y'all something," said Louisa. "I don't believe in Hell. I don't believe that the same God that made you precious children could possibly make a Hell. Or punish people who are too sad to live. I just don't believe that. So if someone tells you that tomorrow, you can pretend you don't hear, or tell them it is none of their business."

Louisa felt a lot better after she got that off her chest. And the children seemed to feel better too. In the ensuing days the children were still the target of some mean comments, but less and less often.

Meanwhile, Louisa met Celia and hired her to come every afternoon after school. Celia was warm and immediately comfortable with the children. One of the first things she did was to make butter cookies with them. When Wally told her that boys probably shouldn't bake, Celia dismissed that as nonsense. "I been bakin' with my brothers all their lives," she said. When the children went out to play, she told Louisa she needed some housework to do. She said she wasn't used to doing nothing. "Mama taught me to make myself useful as well as ornamental", she said. Louisa laughed and suggested she could work on keeping the kitchen cabinets and walls clean, since they were always getting spattered. Or she could do some dusting or sweeping. She could do these jobs any time while keeping an eye on the children.

Occasionally Ada was still there when Celia came. One afternoon Ada was showing Louisa more about how the wood stove worked, when Celia arrived. Then both of them started giving her advice on how to cook different foods on it. Ada explained the best way to cook collards and then, with a twinkle, Celia said she knew an even better way. The situation took Louisa back ten years, to when May Belle and Sally were teaching her, Ellen, and Mary to cook. She was reminded of the same kind of easy joking between mother and daughter as they worked together. Her eyes filled, remembering Ellen, remembering May Belle, both dead now. Ada noticed and said as she nodded her head, " You be grieving'. It'll be a while, Miz Louisa." Louisa wiped her eyes and said, "I spose so."

The days passed with the children going to school, Sam going to work, and Louisa managing the household. Having Ada three days a week until after midday dinner, and Celia every day after school was a very big help. As Louisa got to know Celia, she observed how bright and capable she was. One day she asked her why she didn't go to school.

"I work," Celia answered quickly.

"But you can go to school if you want and still work here for Mr. Sam. You are smart, Celia."

"Thank you for sayin' that Miz Louisa. But I'm too old to go to school. All the children my age have already learned to read and write. I was takin' care of my brothers and sisters when my friends was learnin'. I'm glad I could care for 'em. But now I would have to be in a class with little children."

"I understand better now," said Louisa. "I appreciate your telling me. Would you like to learn to read and write and figure?"

"Yes Ma'am. I surely would."

"I can teach you. I taught my own children and grandchildren."

"Yes Ma'am."

"Can you come an hour earlier every afternoon, so that we have that time before the children get home?"

" I have to ask my Mama. Since all my sisters and brothers have been in school, I been takin' in laundry. Maybe I can let another of those accounts go, but I have to ask Mama."

"See what she says," said Louisa, thinking about Ada raising six children on her earnings. She knew that Ada worked three days from six to six when she was not at Sam's, but Celia's contribution was important.

The next day was one that Ada came. She was smiling. "Celia tol' me you offered to teach her, Miz Louisa. The answer is yes. I just wanna say thank ya." Ada went on to tell Louisa that she had been worrying about Celia not learning how to read or write. She felt bad that she hadn't made her go to school years ago when the Freedmen's school opened, but had needed her to take care of the little ones while she was working. When her husband died at the end of the war, she had depended on Celia even more.

"I can understand that Ada. And I'm very glad I'll be able to teach Celia. She's a fine girl, very smart and resourceful. Would you like to learn with her?"

"Oh, no Ma'am. I don't need learnin' to cook and do housework. It's my children that need to know. Their lives are gonna be different. I grew up, held on a plantation down in Halifax County. My husband too. I jus' wish he could see our children now. He would be proud."

"Indeed he would," said Louisa, struck by what an enormous change Ada had experienced in her lifetime.

Louisa had had enough experience teaching basic skills to create the materials she needed to start with Celia. Then she wrote to Mary with a request to send more materials as soon as she could. In her first session with Celia, she found out that she already knew the alphabet and many of the letter sounds. Celia laughed and said that she had heard her brothers and sisters sing the alphabet song so many times that she couldn't help but pick it up. And she listened to them sounding out words all the time. She had also had to learn to count to keep track of napkins and shirts in her laundry orders.

She was eager to learn and made rapid progress. Louisa enjoyed teaching her and was always sorry that their hour flew by so quickly. But she was glad to see that the children's faces lit up when they saw Celia there when they got home from school. One afternoon they opened the door looking miserable though. "Miz Dillard up the street stopped us just now," said Henry. "She said she knew who we were:

the children whose mother took her own life and is burnin' in Hell now."

Wally broke in. "She said it was no wonder, since our grandmother and aunt are sinners too, teachin' no good Negroes to read and write. I'm sorry Celia", he said, looking at her.

Louisa spoke up quickly. "Miz Dillard must be a very foolish woman, speaking to you all that way. If she approaches you again, just turn around and go the other way. Run, if you need to. She doesn't look like she can run. And as for teaching Negroes, I am very proud of your Aunt Mary and just hope I can do a good job too."

"Oh you do, Miz Louisa," said Celia, smiling.

"Why do people keep talking to us about Mama?" Laura asked.

"Maybe they just don't have enough to do, so they mind other folk's business," said Louisa.

After a few more weeks Sidney wrote and asked Louisa to come home. He said tobacco was bringing a good price, John and Amy were expecting a third child, George and Eliza wanted her to come back to teach their children again, and he loved and missed her. "As good a grandmama as you are, you are my wife and belong by my side," he reminded her.

Louisa was torn about leaving. When she talked with Sam about it, he urged her to go, but told her he hoped she would come back at least one weekend a month. The children didn't like the idea of her leaving at all. Laura loved sharing her room with her grandmother and said she would sleep on a pallet the rest of her life if she would stay. The boys were less expansive, but made it clear they liked it better when she was there. "Mama was so withdrawn for a long time. It was almost like she wasn't here" said Henry. "When you're around, we know it."

Louisa nodded. She swallowed and said, "I'll be back."

It was hard to tell Celia she was leaving, since she was approaching her lessons so enthusiastically. When she did tell her, Celia looked down, disappointed, and said, "Yes Ma'am."

"You are doin' very well Celia. And I want you to keep on learning. I'm leaving all the materials my daughter Mary sent for you. They are in order of difficulty, so please use them that way."

"Yes, thank you Miz Louisa."

"You can work through them at your own pace. When I come back for weekends we can set some time aside on Friday or Saturday afternoon to work together. Do you think that will work?"

"Oh yes Ma'am, I think it will!"

At the end of the week Louisa took the train to Danville, where Sidney was waiting for her in the new carriage he had bought for far too much. The smooth velvet seats were covered in the same color green that had been used in their old carriage, which Sidney pointed out right away.

"Finally you can travel like a lady again," he said proudly. "What do you think of it?"

"I hate to think what this buggy must have cost, Sidney."

His face fell. "Just appreciate it, Louisa"

"It's very comfortable, I will say that, Sidney. "

Sam
Winter 1871

When Louisa left, it all hit Sam: the shock of Ellen's death, the finality of losing her, the reality of being alone, and the responsibility of being the children's only parent. For months he had been looking after them more than Ellen did, but they had always known she was there, as he did. As Ellen had become more and more withdrawn during the Fall, he had gotten used to quiet nights. Now he asked himself over and over what he could have done. She had refused to see a doctor, insisting there was nothing wrong with her. She was ashamed at any implication that her problems might be other than physical, and flew into a rage at any such suggestion. Should he have made her see Dr. Smith? Could he have made her?

Sam stood at the window and looked into the darkness, imagining Ellen standing under the streetlamp. He was desolate. After a while he picked up the book Mary had brought him and opened it. It was David Copperfield. Getting engrossed in a novel was some comfort, at least.

The children too felt the loss of their mother anew when their grandmother left. Again they asked how their mother could have left them, which made Sam's heart ache. "I don't know," he said. "She loved you with all her heart. But her sadness was like a sickness. She couldn't overcome it."

"I wish she had gone to Dr Smith. Maybe he could have helped her," said Laura, and Sam's heart sank.

During dinner Sam and the children usually talked about school. A few days after Louisa left he told them he wanted to talk about a problem he needed help with. "After dinner, you have to go back to school and I have to get back to the store. When Ada isn't here it would really help if we could all clean up together before we go."

They all nodded.

"One can clear and clean the dining room table and put the leftovers away. One can wash the dishes, one can dry them and one can wipe down the kitchen table and cabinets. With four jobs, we can switch off every week. What do y'all think?"

"I think it will work fine," said Henry right away. "I'll wipe down the kitchen."

"I'll wash," said Wally.

I'll do the dining room table," said Laura.

"So I'm the dish dryer," said Sam. "We can switch off in a few days."

They all got to work.

"I wish I had thought of that before," thought Sam when they finished and he walked back to his store. "Ellen did all that herself when Ada wasn't there."

The woolen fabrics from Rhode Island had arrived that morning. His clerk was unpacking and sliding the heavy bolts of fabric into the upper shelves. A number of customers came in to look at the new fabric, planning to use it to make cloaks and coats for themselves and their families. One of the ladies held Sam's hand and gave him her condolences. Sam thanked her and then had to look down as his eyes filled.

When he came home from work Celia was making soup with the children. They had used leftover vegetables and gravy with extra onions. It smelled delicious and Sam was so grateful he almost cried. He had completely forgotten about supper until he got to his front steps. Celia and the children were delighted at his surprise.

"We make lots of soup like that," Celia said before she left. "See y'all tomorrow."

"She is a Godsend," said Sam.

"That's for sure Mr. Sam," said Wally. "Tomorrow we're making sugar cookies."

A few days later Sam and the children were sitting at the breakfast table. Sam and Henry had made hotcakes, since it was Sunday. "I was brought up to go to church on Sunday," said Sam. "Do y'all want to go to church?"

"Well, certainly not to the one Mama made us go to with her," said Laura. "It was cold and unfriendly."

"I know," said Sam. "This afternoon we're invited to Uncle Matthew's and Aunt Emily's for dinner. I think they like the church they go to. We can ask them about it."

"Why do we need to go to church?" Henry asked.

I've been thinking about it," Sam said. "Maybe it just gives us a chance to stop and think about how we're living our lives. But I do know it meant a great deal to my parents. They were too far away from town to attend a real church more than a few times a year. So the rest of the Sundays my grandfather himself conducted a service for everyone on the plantation."

The field hands and house servants and everyone?" asked Wally.

"Yes indeed Wally. And then in the afternoon you could hear the folks down in the quarters singin' their hearts out, singin' the most beautiful songs they seemed to make up and add to while they were singin'."

"That must have been amazing," Henry said, and they all nodded.

"Can I ask you something completely different, Mr. Sam? said Wally.

"Certainly," Sam said.

"What was it like being a soldier in the war?"

"It was terrible. In battle there were men everywhere, shooting and getting shot. It was confusing and extremely loud."

"Were you scared?" asked Laura.

"Of course I was scared. Everyone was scared, I think. Did you ever ask your grandfather about it?"

"Grandpapa won't talk about it," Wally said. "His son, our Uncle John, was killed in the Battle of Sharpsburg."

"I'm sorry. My youngest brother was also killed in that battle. He was right beside me."

"That's awful," Laura said.

"Did you kill anybody, Mr. Sam?" asked Henry.

"Yes I did, but I'm not glad about it."

"Why not?" asked Henry.

"Those Union men were just like us, doin' their duty and longing for home. Killing each other didn't heal our division at all. Think about it: Most white folks around here still want Negroes to be servants or sharecroppers, if not slaves. From what I have read, folks in the North were all for abolition, but few seem to be interested in helping to make it work. It was good that Lincoln emancipated the slaves, but we should have done it without a war."

"Uh oh Mr. Sam. Did Mama know you feel that way?" Henry asked.

"We didn't talk much about the war and the Negroes. I knew she felt differently."

"She sure did. She thought Aunt Mary was wrong for teaching Negroes," said Laura.

"I remember how angry she was when we found out that thousands of escaped slaves had joined the Union army," said Wally. "And she even hit Ada when she found out her husband was one of them."

Sam swallowed hard. "You know, your Mama saw herself as part of an earlier time that had a different way of looking at the world. She was still precious."

"You're even older than she was, Mr. Sam. What changed your outlook?" Henry asked.

"Fighting in the war. Starting to see what slavery had done to us and then seeing what it did to the slaves."

Henry looked thoughtful.

That afternoon they walked over to Mathew and Emily's for dinner. It felt good to be there. Emily's warmth and genuine hospitality always put them at ease. The food was delicious–juicy pork roast with mashed sweet potatoes and collards. Sam noticed that Wally was talking with his mouth full and made a mental note to speak to him about it later. The duties of parenthood continued to take him by surprise. After swallowing a bite of sweet potato, Sam said, "I was hoping you could tell us about your church, Matt."

"Well today our minister was quite riled up," Mathew said. "Evidently the Ku Klux Klan has been terrorizing the Negroes who attempted to vote in the recent local elections."

Laura, Wally and Henry looked at Mathew in surprise.

"Oh, he tied that into scripture, as a contrast to the story of the good Samaritan," Mathew continued. "Some of the members of the congregation who have a good deal of sympathy with the Klan, must have felt a bit uncomfortable. I was glad to see them squirm a little."

"How do you like your church, Emily?" Sam asked.

"I mostly love singin' the hymns," she replied.

"And I'm in the choir," Micajah offered.

"I'd like to be in the choir too," Henry said.

"Maybe we should try it," Sam said. "What do you think, Wally? Laura?"

"I'll try it," said Wally without much enthusiasm.

"Not me," Laura said. Everyone looked at her.

"Well, we don't have to decide right now," said Sam. "Did I smell apple pie?"

On the walk back home Sam asked Laura why she didn't want to go to Aunt Emily's church.

"I just don't want to go," she replied firmly. "I don't want to hear about Hell and Damnation."

"I don't like that much myself, but I have the impression that the Episcopalians don't talk about that all the time like the Baptists do."

"Well that is a good thing, but I still don't want to go, Mr Sam. Y'all can go without me. I'm old enough to stay by myself for two hours and read."

"I suppose you're right Laura. We'll give it a try next week."

The next Sunday Laura curled up on the couch in the parlor with Oliver Twist and said goodbye to Sam and her brothers. On the way to church Henry told Sam and Wally that Laura had asked him to count the number of times the minister mentioned Hell or Damnation. After the service Henry noted there were none to report to her. Then he asked to join the choir and stayed behind to join in practicing for the following week. On the walk home Wally told Sam he understood why Laura wouldn't go to church.

"Jane Turnbull told her that her mama was burning in Hell and was damned for eternity because she had taken her own life. Grandmama told us she did not believe in Hell, but Laura still worries about it."

"I think your Grandmama is right," said Sam. "There are too many things that show God's love for His creation for me to believe in Hell."

"That makes sense to me. I think what made such a big impression on Laura was that Jane Turnbull seemed so sure, and backed up her claim with the Bible. It made Laura want to avoid anything that might remind her of that, like church."

"Thank you for helping me understand what Laura is feeling, Wally. It seems like you have done some thinking about these things yourself."

The following Sunday afternoon Sam was relaxing in the quiet house while the children were over at Matt and Emily's. Hearing a knock at the door, he reluctantly laid down his newspaper. There stood Olivia, whom he had not seen since before Ellen's death.

"I came to extend my condolences Sam. But I can still not forgive Ellen for what she did to you and the children." Sam was speechless. He held the door open and Olivia sailed in. She looked around at the books and newspapers on the sofa and side tables and the wet shoes abandoned beside the door.

"You poor boy, having to live in such disorder," she said. By this time Sam had gathered himself enough to put on the kettle and offer her a cup of tea. "Oh, you poor boy," she said again. "No one to take care of you."

"Actually Sister, we're doing quite well, except we miss Ellen, because we loved her so."

"I can't even talk about Ellen, after what she did," Olivia sniffed,

"Well then, that's just as well, Olivia. Don't talk about her."

"The other reason I came is to offer you help with Laura, before it is too late."

"Too late for what? Is she in danger?"

"Is Laura headstrong?"

"No, but she has always been able to think for herself. Why?"

"Well, I'll just tell you. But you are not to tell another livin' soul. I even hated to tell Adam."

"Really." Sam handed her a cup of tea. She looked at the tarnished silver sugar bowl with disgust, and then served herself three spoons full.

"Being a man, you may not know about this particular sin, but it can happen. Just the other day I walked into Amanda's room when she thought I was out at the Ladies Auxiliary and found her on the bed with her best friend Cora. They were kissing and rubbing up against each other. I was horrified! It was disgusting! I made Cora leave immediately, and forbade her ever to speak to Amanda again. Amanda started crying even before I strapped her. Then I made her stay in her room until she was ready to come out and promise me that she would never behave unnaturally again, with Cora or any other female person." She sipped her tea and put the cup down.

"I don't see why you are telling me about Amanda's private business. What does that have to do with Laura?

"Because, don't you see, any young girl could be lured into such a path of evil. And I am offering my help, since she has no mother."

"I appreciate your concern Olivia, but I think Laura will be fine."

Don't fool yourself Brother. I'm watching Suzanna like a hawk now too. I'll have no more of this disgusting perversion."

"Thank you for your visit," Sam said, rising to his feet. "There are a few things I need to do before the children come home from Mathew's."

"I knew they were over there now. I heard them planning together after church. But where was Laura? She wasn't at church last week either."

"Laura is deciding whether she wants to go to church."

"I never heard such nonsense!" Olivia stood up. "That is your decision, not hers. You see, it does seem that she is a stubborn child, just like I feared."

Sam walked to the door, opened it, and said, "Have a pleasant walk home, Olivia."

It was all he could do not to slam the door. Furious, he strode out the backdoor and into the yard. As soon as he was sure Olivia was out of sight, he nearly ran to Mathew's. By the time he got there, he had worked off enough steam to go in. The children were up in the trees in the backyard. Mathew was glad to see him. At first they sat together sipping whiskey and talking business. Then Sam told him about Olivia's "condolence" visit, but not about Amanda. "I don't know who made Olivia world judge and jury," Mathew said, referring to her judgment of Ellen.

"I think she's always been that way," said Sam. "When we were young I used to argue with her, but she could never see things any differently from where she started."

"I sympathize with Adam," said Mathew.

"And with Amanda and Suzanna," Sam nodded.

Monday was one of the days Ada came. She usually arrived after the children and Sam had gone, did some cleaning or laundry, went to market, and prepared dinner. So when Sam and the children came home for dinner and no one was there, they were worried. They were also hungry, so Sam fixed up some eggs and leftovers. He sent the children back to school early and walked down to Ada's house in the Negro neighborhood two blocks over. No one was there, but the woman next door knew who Sam was and called to him. "Over here, Mr. Roberts. Ada tol' me about you. Ada's son Harold got beat up bad this mornin' Sir. Ada's with Harold at the doctor and she still not back. She had me send the children back to school after I gave them dinner."

"What happened to Harold?"

"He been workin' on rebuildin' the bridges that were damaged by the flood, Sir. It's a good job and most a the fellows workin' there are Negroes. This mornin' Harold left here with two friends. They was just walkin' to work when four young white men jumped em and beat em up. They used metal bars, and hurt em bad."

""'How did they get to the doctor?" asked Sam.

"Some of the other men who were workin' on the bridge came lookin' for them when they didn't show up. When they found them, they took them all to Doc Findley. Thank the Lord we have a colored doctor now."

"Please tell Ada and Celia how sorry I am, and ask them how I can help. Make sure they know I understand they can't work right now."

"She tol' me you a nice man, Sir. I see that and I'll tell her what you said."

When the children returned home after school, they were surprised to find Celia there. The students at their schools were all talking about the attack, so they had found out that Celia's brother was one of the victims. "How is your brother?" they all asked at once.

"He's hurt bad. Mama can't leave him. One leg is broke and his head and ear are all bloody. Mama says we all have to be brave to help him be brave."

Laura and the boys tried to comfort Celia, but it seemed to make her cry. "Y'all sweet," she sniffled. "I'm spose to tell ya your Papa left a message that Mama and I didn't need to come today 'cause of Harold. Are y'all gonna be alright?"

"Yes, Celia," they assured her.

"Just wanted to be sure," she said, and left to go home.

When Sam arrived home he found Laura and Henry making what they called "Celia's soup". No tellin' what's in it," said Wally.

"But it tastes fine," Laura grinned.

Sam told them what Ada's neighbor had said about Harold and his friends being attacked and hurt and they told him what they had heard at school and from Celia.

"Why did those white men attack them?" Henry asked as he ladled soup into the bowls Laura held.

"I can't say for sure, but I hear the jobs rebuilding the bridges over the James River pay pretty well. Maybe those men don't want Negroes to earn so much money." Sam said.

"Can't white men work there too?" asked Laura.

"Yes, they can. And there are a few white men workin' in those jobs. But some white folks don't want to work with Negroes."

"That is just plain dumb, Mr Sam. Why?" asked Wally.

"You know, Wally. They think they are better than Negroes," said Henry.

Sam nodded. "A lot of white people think that."

"I want to help Ada get through this," Sam went on. "She needs to be with Harold to take care of him, so she can't work.

Sam wrote some figures down on an envelope.

"I expect Celia will need to cook and take care of her younger brothers and sisters when they get home from school this week. So she can't come to us. She has a laundry business she does in the early part of the day, so she'll still be bringing in some money. But what will be missing?"

"Ada's and Celia's pay from you," said Henry right away.

I think the right thing is to pay them anyway, because they are good to us and they need the money," Sam said. They all nodded.

The next Monday when Ada came back to work she was still worried about Harold. His head and ear were healing nicely on the outside, but he was still having severe headaches. Doc Findley didn't know what else to try to ease them. He had set Harold's broken leg and it seemed to be healing well. It was going to be hard to keep Harold off his leg for the seven more weeks that Doc Findley had ordered. He had given Harold a pair of crutches and all the children enjoyed using them, so they were often not at hand when he needed them.

Although Celia was glad to see Sam's children, her concern for Harold stayed in her mind. With his hurt leg, it would be a while before he could work again. Also, he had told her that he was having trouble seeing now. And she was angry, because she had learned that the young white men who had attacked Harold and his friends got away with it completely.

"The police took three of them into custody the day of the attack", she said. "They brought them into the police station and let them go in less than a half hour."

"That's terrible! Wally said.

"The fourth man didn't even have to go to the police station. We think he knew somebody important or somethin'," Celia said.

"It makes me sick," Laura said.

"What happened to Harold's friends? Did they get hurt as bad as he did?" Wally asked.

"Oh, yes." Celia said. "Each of them got a broken leg. Had to be on purpose. And they beat their backs with those metal bars too. Poor fellas. None of them will be able to walk for months. So they can't work, which is what these white devils want." Celia stopped and covered her mouth with her hand. "Shouldna said white devils."

"We understand. Those men are devils," Henry said.

That evening at supper the boys told Sam about the white men not being punished for attacking Harold and his friends. Laura was quiet and didn't eat much.

Wally asked, "Mr. Sam, how can they get away with hurting those boys like that?"

"They should end up in jail." Henry said.

"Sometimes the police are not just," said Sam. "If the police don't like Negroes, they might look the other way if white men beat them up. I have heard that the police in some places in Virginia know who is in the Ku Klux Klan, but when there is a lynching, they just play dumb. And in some towns members of the Klan are actually in the police force.

"I hate that! It's not fair," sobbed Laura.

"You're right, Laura. It's wrong." Sam knelt beside her with his arm around her and handed her a napkin. "Too many sad things going on. Let's finish up and read something fun together tonight. Who wants to pick it out?"

In the middle of the night Laura woke up sick to her stomach. She vomited, but her stomach still hurt. By morning she was burning up with fever. Sam fixed breakfast for the boys and they went off to school. Concerned about Laura's high fever, he decided not to go to the store. When Ada arrived and saw her, she said Laura probably ate some spoiled food. "But we all ate the same thing," said Sam. Laura burst into tears and said, "No, I ate a piece of my friend Katie's venison after school yesterday." She took a big breath. "It tasted awful, but I didn't want to hurt her feelings so I ate the whole hunk."

"Bad meat. All kinda diseases come from bad meat," Ada grumbled. Then she made some herbal tea and asked Sam to make sure Laura drank it. Laura slept heavily and woke up with a bad headache in addition to a stomach ache and fever.

There was no improvement by the next day, so Sam walked over to get Dr. Smith. The doctor came and examined her. He said it could be typhoid, but it was too soon to tell. He recommended herbal teas and a bland diet and said to let her sleep as much as she could. Sam stayed home another day, and went to his store when Celia came. Wally and Henry were as worried as he was. After school, Henry sat with Laura and read to her when she woke up. When Sam came home, Henry went downstairs, where he was preparing supper. "Mr. Sam, I know you need to be at your store. I can stay with Laura."

"What about school?"

"Wally can pick up my assignments from my teacher and I can do them here at Laura's desk while she sleeps."

"You know, I think that will work. I can write a note to your teacher. Thank you Henry. I'll just check with Laura when I bring her this broth."

Laura smiled weakly and nodded when Sam asked her about Henry staying with her. Then she ate a little broth and went to sleep. The next day Sam went to the store early. When Laura woke up still feverish and achy, Henry heated some chicken soup and brought it to her. She had trouble getting the spoon from the bowl into her mouth, and dribbled it down the front of her nightgown. So Henry asked if she would like him to feed her. She looked surprised at the idea, but then said yes. So Henry fed her, as if it were the most normal thing in the world. Afterward he asked if she would like for him to read to her. "Later," she said, and slid under the covers. She slept for hours while Henry worked on an essay for English class and read ahead in his history book. Meanwhile it was an Ada day. She looked in on Laura as she slept and then made her a bone broth. "This is bound to give her some strength," she said. "You give it to her as soon as she wakes up, Henry." Laura finally woke up, achy, but not as feverish as before. Henry brought her the bone broth and she ate it without dribbling.

"I think I'm getting a little better," she said.

"That's the best news for ages," said Henry. "Tell me, why in the world did you eat that bad venison?"

"Katie lives too far away to go home for dinner, so she always brings something from home. The other girls tease her because her food often has a bad smell. So when she offered me a hunk of her venison, I didn't want to hurt her feelings, so I said yes. Then I had to eat it."

"That was really kind of you Laura. I understand. But please don't eat bad food again."

"I didn't know it was bad. I just thought it tasted awful."

Celia came upstairs to check on Laura and bring her some tea. "Good to see you sittin' up, chile."

"Thank you Celia. And thanks for the tea."

"May we borrow your Grimm's Fairy Tales Celia?" Henry asked.

"Of course, as long as you want. It's really your grandmama's, you know."

In the following days Laura slowly got better. She was very tired and weak, but the fever and aches subsided. Henry read her most of the fairy tales and did his schoolwork whenever she napped. Finally she left her bed during the day and ate meals with the family again. Sam, Henry, and Wally were overwhelmed with relief. In another week Laura and Henry went back to school.

More time passed and life fell into a new rhythm. Ellen was still Sam's last thought at night, but the children's voices were what he heard first thing in the morning. And they all were looking forward to Louisa's return at the end of the month.

Mary

Winter – Summer 1871

Mary could hardly remember the train ride home from Lynchburg to Philadelphia. All the pain of Ellen's death, which she had held at bay to help the children deal with their pain, overwhelmed her. She cried and remembered. Riding together on their first ponies, giggling with Ellen and Sally during their tea parties and endless sessions of make believe, the tension among them when they realized they all shared a father, Ellen's meanness to Sally after that, the surreptitious pinching and whispered comments. She pictured Ellen, the beauty, the belle of the ball, dancing and glowing, and then Ellen depleted and empty after each of her children was born. Groggy with exhaustion, she changed trains in Richmond, and fell asleep.

The conductor woke her in Philadelphia. She was comforted to see Priscilla and Peter there. Mary had sent two telegrams to Priscilla. The first was the day after Ellen's funeral, telling of her death. The second was the time of her return. Mary walked to them on leaden legs and they all embraced. Mary had not been able to put the way that Ellen had died in a cable, but Priscilla and Peter knew, because of what Mary had told them about Ellen's state of mind. It was a comfort just being with them and returning to the Atkins'. When they entered, Mr. and Mrs. Atkins took Mary's hands, told her how sorry they were, and how glad they were that she was back.

Returning to school the next day was difficult. Mary's pupils seemed unruly and forgetful about where they were in their lessons. Mary felt a bit confused herself. When the day was finally over she told

Priscilla how it had been. Priscilla said it was always that way after a break, Mary had probably forgotten. What made it especially hard was that Mary had not had a break herself this time. "Maybe you can come back a day or two sooner next time."

In a few more days Mary felt back in the rhythm of teaching. Her pupils were a mixture as usual, curious, careful, careless. She and Priscilla shared ideas, complained about the lack of books and materials, and made some of their own. On Monday of the next week five pupils were absent. This was unusual, so Mary asked if anyone knew why. The children explained that their fathers worked at a textile mill and had been fired. "I'm sorry to hear that," Mary said. "Do you know why?"

"Yes Miz Turner," Joe said. "They said it isn't fair that they get paid less than the white men, when they doin' the same job."

"So any colored man who complained got fired," Nettie said.

"Do you think that's right, Miz Turner?" Frederick asked.

"I think people doing the same job should be paid the same wage," Mary said. The next day there were three more absent pupils. Their friends said all the absent ones were working as day labor because their families needed the money until the fathers could get other jobs. "Do you know what they are doing for work?" Mary asked. "The boys are probably muckin' out stables and the girls are doin' laundry, said Joe.

"If any of you see them, please tell them I miss them and hope they will come back to school as soon as they can," Mary said.

Priscilla was missing pupils also. In fact every class was. Walking home, Mary and Priscilla talked about how outrageous it was that mill owners had an openly two-tiered wage scale. "How can they say they believe in America when they deliberately cheat people like that? It makes me so angry!" Mary said. "How do we convince men like these mill owners that they will be better off too if they pay everyone a fair wage? asked Priscilla. Can't they see that if everyone had more money they would buy more?

They were still talking about the issue of fair wages when Peter, Ben and Susan came for dinner on Sunday. "Congress simply has to pass a law requiring equal pay for equal work," said Ben. "And lawyers will have to enforce it with lawsuits and prosecutions, a whole new field," said Peter.

After dinner Peter and Mary went for a walk. "How are you Mary? This must have been a hard week," Peter said.

"Yes, it has been," Mary said.

"Do you want to talk about Ellen now? I understand if you do not."

"I do Peter." And she began, pouring out a jumble of memories and feelings, and ending with her week in Lynchburg. He listened and nodded.

"It sounds like Ellen suffered deeply with all the changes the war brought about. And her resentment and guilt about Sally must have been a heavy burden."

"I've been thinking about that. It helps to be able to think about these things with you , Peter." Peter took her hand and squeezed it.

"You're cold, Mary."

"I forgot my gloves."

Peter reached into his pocket and pulled out his gloves. Tenderly, he drew them onto her cold hands.

Toward the end of February there were some warmer days. Mary began to look forward to walks without her long underwear, which was still slightly itchy. One Sunday Peter seemed nervous on their walk. Mary noticed, and asked him if he were working on a difficult case.

"Yes, these contracts can be intricate. But that is not what is on my mind. What's on my mind is you, Mary."

"Why does that make you nervous Peter?"

"I love you, Mary"

Mary smiled broadly and said, "I love you too, Peter."

"You do?"

"Yes," said Mary, and reached up to kiss him on the mouth. They kissed and laughed and kissed some more.

"Will you marry me Mary?"

"I think so. Can we talk about that some more?"

"Of course. What do you want to talk about?"

"I want to keep teaching. Is that a problem?"

"No, in the Negro schools here they are allowing married teachers, because there is a shortage of teachers."

"Are you certain? Did you actually look into it?"

"Yes, indeed!"

"I love that you looked into it."

"I hoped you would."

"Well, so the answer is yes!"

"You mean you'll marry me, just like that?"

"Yes! Yes!"

Mary and Peter decided to marry in the spring when the world would be green and blossoming. The Atkins were delighted to have their "adopted" son marrying their newly "adopted" daughter. Priscilla said she would miss sharing her room with Mary, but was relieved that she would still be in Philadelphia.

Mr. Atkins had invested Peter's money from the sale of his family's house, so the sum had grown. It was now enough to purchase a modest brick row house, which they did. They furnished it from second-hand shops and Mary made curtains for the windows with fabrics that Sam sent from his shop in Lynchburg.

When it came to choosing a location for the wedding ceremony, Mary surprised herself. "You know," she said to Peter, "the place that feels like church to me, is the Episcopal church in Chatham. But I don't want to be married down there. So how would it be to be married in an Episcopal church up here in Philadelphia?"

"That's fine with me," said Peter. "I don't care where the ceremony is, as long as you marry me."

The date was April 4. Sidney, Louisa, Sam and the children arrived the day before. The Atkins had gotten them rooms in a nearby inn, and invited them all to their home for a late supper.

The day dawned shiny and gold. Louisa had brought her lace wedding gown, as Mary had requested. She brought it over early, for Mary to try on. But when she walked into her daughter's room, she found her sitting on her bed in tears.

"Ellen missed out on so many good things. Why Mama?"

"I wish I could understand Ellen. I felt like I should be able to, but she shut me out. But I think she was doing the best she could when she married Sam."

Louisa and Mary held each other. Finally, Louisa said, "Now let's see if this dress fits you like you said it would."

Mary slipped the creamy white dress over her head and pulled it down. It fit perfectly. "Well, I'll be…" murmured Louisa.

Priscilla came in, carrying a short veil. "Mother says you may wear this if you like, Mary. It was hers."

"That's a good reason to try it," said Mary, and did.

Louisa and Priscilla pronounced it the perfect touch.

The wedding was quiet and lovely, the familiar words of the Book of Common Prayer lending their weight and dignity. Mary and Peter looked at each other and smiled throughout. Afterward they all went back to the Atkins' to celebrate. Mrs. Atkins and Mary Lou had prepared a delicious meal and Mr. Atkins had even bought wine. Sidney contributed Virginia whiskey and was its main consumer. He talked so earnestly with Peter about coming to visit at Oak Hill, that Peter agreed they would come in the summer. Ben and Susan were so carried away by the joy of the wedding that they announced they were moving their date up and would be marrying in May. Everyone toasted them and then toasted Mary and Peter again. It was a beautiful day.

Moving into their own home was simple, since neither Mary nor Peter had any possessions except for their clothes and books. Mrs. Atkins had helped them find kitchen implements, dishes and utensils at flea markets. One day she arrived with a brand new soup pot and her favorite soup recipes. "No matter how little food there may be, a pot of soup on the stove makes it feel like enough," she said firmly.

"She was famous on the Underground Railroad for her endless pots of soup," Peter whispered to Mary.

Peter and Mary settled easily into life together. Before they had met, Peter had begun to think he would never find the right woman. Mary had started wondering if she would ever marry. So it was a joy to both that they got along so well.

When Peter told Mary that he had agreed to a visit at Oak Hill in the summer, they might have had their first disagreement. Mary did ask Peter to discuss such things with her first in the future, and he agreed. When he told her that Sam and the children were going too, she became enthusiastic about the visit. They set a time that coincided with school break in both Philadelphia and Lynchburg, and traveled by train to Danville. "Where will everyone stay?" asked Peter as the train rolled through Virginia.

"Oh, there's plenty of room at Oak Hill," replied Mary.

"So your family was able to hold on to the big house. How was that possible when so many plantation owners lost everything when the slaves ran away?"

"We were able to live there and keep the land because three of the slaves stayed a few months before they ran off. Joseph saved a plow horse and showed us how to plow. May Belle and Sally taught us what we needed to know in order to survive—growing vegetables, preserving and cooking food. Then Mama and I also grew and sold corn, while Ellen took care of the children and the house. So when Papa came back at the end of the war, we were still there. He wanted to grow tobacco again but we didn't have any money for seed. So he sold a good piece of land to a Yankee and set up to get sharecroppers to plant the seed and grow tobacco. At first it was questionable whether he would make it, but now he seems to be doing well."

"What a story, Mary. Before now I thought your dedication to teaching Negroes was because it's just and it's necessary. Now I see it's also very personal. So why does your father object to your teaching Negroes?

"He grew up believing that they are not really human beings. Believing that makes it possible to enslave them and use them."

"He told me he hoped I would talk some sense into you about your teaching."

"And what did you say, Peter?"

"I told him I was proud of you and he looked at me quizzically. I had no idea what you went through during the war, Mary. You are one amazing woman."

"It is my mother who is amazing, Peter. She and May Belle. I will tell you all about that in time. I'm glad we have time for these things. We have our whole lives. Look, we're almost in Danville."

Sidney had come to meet them in the carriage. He seemed excited and said he would be sending the wagon to meet Sam and the children, who were arriving on a later train. Mary and Peter were so sleepy after the long train ride that they almost fell asleep on the ride to Oak Hill. When Sidney pulled up to the wide front steps, he called to Louisa that they had arrived.

Louisa ran down the steps to greet them and encouraged them to have a wash and a rest before the others arrived. Mary entered her old bedroom with fondness. "I love having you in my room and my bed," she said to Peter, slipping her arms around his waist. They took off their shoes and lay down in the four-poster mahogany bed.

They awoke to the sound of Wally knocking on the door. Everybody was here and ready for supper, he said. At the table it was evident that the children had enjoyed the train ride from Lynchburg immensely. Sam looked a bit harried, but it was clear that he was enjoying the children's conversation. Mary was relieved to see that the children seemed well. Louisa had written her about the comments the children had endured concerning their mother's death and place in the hereafter. Subsequent letters had been more hopeful, thank goodness. Mary was glad to hear how it was working out with Celia in the afternoons and delighted that she was progressing with reading and figuring, with support from Louisa.

It didn't take long for Wally and Henry to discover the horses Sidney had just bought. "May we please go for a ride, Grandpapa?" Henry asked, running up the front steps.

"Do you still remember how to ride, now that you are city boys?"

Wally and Henry immediately asserted that they did. Laura looked doubtful.

"Laura will ride old Prince until she is sure of herself," said Sidney. "That is, if your father says yes." Sam agreed and said Sidney would be a better judge of which horse would suit each child. So horseback riding became the favorite part of the visit for the children. For Sam, it was the adult conversation.

Louisa was glad for the chance to get to know Peter. He was very different from Sidney. When Mary spoke he looked interested and listened, just like she did with him. He seemed proud of her and she of him. The other men Louisa knew, except for Sam, affectionately belittled the women they loved. They didn't treat them as equals, but they were tender with them and tried to take care of them. Louisa asked Mary about this when they went riding one morning. Mary knew just what she meant. "I love the way Peter assumes I can make decisions for myself. I wish Papa were more like that!"

One warm morning after breakfast Sidney asked Peter to go for a ride around his property. "I want you to see it all while you are here," Sidney said. They rode past field after field of healthy green tobacco plants and Sidney pointed out the cabins where the leaves were dried. He pointed out the sharecroppers' cabins as well. "Two of those families used to belong to me. Now that is what I call loyalty."

Peter wondered about that, but decided not to comment.

"The reason I want to show you all this, Peter, is that I'm offering to give half of it to you now. You and Mary can build a house down here and I can teach you to be a great tobacco farmer. Why should you and Mary have to wait 'til I die to have a fine life here in Virginia!"

"Well thank you Sir. That is mighty generous. But of course I need to discuss it with Mary."

"Nonsense! What does Mary know about these things?"

"Probably a great deal more than I do, Sir. And I do like practicing law."

"Well, you could practice law at night if you had to. "

"What about Sam, Sir?

"Sam will inherit his half when I die. He's completely tied up with his business and his brothers in Lynchburg. We have discussed it."

"I see. Well, I will talk about this with Mary."

"You will have to take a strong hand with Mary, Peter. She has become a stubborn opinionated woman since the war. You should have seen how sweet and beautiful she was as a girl. She didn't worry herself with anything like the Negroes then. She just loved having a good time."

"Well Sir, I do admire the woman she has become."

They rode back to the stable in silence. Mary and Laura were sitting on the veranda, sewing and chatting. When Laura went inside, Peter told Mary all about his conversation with Sidney. Mary groaned. "How like Papa. He intends to be generous, but it never occurs to him to ask what we might want for our lives. What do you think about his proposal Peter?"

"I hope that living down here is not what you want."

"Then we don't even have to consider it, because I don't want to at all."

Later, after the children were upstairs in bed Mary and Peter found Sidney in his study, sipping bourbon as he read about a thoroughbred he was interested in. "We appreciate your generosity Sir," said Peter, "but moving down here is just not what either of us wants."

Sidney looked at them with sad eyes. “After losing John and Ellen, I want to hold our family close. Can you blame me?” he said, reaching for the whiskey decanter.

“No Papa,” said Mary, taking his other hand. “I don’t blame you. And we will write and visit.”

Sidney poured another whiskey and handed it to Peter. “I think you are both very foolish. It’s because of Mary’s job teaching Negroes you don’t want to come. Mary, there are plenty of white children you could teach down here if you would just give up such a pointless mission.”

“Sir, I respect what Mary is doing. It’s important.”

“And I’m proud that Peter is building a law practice with a partner he wouldn’t let down.”

“Oh Mary,” said Sidney. “You’ve forgotten who you are, forgotten where you came from. You’ve forgotten what I fought for and what your brother died for.” He sighed.

“Good night Papa,” said Mary. “Go to bed. Whiskey makes you maudlin.”

Louisa
Spring 1872

It had been almost a year and a half since Ellen's death, and the agony of her loss still weighed heavily on Louisa. Sometimes she would stand in Ellen's room and look in the tall mirror on her mahogany wardrobe, almost glimpsing the reflection of her daughter. Ellen had left two of her gowns inside, and Louisa would hold them to her face, still trying to breathe in her daughter's scent.

She was glad to have Alexa, Max and Robert to tutor, and enjoyed the stimulation of their young minds. Their parents Eliza and George had still shown no interest in their studies and the progress each was making, to Louisa's continued mystification. Even if they had little education themselves, Louisa couldn't understand their almost total lack of interest in finding out what their children liked and were good at. Nevertheless, in late May she invited them for tea and gave them a summary for each of their children. She pointed out that Robert wanted to attend the University of Virginia in another year. He would be well prepared by then, she thought, except for Latin and Greek, so it would be good to get him a tutor for the summer.

"Poor boy, havin' to study Latin in the summer heat," Eliza pouted.

"You can't keep him a child, Eliza," said George. "If Louisa thinks he'll be ready for the University after another year, that settles it. I'll get him a Latin tutor."

Eliza looked resigned and sighed. "I really wish the children could come to you four times a week instead of three, Louisa."

"I'm sorry Eliza, I often go to Lynchburg on weekends, you know. I travel on Fridays and Mondays in order to have the weekend with my grandchildren and Sam. So I hope three times a week will continue to be suitable for your children."

"I know all that. It's just that it gives them something to do, so I can go off with George."

Louisa excused herself and went inside and into the library, gritting her teeth. She stood with her fists clenched and silently screamed, "Was her work with their children just something to fill their time? And how could such feckless people have children who were curious and smart like Robert, Max and Alexa?"

After a few minutes she took some deep breaths and felt calmer. She returned to the veranda and sat down. Sidney had joined them with the whiskey decanter and Lucy soon appeared with glasses, water, tea, and shortbread. George announced that he had news. One of the largest plantations in Halifax County had been bought by a Yankee carpetbagger. The rumor was that he knew absolutely nothing about tobacco, so he had lured an overseer away from a neighboring plantation. Then he had ridden around collecting sharecroppers to work for him by promising them the best deal around, which he had no intention of keeping.

"It certainly will be interesting to see how he does. Was the place in bad shape?" Sidney asked.

"It was a ruin," said George. "The house was burnt near to the ground, and most of the outbuildings too. There were a few colored families living in the old quarters and growin' vegetables, but he cleared them out."

"You be sure and point this Yankee fella out to me if we see him in Danville, George," Sidney said.

"I hate those carpetbaggers," said Eliza. "They're scoundrels, coming down here buying land when people are struggling. Takin' advantage out of pure greed."

On Friday morning Sidney asked Jim to take Louisa in the buggy to the train station. "Overseeing the planting process is critical, you understand, Louisa."

Louisa understood. The train was late, so when she arrived in Lynchburg, there was Wally waiting to meet her instead of Celia. At thirteen, Wally was as tall as Louisa, and proud of it. He would probably grow as tall as Walter and be handsome like him too, with his red hair and strong body.

But thank goodness he wasn't lazy like his father. Louisa thought Walter's laziness and tendency to brag and exaggerate were due to his drinking, but perhaps it was the other way around. She was relieved to see that Wally worked hard at his studies and was responsible in regard to Henry, Laura and his stepfather.

Louisa embraced Wally warmly and he took her small tapestry bag for the walk to Federal Street. She had been leaving a few clothes and necessary items in Laura's room, so that she wouldn't have to bring them for her frequent visits. "How was your trip, Grandmama?" Wally asked.

"First the train was late, and then it stopped almost at the Junction, and we just sat, for a long time. No one explained why. There was a great deal of smoke and soot though. Am I all sooty?" she asked, wiping off her shoulders.

Wally brushed off her back with his hands. "Not any more Grandmama."

"How is school, Wally?"

"It's alright. I can't wait for summer break, when we go down to Oak Hill. How are our horses?"

"I expect they will be very glad to see you and get ridden. Your grandfather and I can't ride them all enough."

"Could we stay there with you and Grandpapa for a while when Mr Sam comes back to Lynchburg?"

I don't see why not, but it's really up to Mr. Sam. Why don't you ask him?"

"I will," said Wally.

When they reached the house, Laura and Henry were making biscuits with Celia. Celia had just taken a pan of them out of the oven and Henry was buttering them. Laura put some biscuits on a plate and passed them around, embracing Louisa along the way. "They melt in my mouth," said Louisa after she ate one. "They almost as good as my Mama's," said Celia.

Celia had written some pages for Louisa to read, but they had missed their lesson together because the train was late. Louisa could tell she was disappointed, and suggested she come for an hour on Sunday afternoon.

"Yes, Ma'am, I'll be here", she said right away. Celia had made good progress in reading, writing, and figuring in the past year and a half. She particularly enjoyed writing stories for her younger sisters and brothers. Louisa found the stories delightful and helped Celia with punctuation, spelling and clarity, but tried to never edit away the tone. She gave Celia stories to read that encouraged her imagination and awareness of the world, and they talked and laughed and groaned over them.

Shortly after Celia left, Sam arrived home, tired and smiling. "Hello Grandmama," he said as he embraced Louisa. "I'm not your Grandmama," she said quickly. She was feeling sensitive as she approached her fiftieth birthday. "I'm only five years older than you," she said, smiling.

"Mr. Sam, wait til you taste the biscuits we made," said Henry. "They melt in your mouth."

"Well let's have supper then," said Sam.

After supper, while they were still sitting at the table, Sam said, "I know you will hear about this at school on Monday, so I'm telling you myself. There was a double lynching last night, in the woods by the river. Two young colored men were found hangin' down there early this morning. The word in town is that it was the Klan again." Sam looked at the children sadly, seeing their horror. "I hate to tell you about such terrible things."

"Why Mr. Sam, why would anybody do that?" Henry asked.

"They hate Negroes. Maybe they think they will take away their jobs or marry white women," Sam said.

"Will they?" asked Laura.

"Nobody knows what the future holds. But are those reasons to lynch people?"

"There are no reasons to lynch people," Louisa couldn't help interjecting.

"Mr. Sam, is lynchin' where Lynchburg got its name?" Wally asked.

"No, actually the city is named for a man named John Lynch, who founded it," said Sam. "But there is one piece of hopeful news. President Grant is enforcing measures to clamp down on the Ku Klux Klan. We must pray he'll be successful."

"I wonder if Ada and Celia know the men who were lynched," said Henry.

"You can ask them, of course. Just remember that a lynchin' is a shocking tragedy for their whole community, whether they knew the victims or not."

The children nodded seriously.

When they were all cleaning up from supper, Louisa noticed how easily it went and how comfortable the children seemed with their tasks. "You all make light work of this. I'm proud of you," she said smiling.

"Now it's time for you to make light work of your lessons," Sam reminded them.

Later, when they were upstairs, Sam and Louisa sat in the parlor. "I hate for Laura, Henry and Wally to have to find out about the ugliness of lynching. But there is no protecting them," said Sam.

"It's the world we live in. You're preparing them to live in it and work on it," Louisa said.

"I hope so. President Grant has a real challenge here in Lynchburg, to undo the damage President Johnson did throughout the south, by allowing the old families to retain their power. Did you hear about how this city turned out to celebrate Johnson in '69?"

"Yes, Emily told me how Olivia bragged about being invited to the formal banquet in his honor."

Sam groaned. "Yes, she bragged about it to me too."

Then Sam caught her up on how each child was doing in school, what they excelled at and what they struggled with. Louisa reveled in hearing the details and was especially grateful after Eliza and George's lack of interest in such things.

Louisa retired to her new bed in Laura's room. When Ada's son Harold had recovered from the terrible beating, his leg had not healed properly. He could still walk but couldn't manage the climbing and carrying necessary for heavy construction. Fortunately Sam knew a carpenter in town who was looking for a young apprentice in furniture building. Harold was a good fit. One of his early projects was Louisa's new bed. It was well made and sturdy, if not a piece of fine furniture. After Sam paid for it, Ada told him that Harold had proudly presented his portion of the earnings to her. Louisa was glad that Laura would no longer sleep on a pallet when she came. Last month she and Laura had gone to Sam's store and picked out some remnants to make quilts for their beds. They were looking forward to laying out their designs on Saturday.

On Sunday morning they all went to church. Laura had been reassured enough times by her brothers that she wouldn't have to hear about hell and damnation that she wanted to go. She also longed to join the choir, which she did. Louisa enjoyed singing too and found herself wishing she could join the choir. "Silly to think about it," she thought to herself.

Emily and Mathew invited them for Sunday dinner after church. Micajah and Emmy, who looked up to their cousins, greeted them warmly and led them into the backyard where the large old trees were, perfect for climbing and playing in. The adults sat on the porch and talked quietly about the lynchings. Emily said she did not want her children to know about them. "Such things give them bad dreams."

"I told mine about it because I know they will hear about it in school tomorrow," said Sam.

"I don't want Emmy and Micajah to be frightened, Sam"

"Do you want me to call Wally aside and ask him not to talk about it?"

"Yes, I do Sam."

So Sam went to the backyard and called Wally aside to ask him if they had talked about the lynchings.

"No, Mr. Sam."

"Will you avoid it today and head it off if Henry or Laura start to?"

"Yes Sir, but why?"

"That's the way Aunt Emily wants it."

"Yes Sir."

Sam returned to hear Louisa finish telling what she had read about Grant's measures against the Klan.

"I have no love for the Klan or for hangin' Negroes, but neither do I want them sitting in the same train car or goin' to school with my children," said Mathew.

"I just want our children to have a happy life," said Emily. A carefree childhood. The war has been over for seven years. Can't we just leave it all behind us and be happy again?"

"But everything has changed since the war," said Sam. "Don't we have to figure out how both we and the Negroes can live in the world as it is now, Emily?"

"And shouldn't all children have a chance to have a happy life, Negro children too? Louisa added.

"I don't know if that's up to us. It's all so confusing." Emily looked troubled.

"I do see that having Negroes be free changes everything," said Mathew. It still takes gettin' used to. I can't imagine what it will mean if the Fourteenth Amendment actually gives them equal civil and legal rights."

"Oh please Mathew, let's not get into all that today." Emily said. "It's such a beautiful spring afternoon."

It was, especially with the lilacs and wisteria blooming. Louisa decided she should hold her tongue until a better time, took a deep breath, and let the intoxicating scents relax her.

After a delicious chicken dinner prepared by Mathew's cook, Sam, Louisa and the children walked home. Celia was sitting on the back steps, looking dejected. Sam and the children went around to the front door and Louisa sat down beside Celia. "I'm so sorry to hear about the lynching Celia."

"How can anybody treat other people like that, Miz Louisa?"

"I don't know Celia."

"They Mama lost her mind with grief."

"Oh no, they were brothers. Do you know them?"

"They went to our church. You know what makes it even more horrible?"

"Tell me."

"The white men who lynched them will never be punished."

"I hate that you're right, Celia."

"Miz Louisa, I just can't work on my story today. Is that alright?"

"Of course, I understand that. How about if I get you Aesop's Fables to read for next time?

"That would be fine."

So Louisa went inside and got the book. "Please tell your Mama I'm sorry about the awful news and tell Harold I certainly appreciate my new bed," Louisa said when Celia was leaving.

Early the next morning Laura and the boys walked with Louisa to the train station. "How soon can you come again?" Laura asked.

"I wish you came every weekend," Henry said.

"Remember to ask Grandpapa whether we can stay on this summer when Mr. Sam has to come back to Lynchburg," said Wally. "Mr. Sam says we can stay if it is alright with both of you."

"Goodbye Grandmama. I'll miss sharing my room with you," Laura said.

"It's getting harder to leave every time," Louisa thought as she climbed onto the train.

Mary

Spring – Summer 1873

Mary's breasts were tender again, but she was waiting to tell Peter. They had both been so very excited the last time it had happened, and then so very disappointed when she lost the baby. She had tried to look on the bright side and focus on what a good year she had had with her pupils. And how she loved living with Peter.

She and Peter continued to go to the Atkins every Sunday for dinner. They were both fond of them and it felt like being with family to be there. One Sunday in March Mary and Peter hosted the family, serving up one of Mrs. Atkins' chicken recipes with fanfare. Ben and Susan came, along with Priscilla. The conversation was about President Grant's continued problems with Congress, which was resisting implementing the measures for Reconstruction. "How can they justify opposing the amendments that they just passed?" said Peter.

"Remember, they've already replaced many of the congressmen who voted in favor of those amendments," said Ben.

"And too many white people are looking the other way, even in Pennsylvania," said Mary.

Later in the afternoon Priscilla joined Mary and Peter for a walk along the Schuylkill. She told them she was looking for a teaching job at a Negro school in Baltimore and if she could find one, would be leaving when school was out to find a place to live. Mary was surprised, since Priscilla had said nothing about it before. "Why Priscilla? You have a good job here, and you can live with your parents."

Priscilla looked serious. "That's just it. I don't want to live with my parents any longer, even though I love them dearly."

Peter nodded. "We didn't want to live close to Mary's parents in Virginia either, even if we had our own house."

"I understand, Priscilla," said Mary. "I'm just sad because I'll miss you so much. I guess I'm being selfish."

"I'll miss you too Mary. I'll even miss you too Peter," she said with a grin.

"We'll come visit you in Baltimore. Would that be alright?" Peter asked.

"Of course, and I'll be coming back to Philadelphia to see my parents."

Shortly after school ended Mary and Peter took the long train ride to Danville. Much to their surprise, Louisa met them in the buggy alone, looking grim. They all embraced and started back to Oak Hill. "Where's Papa?" Mary asked.

"He's sick," said Louisa.

"What's wrong with him?" asked Mary.

"He drank so much whiskey last night that he was ill. He was raving and vomiting and then fell asleep on the floor, so I couldn't get him to move. Thank goodness he is in his study instead of the drawing room or the dining room. I cleaned up the mess as well as I could and then closed the door tight. I told Lucy not to bother with it, or with him," she added with disgust. "She shouldn't have to do that."

"Nobody should, Mama."

"I'm glad Sam and the children won't get here until tomorrow," said Louisa. "He should dry up and clean up by then."

"I'm sorry about this, Louisa." said Peter. "Has it happened before?"

"Yes, but not this bad. He's been drinkin' more and more lately."

When they arrived at Oak Hill, they were relieved to find that Sidney had gone upstairs to bed.

Mary opened the windows and cleaned up the study with soapy rags. Then she washed herself and changed her dress.

Lucy served supper, which they ate on the veranda in the fresh air.

"What is happening with Papa?" Mary asked.

"He's dissatisfied and irritable much of the time," Louisa said. "He wants to be wealthy again. He wants his life before the war. He was comfortable owning his workers. It's much less comfortable for him to negotiate with them, so he still tries to treat them as if he owned them."

"I was hoping he would learn from experience," Mary said.

"He doesn't have his old friends to talk to about things, since they were lost in the war. Young John Stanton is a spoiled fool and George Willis is a nice buffoon, though Sidney would probably not admit that about either of them. So he is lonely. So he drinks. And spends money he doesn't have, like buying such a luxurious carriage or another thoroughbred. So then he is anxious. So then he drinks."

"It must be hard for you, Louisa," said Peter.

"To be truthful, it is," said Louisa.

"Do you get lonely too Mama?" asked Mary.

"Sometimes, yes. But I go to Lynchburg every weekend I can. I love being there with Sam and the children."

"I can't wait to see them tomorrow," Mary said.

The next morning Mary awoke early, when the house was still. She looked at Peter sleeping beside her, thinking how much she loved him. She leaned over and kissed him softly on the lips. He stirred and reached to fondle her breasts. She shrank away at his touch. Peter opened his eyes and they looked hurt. "What is it, Darling?" he asked.

"My breasts are sore, because I'm pregnant."

Peter sat up and beamed. "Are you sure?"

"I'm sure and I feel different this time. Better."

"Mary! We're going to have a child! Our child! " He kissed her tenderly. "When will it be?"

"Well, I think the baby should come around Christmas time."

Peter kissed her again. "When do you want to tell the family?"

"Not yet. Let's just make sure everything is alright."

"And what will we do about our smiles?"

When Mary and Peter went downstairs, Louisa was sitting on the veranda drinking tea. They kissed her and wished her good morning. "Where's Papa?" Mary asked.

"I'd like to go see the horses," Peter said before Louisa could answer.

"They'll be glad for the company," said Louisa as he descended the steps.

"How are you and Papa?" Mary asked.

"I couldn't get into bed with him last night because he smelled foul and was filthy. So I slept across the hall in John's old room. This morning he woke me up, climbing into my bed. He had taken off his dirty clothes and was naked. He said he was truly sorry and wanted to show me he loved me. I just couldn't. I couldn't. I was still disgusted. I probably shouldn't tell you all this, Mary. He's your father."

"I understand though, Mama."

"So I suggested he take a bath and asked Caroline to bring up some warm water. He'll probably be down soon."

"Oh Mama, I'm so sorry." She squeezed Louisa's hand.

"I hope he won't drink too much while the children are here. They love their Grandpapa. I think they would be awfully disappointed to see how he is when he's drunk."

"I agree. Papa has always been a drinker, but he seemed to keep it pretty much under control. Now it seems to be controlling him."

"I think he drinks to feel better, as I was telling you yesterday. But it only makes him feel worse."

"Are Laura, Henry, and Wally staying on for a few weeks after Sam goes back to his store?"

"That is the plan if things go well with Sidney, but I will have to have a private talk with Sam about it. Then he'll be prepared if I bring them back unannounced."

Sidney appeared on the veranda, clean, combed, and dressed in fresh clothes. Lucy served them tea and hot biscuits with butter and jam.

"Sorry I missed you and Peter last night, Mary. I was a bit under the weather", he said."

"I'm sorry too," said Mary. "Do you want me to go to Danville and pick up Sam and the children?"

"Why no, Mary. I want to go. But thank you."

Sidney returned with Sam and the children early in the evening. Sam visited with the other adults on the veranda, while Laura and the boys went down to the stables to see the horses. They could hardly wait to ride again, including Laura, who had become a passable rider by the end of their visit last summer. They planned to ride every day, unless it rained very hard.

Peter
Summer 1873

The adults fell into a routine too. Mary and Louisa enjoyed long walks and talks after dinner, while Sidney, Sam and Peter liked sitting on the veranda and talking. Peter was still getting to know Sam and Sidney and was especially fascinated to hear their views as Southerners, since Mary was the only other Southerner he knew well. He learned things even Mary didn't know, and told her everything. One afternoon Sam asked Sidney, "How old is Oak Hill?"

"Well, my father inherited it from his father, my grandfather. My grandfather inherited it from my great grandfather, who built it in 1751. I inherited it from my father. We were all named Sidney Turner. Maybe now you can understand what this place means to me. It has been held in trust for four generations in our family. It's my duty and my honor to be the steward of Oak Hill and keep it goin'. You understand, don't you Sam?"

"I understand why you feel so connected to Oak Hill, Sidney. I just wish the stewardship of land in the South had not depended upon slavery."

"But of course it depended upon slavery. The economy of the whole South depended on slavery. And it flourished. I'm afraid you have been influenced by my wife and Mary, Sam." Sidney got up to get the whiskey decanter and some glasses.

"Sam," said Peter as they rocked, "Mary told me you grew up on a tobacco plantation too. Where was that?"

"It was over in Halifax County," said Sam. " I grew up there with my two brothers and my older sister. It was burned down in the war in a terrible fire that killed our parents."

"I'm sorry to hear that," said Peter.

Sidney handed Peter and Sam each a whiskey, sat down again, and said, " I have to hand it to you Sam, how you have adapted to livin' up in Lynchburg. I certainly could not."

"Actually, Sidney, you know what has happened? I've come to like Lynchburg. I like having neighbors close by, I like owning a fabric store, and I like paying the people who work for me."

"Well, that surprises me, but it's a good thing for you, I suppose. I can't say I like payin' these sharecroppers."

Sam sipped his whiskey. "Something I've been wondering, Sidney, who was Laura named after?

"My mother," said Sidney. "She died in childbirth when I was two."

"Who raised you?" Peter asked.

"My father's mistress, Bess. She was very dark, very beautiful. I loved her. She was always kind to me. She laughed a lot and brought me down to the quarters to play. One of my playmates was Bess's daughter, May Belle, whom you have both heard of, I'm sure. My wife thinks May Belle was a heroine."

Sam and Peter nodded.

"I inherited May Belle along with all the other house servants and field hands when I inherited Oak Hill. It's a small world."

Peter looked at Sam and Sam looked at Peter.

"What happened to Bess?" asked Sam.

"She died soon after my father. She nursed him through typhoid but caught it herself."

After a moment Peter asked, "While we're talking about names, why didn't you continue the Turner tradition of naming the son Sidney?"

"That was Louisa. She had some crazy ideas even then. She said each child deserved to follow their own path and should not be expected to follow the path of their forebears. She never has understood the value and importance of family tradition and honor."

The men continued to have afternoon conversations, which became lively arguments as they got to know each other better. Sidney was increasingly outspoken with them in his defense of slavery and his belief that things would improve if the Negroes would stay in their places. Sam argued for the urgent necessity for education to give Negroes opportunities, and Peter was skillful in advocating for equal rights and voting. Nobody changed anyone's mind, but nobody stopped trying.

Mary

Spring – December 1873

Two weeks went by quickly. Before they left, Mary and Peter told the family their good news. Everyone was delighted at the prospect of a little one, especially Laura, who was hoping for a girl. Sidney had managed not to get drunk for two weeks, so Sam thought, as long as Louisa would bring them to Lynchburg at the first sign of a problem, the children could stay a few more weeks. Louisa agreed.

On the train ride back to Philadelphia Peter told Mary all he had learned in his conversations with Sidney and Sam. "Well the part about Bess shouldn't surprise me," she said. "Papa did the same thing with May Belle, and you know Sally is his daughter. From what Mama has said, I don't think his relationship with May Belle went on for very long though, in contrast to his father's relationship with Bess. It sounds like that was lifelong."

"I wonder if Bess had children by your grandfather."

"She must have. And we'll never know what became of them.

Isn't it amazing that Papa never mentioned to us that his mother died when he was two? I remember before the war when he asked Ellen to name her next child Laura, after his mother, if she were a girl. We thought his mother had died around ten years before, around the time his father died.

I asked him to tell me about his mother and he said he didn't want to talk about her."

They rode along in silence for a few minutes. Then Mary said, "I just can't get over Bess being May Belle's mother!"

"How do you know whether your grandfather was May Belle's father?"

"May Belle was dark. You said Bess brought my papa down to the quarters to play, so she must have wanted to spend time there. Both things make me think Bess had a husband or lover down there who was dark skinned."

They rode in silence for a few minutes.

"You know Peter, Papa has all these secrets about his childhood and about the war. And he keeps his grief about losing John and Ellen locked up inside him. He must feel very much alone."

Peter nodded and took her hand.

"Where is Sally now?" he asked.

"The last I heard she went to Baltimore to teach."

"Maybe Priscilla will run into her doing teachers' business and you could get in touch."

"Maybe, but she wasn't glad to see me in Richmond. I think I see why now."

"Why?"

"Because she is the innocent result of a crime my father committed. You know, so many planters impregnated their female slaves, often by raping them. Not many of those women had the status of mistresses, which might have made their lives a little easier. I hope it did for Bess."

"I know. I've read that some planters had relations with their slaves for the very purpose of breeding more slaves."

"I don't think Papa did that. At least I hope he didn't. But Sally has every right to resent that her father took advantage of her mother, who was already married and loved her husband. And not to want to be around me, his privileged daughter."

"Did Sidney ever treat Sally as a daughter?"

"As far as I know, he never acknowledged her as his daughter. Can you imagine what that felt like to Sally? And Papa doted on John, Ellen, and me. Why would she be glad to see me?"

"The whole system of slavery was rotten to the core," said Peter, shaking his head. "It was so riddled with exploitation and cruelty, that it destroyed natural human relationships."

"And yet Peter, it took us goin' to war and losing our slaves for me to even start to realize that slavery was fundamentally wrong. I'm ashamed to say that, if the South hadn't gone to war, I would have grown up accepting the way things were and enjoying my easy life, without giving it a thought."

"I'm very grateful that you began to think differently and wanted to take action. Not just because it's vital for Negroes to learn, which it is. But also because teaching Negroes brought you to Priscilla in Richmond, and from there to me in Philadelphia."

"I'm grateful too, Peter, for both things."

They changed trains in Richmond and again in Washington. As they went through Baltimore, Mary peered out the window, wondering if Sally were still there. Next came Wilmington and finally Philadelphia. Their little row house seemed smaller after the high ceilings and spacious rooms at Oak Hill, but they were glad to be home. On the train, Mary had started imagining a cradle beside the bed in their room, and now saw that it wouldn't fit. "Let's move the bed to the middle of the wall," she said. "Now?" asked Peter. "We do have a few more months," he teased.

"Well, I was hopin' we could go to that used furniture shop on First Street tomorrow afternoon."

"I need to work at the office all day tomorrow, Mary. Now that Negroes can testify in court we are moving forward with several cases."

"Oh, that is wonderful to hear!"

"Would you like to go down to the shop and look?" he said as they pushed the bed over. "Then if you find a cradle you like, you could ask Mr. Eliot to put it aside for us."

In the morning Peter left for the office right after breakfast. Mary cleaned up the kitchen and finished getting dressed. She walked over to the Atkins' to tell Mrs. Atkins and Priscilla her good news.

When she heard it, Mrs. Atkins beamed and embraced her warmly. "Priscilla will want to know, but she has gone to Baltimore."

"Already?"

"She's sharing a little row house with Amelia Evans, one of her good friends from grammar school. They had to take it right away or the landlord would rent it to someone else."

"Did Priscilla get a job in Baltimore?"

"Yes. Amelia has been teaching in a Negro school there for three years. The school needs more teachers, so Amelia suggested Priscilla. They hired her right away."

"That is exciting," said Mary. "It certainly did happen fast. Please give me her address so I can write to her."

"Of course dear. I'm sorry you couldn't tell her today. How are you feeling?"

"I feel well, different from last time. I had some morning sickness in the spring, but that's over now."

"Then I'd better get started on a quilt for that baby."

"Would you like to walk down to Eliot's Used Furniture and look for a cradle with me?"

"Why yes. It's a lovely day for a walk. Just let me talk to Mary Lou about what we need at market."

"I need to go to market too. May I borrow one of your baskets?"

July was hot and humid in Philadelphia, but nevertheless Mary felt better than she had during the previous months. Toward the end of the month she felt fluttering in her womb. She told Peter it felt like a miracle in her body. A letter came from Priscilla, asking if she could be the baby's aunt and inviting Mary and Peter to visit in Baltimore. Peter was still trying to catch up with work after his two week holiday, so they decided Mary would go alone and right away.

It was a short train ride, compared to her trips to Virginia. Priscilla and Amelia were standing at the station to greet her. Priscilla embraced Mary warmly and introduced her to Amelia, who looked enough like Priscilla to be her sister. Then Priscilla took her valise and they walked the few blocks to their house. Baltimore was even muggier than Philadelphia, but their house and the tiny garden behind it were neat and pleasant. Small boxwoods and bright marigolds grew along the brick wall in the back. Once they were sitting in the garden drinking tea, Priscilla wanted to know whether Mary would be allowed to teach once she had a child. "Only because there is such a shortage of teachers for the Negro schools. I won't go back the first year, but that is my choice."

"And after that?" Priscilla asked.

"Your mother offered to care for the baby when I go back. Do you mind that?"

"No. As a matter of fact, I'm very glad, both for you and the baby, but also for me."

"For you?"

"Yes, it takes the pressure off me to get married and have a baby. You know how much she hopes for that."

"Well, her help will certainly be wonderful for me, and I'm grateful to her."

"How long will you be able to teach before the baby comes?" asked Amelia.

"I don't know. I plan to wear loose dresses and keep goin' as long as I can, unless the principal stops me.

Their conversation shifted to the long friendship between Priscilla and Amelia. "I told Amelia about Sally," said Priscilla. "I hope that was alright."

Mary nodded.

"I inquired at the superintendent's office about where in Baltimore Sally Freeman teaches. I found out she teaches in a school across town and is now called Sally Brown. Would you like to get in touch with her?" Priscilla asked. "I got her address."

"Thank you, Priscilla. I think I should write to her about Ellen's death. She was her half sister, after all."

After supper the three women walked down to the harbor, enjoying the cooler evening breeze. The next day Amelia showed them around the city and then they returned to the welcome quiet of their little garden. Mary observed Amelia and Priscilla together, listening intently to one another, smiling, laughing, gently touching the other's arm. She had never seen Priscilla so completely at ease, so happy. Mary left with a full heart and returned home.

The next day she wrote to Sally:

Dear Sally,

I see that you have a new last name and hope that means you have remarried and are happy. Congratulations to you and your husband!

I have sad news about Ellen. She ended her life more than two years ago with a jump from a bridge over the James River in Lynchburg. Her children are living with their stepfather there.

I understand that you and your family were badly mistreated by my family, and for that I am deeply sorry. Nevertheless, I thought you might want to know because Ellen was your half sister. Can you ever forgive us?

Please write back to me here in Philadelphia if you wish. I am teaching, married, and expecting a baby in December. When I come to Baltimore to see my friend Priscilla, I would like to visit with you, if you consent.

Best wishes,
Your other half sister,
Mary

Mary did not hear from Sally for several months, but then she received a letter:

Dear Mary,

It has taken me a while to write back to you, but I will try now. First I want to say, I'm sorry Ellen's children lost their mother.

What makes it so hard to write back was your question, "Can you ever forgive us?" You asked it so easily, as if you were asking about the weather. What a request! I do not know where to begin. The crime your family committed against mine was part of a monstrous crime committed by this country against millions of innocent people. It's far too big to ask me to forgive.

The crime of slavery has left a terrible legacy—- millions of Negroes who are legally free, but still subjugated by lack of education and the greed of white people in control.

I think being able to forgive depends on what happens now and in the years to come. Will Negroes actually be free, with opportunities for education, work, and ways of living that they choose? Will they be able to vote and hold office? Will they have equal justice under law?

If the people in power let these things to come to pass, then forgiveness and even reconciliation seems possible.

We shall see.
Sally

Mary sat and nodded. Then she put Sally's letter carefully away with a sigh.

By the end of August Mary had let out her dresses as much as they could expand. Mrs. Atkins invited her to bring them over and showed her how to sew in inserts that could expand them even more. Mary was slender to begin with, so with the expanded dresses and a shawl, she thought it was hard to tell she was pregnant. When school started she felt the familiar excitement of meeting her new pupils and starting a new year. After school on the first day, Mary was sitting at her desk, writing plans for the week. Mrs. Tatnall, the principal, knocked on the door and walked in briskly, looking serious.

"Hello Mrs. Tatnall, how are you?" Mary said.

"Oh, I'm just fine Mrs. Stewart. The question is, how are you?"

"I'm well, thank you. The ba-"

Mrs. Tatnall interrupted, "I don't want to hear about your personal business, as long as you are well enough to teach. That way we both stay out of trouble. You may talk to me about your pupils, your teaching, or all the materials we don't have. But no personal business. Do you understand, Mrs. Stewart?"

"Yes, Mrs. Tatnall, I think I do now."

"We are already short one teacher in this school, so when your personal business becomes urgent, please let me know, so I can look for two more. I'm already trying."

"I will let you know as soon as I know."

"Thank you, Mrs. Stewart. I'll take my leave now."

On a Friday afternoon in late November, Mrs. Tatnall made another visit to Mary's classroom. She observed the class for a while and when Mary dismissed her pupils, she announced that she wished to speak to her.

"Your pupils are either blind or exceptionally loyal," she began. "Not a single parent has complained or even mentioned your condition to me."

"I'm glad to hear that," said Mary.

The parents do say that you are a good teacher. And those children love you, even though you are white."

"Well I love them too."

"However, Mrs. Stewart, decency demands a limit. You are mighty big now. I will not have you giving birth on the classroom floor. I have hired another teacher and she will begin on Monday. So please take your personal things with you today."

"I wish I could speak with the new teacher and tell her what we've been doin' and about some of the children."

"She will find out on her own, you can be sure of that. If you want to leave some of the materials you created, you can. She can choose to use them if she wants to."

"I hope they'll be useful," said Mary, disappointed.

"Mrs. Stewart, I want you to know that when you are ready to return, you will be welcome."

"Thank you Mrs. Tatnall. I would like to stay home with the baby for a year, and then come back."

"Good that you want to come back. Negro women with children have always been working. I can't understand why white folks with children find it unthinkable."

"Neither can I."

"Well, best wishes to you and your husband, Mrs. Stewart. And best wishes for the baby, or maybe the babies," she said, looking hard at Mary's belly.

"Thank you, Mrs. Tatnall. We are very excited, but we don't think we're having twins."

The babies were born in less than a week. They named them Rebecca Alice Stewart and Emett Pringle Stewart. Mrs. Atkins and Susan were both in attendance at the birth, since neither wanted to forgo the chance to be a midwife at the birth of Peter and Mary's child. Mary's labor was hard and short. She said it seemed like the babies were in a hurry to see the world. When Susan called him to come in moments after the second birth, Peter was amazed and thrilled. "You never cease to astonish me, my darling Mary," he said.

She lay in bed exhausted and smiling, holding one baby in each arm. Gently, Mrs. Atkins helped them find Mary's breasts. "This is what you can do at first, Peter dear. Just until they learn. And then you do whatever else Mary needs."

"How will I know how?" Peter asked.

"You and Mary will figure it out, I know you will," said Mrs. Atkins.

Susan was preparing a little bed in a bureau drawer. "One thing you need right away is another cradle. Would you like me to get one?"

"Yes please, Susan," said Peter.

Louisa

December 1873 – June 1874

As soon as Louisa received a telegram from Peter, she boarded the train in Danville for the long journey to Philadelphia. She spent part of the train ride planning and writing out reading and writing assignments for Robert, Alexa, and Maxwell. When she changed trains in Washington, she mailed them to the Willis's post office box in Danville. Her plan was to stay for a few weeks to help Mary with the babies and then go to Lynchburg to have Christmas with Sam and the children. Sidney would come up and join them.

Riding along in the train, looking out the window, she thought about how lucky she was to have grandchildren. Wally, Henry, and Laura, so dear to her heart, and now two more. What would Becca and Emett be like? She was sorry not to have been present at their birth, but could tell from Mary's letter beforehand that three midwives would be too many.

After what seemed an endless trip, Louisa arrived tired and dirty in Philadelphia. Peter met her at the train station and they took a streetcar almost to their street. Louisa was still fascinated by the horse drawn streetcars. Arriving at Peter and Mary's home, she washed the train dirt off right away. Mary put Becca in her arms. "She has your eyes!" said Louisa. "I remember you looking up at me with those eyes when you were a baby." But whose mouth is that?"

"It's Peter's, Mama. Just look!"

Peter grinned. Then Mary took Becca and put Emett in her mother's arms. Louisa gasped in happy surprise. "He looks just like John when he was a baby."

That evening they all went to bed early and slept. Becca and Emett woke up to nurse every couple of hours and fell back to sleep afterwards. Until the last time they awoke, as it was getting light and they wanted to stay up. Then Louisa took them so Mary could sleep. She rocked them and danced them around until it seemed like time to nurse again, when she returned them to Mary. During the day Louisa did laundry, went to market, and cooked. Barbara Atkins brought soup, good company, and advice on raising twins that she had gathered from a friend. Peter went back to his office and was able to concentrate on his civil rights cases.

After three weeks Mary was feeling much recovered and encouraged Louisa to go to Lynchburg to be with Sam and the children. But Louisa saw that caring for the twins was demanding in itself, and that doing all the laundry, going to market, and cooking in addition might be overwhelming. She discussed it with Barbara Atkins. "One baby at a time is so much easier," said Barbara. "No doubt about that. I wish I could help more, but I am committed to work as a volunteer at the hospital until Mary goes back to work. I don't want to let them down."

"I'm sure Mary respects that."

"I have a good idea though. If you think Mary will permit it, I would like to ask Mary Lou if her daughter would be interested in working for Mary. She is eighteen and a fine girl. She works for me when I need extra help , so I know."

When Louisa explained Barbara Atkins' suggestion to her, Mary seemed annoyed. "I don't need a maid, Mama. And even if I did, I couldn't pay one."

"You know I have been tutoring Alexa, Max, and Robert. I've saved all that I've earned for something I want to do, and this is it."

"That money is for you, Mama."

"It would make me so happy to think of you takin' a nap when the twins do, instead of doin' laundry and cooking. With waking up so many times during the night to nurse the babies, you need rest to keep goin'. I don't want you to get overwhelmed."

"I won't get overwhelmed, Mama."

"Or if you did, you wouldn't admit it."

Mary's face showed she knew that was true. She looked at her mother and nodded her head.

"Thank you Mary. It will make leavin' you and the babies and Peter much easier."

So it was arranged that Mary Lou's daughter Sara would come to work for Mary and Peter. She was glad to leave her work in a textile mill and pleased to be in a household with babies. As she did laundry and cooked, she sang melodious Irish songs. And lullabies for the babies as she rocked them while Mary slept.

Seeing that the situation was working well, Louisa took the train from Philadelphia to Lynchburg a few days before Christmas. Wally, Henry and Laura had come to meet her. "Mr. Sam is still at the store," Laura said." "We all came to help you in case you had presents to carry," said Wally.

"Well, I'm glad you all came because I love seein' you," said Louisa, smiling. "And I do need you to carry things, even though they might not be presents." She handed Wally one of her tapestry bags.

"We've missed you, Grandmama," said Laura.

"We always miss you when you're not here," Henry said.

"I miss you too," Louisa said as they walked. "Do you want to hear about the babies?"

They nodded.

"Rebecca Alice has Aunt Mary's eyes and Uncle Peter's mouth."

Wally looked doubtful. "Is she funny looking?"

"No, she's adorable and smiles already."

"Why did they name her such a long name?" Henry asked.

'It's a family name, and they call her Becca."

"And what about the boy?" Laura wanted to know.

He is Emett Pringle and looks like your Uncle John, who died in the war. Most of the time he's quiet, but when he cries, he turns beet red."

By the time they got to the house, Sam was home, heating the thick bean and ham soup Ada had made them for supper. He and Louisa were glad to see each other and he wanted to hear all about how Mary and Peter were managing with the twins. The children had put up a Christmas tree and had waited to decorate it. "Mr. Sam says we are in charge of decorations this year. Will you help us, Grandmama?" Wally asked.

"Yes, that will be fun," she said.

Sidney arrived the next day, while Sam was at work and the children were out collecting pine cones. He looked disheveled and smelled of last night's whiskey. As Louisa told him about Mary, Peter, and the babies, he seemed distracted.

"What's on your mind?" Louisa asked him.

"The stock market crash is affecting tobacco prices too. We won't get nearly enough for our crop this year."

"I'm sorry Sidney. Can you still pay your sharecroppers?"

"That's what you worry about, my sharecroppers?"

"Well, if you can't give them enough crop to sell, how can they live?"

"They always manage somehow. And of course I need them to live so they can work."

"Can we talk about this later, Sidney? The children will be back in a few minutes. They're gatherin' pine cones so we can decorate the tree."

"Well, I want to go see Sam's brother-in-law, Adam, anyway. He knows the tobacco business from the top. I want to hear what he thinks of this Panic. Maybe he'll have some perspective to pass on. He's rich enough."

"Before you go, Sidney, did you bring the Emerson for Sam?"

"I forgot."

"That is our Christmas present to him. I know how much he will like it."

"Well, I forgot it." And he left.

When the children returned, Louisa and they made pinecone people to hang on the tree, using bits of fabric and glue to create facial features, hats, clothes and limbs. Sam came home and laughed to see the tree decorated. He examined the ornaments, guessing who made each one. Louisa had prepared a chicken soup for supper and Laura's biscuits were ready. They were just waiting for Sidney to return from Adam's. After an hour, Louisa said they should go ahead without him, which they did. When they were almost finished, the door opened and Sidney entered, clearly intoxicated.

"Helloo children! Helloo Sam! So good to see you! Nice of you to wait for me!" He wobbled across the room and sat down heavily at the table.

"Is there any left for me Louisa? My wife has become a rather good cook, even though I hired a Negro cook for us."

Louisa brought Sidney a bowl of soup. He reached across the table, grabbed a biscuit, and stuffed it in his mouth. Laura, Henry, and Wally watched their grandfather, wide eyed.

Sam said, "Children, I have something to take Aunt Emily from the store. Will you walk over there with me? It's a beautiful starry night."

As soon as they had left, Louisa said, "I'm sorry for your grandchildren to see you like this."

"When did you become such a prude, Louisa?"

Louisa looked at him sadly and carried the dishes into the kitchen. When she finished washing them, she found Sidney asleep on the sofa. She tried to wake him up. "Sam said for us to sleep in his room and he'll sleep with the boys." Sidney didn't move. When Sam and the children returned, Louisa was mortified that Sidney was still on the sofa. But she knew that Sam would have talked about Sidney's drinking problem with them while they walked, and would have answered their questions. That was a real comfort. So she embraced them and said, "I'm sorry."

"You didn't do anything wrong," said Sam.

"But I don't know what to do," she thought.

The next day was Christmas. Sam had given Ada a large ham and the day off with pay. He gave Celia the day off with pay and some beautiful fabric. He got up early and prepared sausage and eggs while Laura made biscuits. Louisa and the children put a few presents under the tree. After breakfast the children opened their presents. Louisa gave them each a Dickens novel from the library at Oak Hill, since he was their current favorite author. Sam gave the boys new shirts and Laura a new dress, made by a local seamstress from fabric each had selected. Sidney pulled three silver dollars out of his pocket and gave one to each of them. "You'd better spend them soon, before President Grant's gold standard makes them worthless." The children were especially pleased with their money, and wanted to take it to church with them to show their cousins and their friends.

"I don't think you should take your silver dollars to church," said Sidney. "They'll want you to put it in the collection. And then they'll give it to their missionaries in China"

"What's wrong with that, Grandpapa?" Laura asked.

"We need a collection for the white folks in the South, whose lives were ruined by the Yankees, not the Chinese."

They walked to church in the cold morning air. Henry and Laura had gone early for choir practice before the service. Sam and Wally walked ahead of Sidney and Louisa. Sidney complained of the cold, having forgotten to pack warm clothes. " See how it is, I need you to look after me, Louisa. I don't do well without you. Will you come home with me tomorrow?"

"I just got here, Sidney. I want to spend some time with the children while they have winter break."

"But you were gone so long already, at Mary's."

The service was lovely. Louisa loved the timeless story of Mary and Joseph, the Christ Child and the shepherds. Watching Laura and Henry sing with the choir, their faces lit with joy, Louisa felt her heart bursting with love. She looked at Sam, who was smiling at them. He looked at her and nodded. She knew he was thinking the same thing– what a blessing Ellen's children were. While they were singing the beloved Christmas hymns, she realized that Wally's voice was changing. She squeezed his arm and he looked down at her and grinned. When had he gotten so tall?

Christmas dinner felt festive. Laura had decorated the center of the table with greens and nestled pine cones around the candles. Louisa and Henry had made chess pies the day before and Wally and Ada had killed and plucked two plump hens. As soon as they returned from church, Louisa stuffed the hens with cornbread dressing and put them in the oven to roast in a pan of root vegetables.

"I'm very proud of how you have all learned to cook," Sam said to the children at dinner time, as he stood at the head of the table and carved the chicken. "It makes you quite independent."

"Well, of course it's nice that they help," Sidney said. "But it saddens me that they need to. They will never know the elegance of our old Southern way of life."

"But remember the price for that old way of life, Sidney. The slaves paid for it," said Sam.

"Having slaves was not the terrible thing the abolitionists made it out to be. Our slaves were happy because we took good care of them," Sidney said.

"I know it is important to talk about slavery, said Louisa. "But I would like to do it later, and just enjoy Christmas dinner now."

Henry, Laura, and Wally were listening intently. "Please don't wait til we're in bed to finish talking about slavery. We need to know more about it," said Henry. Laura and Wally nodded.

"I know", said Sam. "We'll talk more."

Dinner was delicious. Afterwards Matt and Emily, came over with Micajah and Emmy. Henry sliced and served the chess pies, while Louisa served raspberry tea made from Oak Hill raspberries. Sidney brought out his bourbon and insisted that Sam and Mathew join him for a drink. "It's Christmas, so you must. After all, President Grant has made it a Federal holiday. We have him to thank for that too, the Yankee bastard."

"Sidney, please remember the children," Emily whispered as she joined him in the dining room.

"Yes, I remember, Miss Emily. Do you know why he made Christmas a federal holiday?"

"No, why?"

"He thinks having a shared holiday will bring North and South together. Do you think that is happening?"

"I really don't know, Sidney,"

"Well I know. It's not happening! The only thing that will bring us back together is for the North to stay out of our business. And that bastard Grant won't do it." He went to the sideboard to pour himself more whiskey.

"The children, please Sidney." Emily returned to the parlor. She said quietly to Louisa, "I think Sidney must have had some bourbon before we arrived. He's pourin' himself more now, if you want to go and stop him."

"I've learned that I can't stop his drinking," Louisa said. "But I'll try to get him to slow down now, for the sake of the children." She went into the dining room with a heavy heart.

Sidney looked at her with a crooked smile. "I know what you are goin' to say, Louisa. But just for once, won't you be on my side?"

"I am on your side. And I hate to see your grandchildren embarrassed by you in front of their cousins."

"Why should they be embarrassed by me, Louisa? When did they become so prudish? Did you and Mary make them self righteous, like you both are?"

"It's very hard to talk to you when you have been drinking, Sidney. Do you think a walk in the fresh air would do you good?"

"Yes, Louisa dear, if you will accompany me."

Mathew appeared and interrupted, "There you are Sidney. I'd like to talk about this Panic in the markets with you. Let's walk outside a bit and talk."

Sidney nodded and they left. Louisa was relieved not to have to take a walk with Sidney when he had had too much to drink. She was tired of having that same conversation, tired of seeing him deal with every difficulty by drinking bourbon. She was tired of never being able to talk a problem through together. And she was shocked at the depth of her tiredness about all of it.

When Mathew and Sidney returned, Mathew went home with his family. Sidney excused himself and went upstairs to bed. As they were cleaning up the tea things, Henry asked, "Can we talk about slavery now Mr. Sam?"

"What do you think, Louisa?" Sam asked. She nodded, shaking off her tiredness. "And Wally and Laura?" They nodded too. They all sat down in the parlor.

"How did our family get slaves to begin with?" Henry started.

"Both of your great great grandfathers bought Negroes who were captured in Africa and brought by ship to Charleston South Carolina. They bought them to clear their land and work in their fields, their houses, their stables," Louisa said.

"But how could they buy people? How could it be allowed?" asked Laura, looking like she was going to cry.

" It was legal then," said Sam. "It is monstrous. Many people in the world thought slavery was alright in those days. They believed that white people were better than other races and thought white people should rule the world and force people who weren't white to work for them."

"So maybe they thought it was alright because they wanted to use the people," Wally said.

"I think you have it, Wally," said Louisa.

"And maybe the next generation knew it was wrong and just said it was right so they could keep doing it," said Henry.

"That might be why Grandpapa likes to talk about how he took such good care of his slaves," Laura said.

They continued talking and Sam and Louisa tried to answer the children's questions honestly.

"Do you understand now why it was so important for the slaves to be free, that our country fought a war over it?" Sam asked.

"I think so," said Wally. "But why didn't you fight on the Union side, Mr. Sam?

"I was defending my home, my parents, my livelihood, and my friends. I wasn't thinking about slavery being immoral. I was wrong."

The children looked troubled.

Louisa was moved by Sam's honesty and courage in admitting being wrong. "Do you realize how brave Mr. Sam is to say that?" she asked them. "If only more Southerners thought that way."

They nodded.

"All slaveholders were wrong, including me." Louisa said. "I never questioned the whole system of slavery until after the war. That's why it's our responsibility to make sure Negroes have opportunities to live as free people now.

"That's why you teach Celia and Aunt Mary teaches in a Negro school," said Henry.

"And that's why Uncle Peter defends Negroes' rights at court," Wally said.

"That's right," said Louisa. "Tell me, how did you three figure out so much about all this?"

"Well, you and Aunt Mary talk about our responsibilities to the Negroes a lot when you're together," said Laura, "and we listen."

"And Mr Sam tried to explain to Mama why life is better now, when she would long for the days before the war," Henry said.

"I didn't know you were listening," Sam said to Henry, smiling. "We can talk about these things more if you like. Grandmama and I don't have all the answers, but we are learning all the time. And Grand-mama can suggest some good reading about this for you. I know that."

"That's for tomorrow," Louisa said. "Now it's time for bed."

"I don't need to go to sleep when Laura does," said Wally.

"You're right. So read until you're sleepy," said Louisa.

The next day Sidney took the early train to Danville. Celia came to work with Ada, shortly after Sam left for the store. Ada said they had enjoyed the Christmas ham, with the children and all the relatives taking turns sitting down to eat in her small house. Her sisters and cousins had brought mountains of mashed yams, collards, biscuits, cornbread and several different kinds of fruit pies. And there was plenty of talking and laughing. Ada was glad to say that her son Harold was doing well, had completely recovered from the beating. He was still working for the carpenter, and "gettin' too big for his britches." Ada and Celia were curious to hear about the twins, but Louisa could see from their faces that they didn't approve of the names Mary and Peter had chosen.

"I know those names from somewhere. Those are planter names," said Ada.

Celia said she was there to do laundry and go to market with Miz Louisa if she wanted her to. "That would be a help, Celia," said Louisa. "And after dinner we can have an extra long lesson. Did you bring your books?"

"Yes Ma'am. I was hopin' we could have a lesson."

That afternoon Celia could hardly wait to read aloud for Louisa. Her fluency had improved markedly.

"You're doin' much better, Celia. What have you been doin' since our last time?

"You remember the story books you gave me to read to my little sisters and brothers? Well, they wanted me to read them over and over. Each time it was easier, until it got so it was just plain easy. Then I started readin' the fables for my lesson, and the same thing happened. It was hard at first and each time it got easier."

"That is wonderful Celia! Now let's keep going."

The afternoon sped by, as did the rest of the children's winter break. The day before she was to return to Oak Hill, Louisa had another long lesson with Celia. She left her with the multiplication tables and some reading, planning for a writing exercise on the reading when she returned.

At supper Wally asked when she would return. "Probably in two weeks," she said. "That's good," said Laura. "I was afraid you'd always have to go help with the new babies, and wouldn't come very often any more."

"We want you to come as often as you can, Louisa," Sam said, smiling at her. "We all love it when you're here."

In the morning Louisa left reluctantly and walked to the station with Laura and the boys. Waving at them through the train window, she realized that she was dreading her return to Oak Hill. Except for her students Alexa, Max, and Robert, there was little drawing her home any more. Sidney was her husband though, and she had once loved him deeply. She would have to try. That was all there was to it.

Sidney met her at the train station in the carriage. He smelled like soap and looked neat. He embraced her and kissed her tenderly. As soon as they were underway, he said, "How would you like to be very, very rich?"

"What are you talking about, Sidney?"

"Remember I told you that young John Stanton had lost his head and was investing more and more money in the stock market? I kept telling him it was too risky, but he didn't listen. Eventually he even borrowed money to invest, a lot. When the stock market crashed last year, he lost everything and couldn't pay his debt, which was enormous. So he had to sell his property. He offered it to me, since our land adjoins his. Property prices are down since the crash, but it was still too costly. So I borrowed against this year's crop for the down payment, and borrowed the rest to pay back over time."

"Are you saying that you own all of John Stanton's land now, although it's heavily mortgaged?

"That's what I'm sayin'."

"I wonder if he hopes you'll default on your loans and he'll get his land back."

"Why would you say such a mean thing about him? He's a friend."

"I hope so."

"Can you imagine what a huge tobacco crop we will have? I have more than doubled our tobacco fields. And we need more land so we can start to let some of it lie fallow and recover. You know how tobacco depletes the land."

"Will John's sharecroppers stay on to grow the crop?"

"Yes, he assured me it was part of the deal."

"I hope they think so too."

"Of course they do. Why wouldn't they?"

"Maybe they weren't gettin' a fair share with John."

"Of course they were, Louisa. Aren't you happy? We'll be rich again."

"I'm a bit uncomfortable about your goin' into so much debt for John's land."

"Oh Louisa, if only for once you would be happy about something I do."

"I'm sorry Sidney, I truly hope it works out well."

"That's as much as you will concede? You are a difficult woman, Louisa."

As they drove up the slope to Oak Hill, Louisa looked up at the ancient oaks standing behind the house and reaching their thick branches into the sky. While Sidney went to the stable, she walked up the stairs, across the veranda, and into the house. She walked through the center hall into the spacious rooms, looking at the lovely old mahogany furniture and Persian carpets they had inherited from Sidney's ancestors. How had she and Sidney avoided thinking about how those ancestors came by this house and these things? Everyone knew they had earned their money by raising tobacco with slave labor. She walked through the library looking at the precious books and then studied the Townsend Goddard desk and bookcases Sidney's father had ordered from Newport, Rhode Island. She stood in the dining room and ran her fingers over the fine inlay at the edge of the Federal table, studying the silver candelabra in the center. Then she walked through the pantry and out to the kitchen house. She could almost see May Belle cooking in front of the fireplace. When she turned around, there was Sidney, looking at her, "What are you doin', Louisa?"

"Just thinking. I forgot to tell you at Sam's, Mary learned that Sally is teaching in Baltimore. She's married again and her last name is Brown. Mary wrote her to ask if she could visit, but Sally didn't invite her."

"Why Mary bothers, I don't know," Sidney said.

"She's her sister, for one reason."

"Half sister, and ungrateful."

Alexa, Max, and Robert arrived for their lesson the next day, rosy from the cold. Louisa had given them Thoreau's Walden to read, and they sat before the fireplace in the library to discuss it. They were intrigued with Thoreau. "He didn't care a whit what people thought of him," said Alexa wistfully. "I wish I could be like that."

"How could he be so sure he was right?" Max asked.

Louisa explained a little of what she had learned about Thoreau's philosophy, and suggested they read some Emerson. Again she realized how fortunate she was to have such an extensive library, and silently thanked their fathers and Walter. Lessons like this, exploring great ideas with deep thinkers like Emerson and Thoreau, challenging and encouraging her students to think, this was what Louisa loved best. Lately she had become aware of wanting more education for herself. As she continued to read and learn, she had questions, and wished she could ask them of a teacher. She would imagine how it would be to be in a class, talking about ideas with other students. Then she would remind herself that she was being "just plain silly." Robert would be going to the university next year. How she envied him! He had a tutor for Latin and Greek now, it was good to know. She was glad that her lack of knowledge in those areas wouldn't be an impediment to him.

When their lesson was over, Robert said, "I appreciate all you have taught us, Miz Turner, and I'm glad we have a few more months with you."

"Well, I'm glad too, Robert. It has been a pleasure to work with you three. You have such curious and active minds." She looked at Alexa and Max. "I'm glad I'll still have you two."

"Father wants to send me to a boys' school in Charlottesville next year, to take Greek and Latin and get me ready for the University," Max said.

"And he wants to send me to the Hollins Institute in Roanoke," Alexa added, "to make a lady out of me."

"Well, what do you know!" said Louisa, surprised, and trying to hide her disappointment.

"I don't know how they turn you into a lady, do you Miz Turner?" Alexa asked.

"I'm not sure, but I think it involves learning how to set a formal dining table, speak in a soft voice, do needle work, and dance gracefully."

"That sounds boring, except for the dancing," Alexa said.

"Mama has a pamphlet about the Hollins Institute, and I read it," Max said. "It says 'the founder based his pedagogy upon the Southern sensibility that a lady was to be trained to submit to the order of men'."

"What in the world does that mean?" Alexa asked.

"That just means they teach you to obey men," said Robert.

"What do you think it means, Miz Turner?" Alexa asked.

"I think Robert is right. It probably does mean that a woman should let a man, presumably her husband, decide what she should do with her life."

"Do you agree with that?" Alexa asked.

"No," said Louisa. "I think women should decide for themselves. What do you think, Alexa?"

"I think so too."

"I was going to tease you about going there, but I just changed my mind." Robert said. "I wonder if Mama read that pamphlet. She sure doesn't like it when Papa tells her what to do."

"Mama said she is not a real lady, since her parents were poor farmers," said Alexa. "So she wants me to be a lady. She said she never wants me to be embarrassed in a social situation the way she has been."

"Well my budding scholars," said Louisa, "it's time for you to ride back home. Dig into that Emerson for Wednesday, and come back with lots of questions."

Louisa felt uncomfortable about Alexa telling her that her mother was not a real lady, thinking that Eliza wouldn't like it. But even more, she was concerned about the effect of the "finishing school" on Alexa. Alexa was curious and open. She loved learning. What would happen to her mind and spirit in such a place? What's more, even though Eliza was not the least interested in education, it did seem as though she made her own decisions. She certainly was not a typical planter's wife. Did she want Alexa to be? Mary had been sending Louisa articles by the suffragists, which had reinforced her feelings about women being independent. So how to handle this?

Deciding to bide her time about Alexa's school, Louisa devoted herself to making the remaining months with her pupils as full and effective as she could. They read more Emerson and Thoreau and wrote essays on their reading. They read several of Dickens' novels. They divided The Rime of the Ancient Mariner into three parts and memorized them and then performed all of it for Sidney and her. They studied more history and geography. They studied botany, learning about the plants growing around the house, in the woods, and along the creek. They learned about the birds and animals they encountered, Louisa learning right along with them. To her chagrin, she said, they had gone as far as she could go in mathematics. As a final assignment, Louisa gave them Douglass's speech, "What, to a Slave is the Fourth of July?" to read. She asked them each to write an essay explaining the significance of the piece to them. At their last session they would read their essays aloud.

When they arrived that last day, they were excited and nervous. Louisa asked that they wait until they had heard all three essays to discuss them. Robert stood up formally and read first. Max and Alexa followed suit. Alexa began the discussion with the comment, "If people had listened to Douglass in 1855 and freed the slaves, there wouldn't have been a war. Why didn't they listen?" Louisa asked Robert to answer Alexa's question, and then she asked Max. The discussion was lively and showed that they had learned a great deal about what slavery had meant for Negroes and white people. Louisa felt proud of them and told them so. They were pleased to hear that, and sorry that their lessons with Louisa were ending.

Alexa asked. "Miz Turner, will you talk to Mama about my goin' to the Hollins Institute? I tried to, but she said she was too busy then. When I tried again, she said it was all decided and I would love it once I got there and made friends. Will I Miz Turner?"

"I don't know Alexa, but I will talk to your mother when she and your father come for dinner next week. I hope you understand that she may not pay any attention to what I say."

Alexa nodded and tears welled in her eyes.

Promising to visit, the three siblings rode away. Louisa's eyes filled up too.

Sidney was pushing his sharecroppers to cultivate, thin, and weed the young tobacco plants faster on his old land, as well as on the new acres he had bought from John Stanton. The field hands seemed slower than usual, which irritated him mightily. It seemed the harder he pushed, the slower they got. And as usual, the more irritated he became, the more whiskey he drank. On the day that Eliza and George were coming to dinner, Louisa turned to Sidney while they were dressing. "Would it be possible for you not to drink so much today?"

"Sorry my dear," he said, "It will be such a pleasure not to drink alone. I wouldn't miss it."

After their guests arrived and they were sitting on the veranda, George thanked Louisa for teaching their three children.

"I'm amazed that they actually enjoyed it," he said. "I hated my lessons with my Grampaw. They were dreadful."

"Mine were awful too," Eliza said. "I've told you that, Louisa."

"I remember," said Louisa. "Well, I have certainly enjoyed workin' with your children. They are smart, curious, and want to learn. The best combination."

"I don't know where they get that," said George." Eliza and I are dumb as posts when it comes to book learnin'. But give us tobacco business and we're damn clever!"

"I can see you're doing mighty well," said Sidney. "Looks to me like you rode over on some new horses. How about if we all go take a look? "

As they walked to the stable, Louisa mentioned to Eliza that Alexa and the boys had told her about their plans for next year.

"How 'bout that. Hard to believe they are all growin' up," said Eliza.

"The boys seem to be lookin' forward to September," said Louisa. "But I'm sure you know Alexa is not. I want you to know I am glad to keep on teaching her if you want to keep her home."

"That's just it. I'm lookin' forward to having no children at home so I can go along with George on business. Imagine, we'll be able to stay overnight in Danville or Lynchburg whenever we want."

"Eliza, Alexa is intelligent and curious. She thinks for herself, like you do. Do you think Hollins Institute will be an encouraging place for her mind and spirit?"

"I really don't know about those things Louisa. But I do know they will teach her how to be a lady. And I know that matters."

"But what if they teach her to be submissive instead of being herself?

"I guess that's my worry, Louisa, not yours."

"Oh Eliza, I'd hate to see Alexa lose her independent spirit."

They fell silent as they arrived at the stable and admired the handsome thoroughbreds George had bought. When they returned to the veranda, Sidney was especially cordial in offering and serving whiskey to his guests. He winked at Eliza when she accepted a glass. Then Lucy served dinner in the dining room. Eliza was amazed to learn that Louisa grew the greens and other vegetables she served. "I wouldn't know a thing about growin' a garden. Our cook does all that, thank goodness." Louisa told Eliza and George that she had written a summary for each child, telling about the books and subjects they had covered and had included some comments specific to each, pointing out their areas of strength. George and Eliza nodded and said they would take them home. Then they went back to discussing how they were training the new horses.

As the visit was ending, Louisa handed her summaries to Eliza, relieved to see the couple say goodbye. "Why were you so quiet, Louisa?" Sidney asked as they rode away. "Can't you make more of an effort to be a pleasant hostess?"

"I still do not understand them. Did you see how little interest they have in their children's education? In their children?

"Not everybody is a bookworm like you, Louisa. Some folks just like to have a good time."

"I didn't change Eliza's mind at all about sending Alexa to Hollins. I wish I could have."

"Well, it's really none of your business."

Needing to get away, Louisa went for a ride on Sadie. When she returned, Sidney was sitting in his study, worrying over his figures and drinking bourbon. "We're gonna need every single leaf to be good… to make the payments on the mortgage," he said, slurring his words. Louisa went upstairs and read until she was sleepy.

She awoke early and went to the open window. She stood listening to the blue birds and wrens chirping and singing in the oaks around the house, trying to link the birds she saw with their sounds.

Sidney was snoring, insistently oblivious. Louisa dressed quickly and went downstairs. In the pantry she ate a piece of yesterday's cornbread. Then she pumped cool water into a bowl, drank deeply, and sighed. She walked to the stable, where Sadie greeted her. She saddled her and led her to the water trough to drink. Then they rode off, following a faint path towards the creek.

The undergrowth had come back since the children had worn it away the previous summer, but Louisa was familiar with the way. Morning sun poured dappled light through the trees and sparkled in the dew on their leaves. Louisa stopped Sadie so that she could drink in the beauty of the morning. Then, after continuing some distance, she heard the sounds of singing and laughing. "Oh Mary don't ya weep, don't ya mourn…" She kept riding toward the creek. When she reached the bank, she saw four women she recognized as the wives of Sidney's sharecroppers. They were washing their laundry, scrubbing it on the rocks, and spreading it on the bushes to dry. As soon as they saw Louisa, they stopped singing and stared. "Good mornin''!" Louisa said. There was silence and the women nodded. Finally one woman said, " Good mornin' Miz Louisa."

Louisa suddenly recognized her as one of their former slaves. "Hello, I remember you," she said.

She heard giggling and saw several very young children peeking out of the woods behind their mothers. "Hello, I 'member you," one of the little girls mimicked her.

"Hush, chile," said the mother Louisa recognized. "Don't pay her no mind, Miz Louisa."

"Well, I'd best be getting back," said Louisa. "A pleasant day to y'all."

Riding back through the woods, she felt left out, isolated from the life around her. She didn't belong with those women, but she didn't belong at Oak Hill anymore either.

Mary
June 1874

The twins were thriving at six months old. Becca now had curly brown hair like her mother and was very active, crawling everywhere to explore. Emett was a quiet baby with smooth blond hair, content to study the world. If Becca wanted to cross to the other side when he was lying in the middle of their blanket, she would crawl right over him. Emett would remain serene, and Peter and Mary would laugh. Peter wished he could spend more time with the babies, but civil rights cases were taking more and more time. By the time he got home in the evening, Mary was bathing them. Then he would rock one baby while Mary nursed the other. Then they would switch. Peter and Mary savored that time every evening. And then the babies slept.

They were grateful every day for Sara, who had an easy way with the twins and seemingly inexhaustible energy for housework and laundry. Mary loved hearing Sara singing Irish songs in her high pure soprano. Even though she sang the same songs often, there were still some words that Mary couldn't comprehend. When she asked Sara to write down a word she couldn't get, she blushed pink and said she couldn't write, or read either. "That is nothing to feel shame for," said Mary. "You probably never had a chance to learn."

"That's right, Ma'am. I've been workin' most of my life."

"Would you like to learn?"

"Of course I would. But I can't go to school. I need to work."

"I can teach you if you like."

"I'd like that Ma'am. I know you are a teacher."

"When you come tomorrow, I'll have some things together and we can start."

"Just like that, Ma'am?"

"Just like that. We'll find some time."

After that Mary and Sara found time every day to work on reading and writing. Sometimes they sat on the floor with the babies and worked on writing while they played. Sometimes they each rocked a baby as they read together. And sometimes they worked a half hour while the babies slept, and then Mary would sleep too, while Sara practiced on her own. Sara was excited to learn, and soon she was able to read the words to her beloved Irish songs. "I din know the words looked like this," she marveled. It took longer to read unfamiliar texts, but she made steady progress.

One morning Sara came late, her face pale with bad news. Her mother Mary Lou had been stricken during the night. It was a heart attack. Mr. Atkins had sent their doctor to examine and treat her. The doctor said she would need complete bed rest and someone to care for her. "I am all my mother has," Sara said. "I need to stay with her. Do you understand, Mrs. Stewart?"

"Of course I understand Sara. You have been such a help to us, but we will manage now, until your mother is better. Go now, and my husband will come to you at your mother's to bring your pay. He is already at his office now."

"I thank you Ma'am, also for teaching me. May I kiss the babies before I go?"

'Yes. I know they will miss you. And thank you for all your help Sara."

As soon as Sara left, Becca and Emett woke up crying. Mary tried to nurse them both at once, but now that they were bigger, it was hard to hold them both in the right position. So she nursed Becca first, and feeling guilty, let the usually calm Emett cry. Then she nursed Emett. When it was time to change diapers, she found the stack was low and realized she had to wash some right away. When she finished that, she looked at the clock, hoping it was almost time for Peter to come home. It was only ten o'clock in the morning! It would be hours until he came. She needed to go to market, since they were out of bread and eggs. Remembering the women working in the fields at Oak Hill with their babies tied onto their backs, she put Becca into a shawl, and tied it onto her back. Becca howled loudly until she finally fell asleep. Meanwhile Mary put Emett in her market basket and set out. At the market she bought butter, eggs, cheese, and bread. She had to put them in the basket, which meant she had to carry Emett in her other arm. Becca woke up and both babies cried and wriggled. By the time Mary got home, she was totally spent and her arms and neck were screaming with pain. Then it was time to change and nurse the babies. The day was endless. Finally Peter came home. Their little house was a mess, the babies were crying, and Mary looked drained. Peter took her in his arms and kissed her. Then he picked up Emett and Becca and held them while he led Mary to the sofa.

"Tell me what is happening," he said.

When she finished explaining, she said, "It was terrible, I was terrible." Tears streamed down her face. "Mothers manage these situations all the time. Why couldn't I?"

"Mary, having twins is hard. Everyone tells us that. Your mother made it clear that she wants to come whenever we need her. This is what she was talking about.

"She would be a Godsend," Mary agreed.

"I'll cable her in the morning."

Louisa came as quickly as she could, glad to be able to help, and delighted to see how well the twins were developing.

"I hope Papa will not mind your being gone a while," said Mary. "Sara's mother is still very weak. The doctor says she may need several weeks of bedrest."

"Sidney minding this is not so important, Mary. He seems to mind almost everything lately."

Louisa soon fell into a rhythm with Emett and Becca, rocking, changing, holding and playing with them, and in between doing laundry, going to market, and cooking. She loved watching Mary and Peter play with the twins and marvel at each of their new accomplishments. It felt like a gift to her to have the time to get to know these new grandchildren and see Mary and Peter as parents.

At the end of Louisa's third week in Philadelphia, Sara paid a visit. Right away she kissed the twins and exclaimed at how they had grown. She said her mother was feeling much better and the doctor said she could stay by herself during the day for one more week of rest before going back to work at the Atkins. So Sara could come back, if they still wanted her.

"Yes, we want you!" Mary and Peter said together.

"I missed these babies! And I missed my lessons with you, Ma'am."

"I'm not surprised you found a chance to teach," Louisa said, smiling at Mary.

"And Sara is doing quite well," Mary beamed.

Hearing how well it had worked to have Sara, Louisa was pleased that she was able to pay for her. And now she felt comfortable leaving, the day that Sara came back.

Louisa
July 1874

The thought of returning to Oak Hill and Sidney made Louisa's heart sink. Realizing that made her sad. She decided to put off her return with a visit to Sam and the children in Lynchburg. It was always a joy to see them. She just had to change to the South Side train at Burkeville Junction. So she cabled Sam to ask if it were convenient. Immediately he cabled back, "always convenient for you to come." She left Mary, Peter, and the twins with many embraces and kisses and boarded the train to Lynchburg.

On the train the feeling of sadness returned. What had happened to their marriage? Looking back, she saw that things really hadn't been right between them since the war. She had changed. She was more independent, and he didn't like it. She was introspective now and concerned about justice. He had changed too, in ways she didn't like either. He was more critical, more impatient, and more often angry than he had been before. And she had watched him deal with his disappointment and anger by drinking more and more whiskey.

She remembered how they were before the war, how they had fun together, dancing, riding and making love. How they enjoyed their children. They were carefree and hopeful, but also careless. They assumed their comfortable lives would go on uninterrupted. They never thought about their comfort being dependent upon slavery. How could they have been so oblivious? They just didn't think about it. But with the slaves freed and gone, Louisa had started thinking about it a lot. She had finally started to realize the enormity of the crime of slavery. She had begun to see clearly that white folks have a responsibility to assure that Negroes can get education. Why hadn't Sidney and Ellen realized those things? Both of them still longed for the past, the gracious Southern way of life.

Thank God for Mary! She had awakened to the issues that slavery had created before Louisa did. And she had devoted herself to doing what she could to bring opportunity to Negroes by teaching. Louisa realized that Mary had had a big influence on her, and through her, on Jewel and Jim's three sons, and then Robert, Max, and Alexa. And then Celia. And Mary had directly influenced Peter, Sam, Wally, Henry, and Laura. And all those children in her classes. Louisa thought with regret that Ellen would not approve. Ellen had been afraid of the new world that was coming.

Louisa changed trains at the Junction and tried to nap the rest of the way to Lynchburg. But her mind returned to Mary and her family in Philadelphia. What a joy it was to see them all together, Peter on the floor playing with one baby, while Mary nursed the other, all the while discussing Peter's ongoing civil rights cases to win equal pay for Negro workers in the textile mills. He was excited about these cases, and Mary followed every detail and asked questions. How long had it been since Louisa and Sidney had shared mutually interesting conversations about what they were doing? Louisa sighed.

Wally and Henry met her at the train station. Laura was at a ballet lesson with Emmy. "It's ridiculous, Grandmama." Wally said, "Can you imagine Laura doin' ballet? She's as graceful as a cow."

"Actually, I can easily imagine it Wally. You never can tell what folks can learn if they want to. What are you boys doin' this summer?"

"Playin' baseball, mainly," said Henry.

"What's baseball?" Louisa asked.

"You have to hit a ball with a bat and run the bases," said Henry.

"Do you mean cricket?"

"No, that's English. Baseball is American."

"It's the best! All the boys are playin' it," Wally said.

They talked about baseball most of the way home. Sam and Laura were there when they arrived. Laura embraced her and did a pirouette. Sam looked up smiling from the chicken he was frying. "So glad you're here, Louisa. Such a nice surprise."

"That's why we're having fried chicken for supper, to celebrate," said Laura.

"It's so good to be here," Louisa said as she washed, and then she started helping Laura set the table.

During supper Louisa found out about the end of the school year and how Sam's business was finally starting to grow. "I've had to hire another clerk to sell all the new textiles I've been buyin'. We need the good business, but I don't see how I can leave and go to Oak Hill this summer.

Oh Mr. Sam, we didn't know that," said Wally, disappointed.

"I wanted to talk with your Grandmama first," said Sam.

"We don't need to talk about it, Sam. I'd love for them to come back to Oak Hill with me. That is, if they would like to."

"Of course we would like to!" Henry said right away.

"When can we leave?" Laura asked.

"I will write to Grandpapa tonight asking him to pick us up at the station. My letter will go on the train to Danville tomorrow. We have a post office box there now, so he'll get my letter the next time he goes to Danville. Let's say he gets my letter by the end of the week at the latest, I think we can go to Oak Hill on Saturday."

The next morning Louisa dropped her letter at the post office and went to market. When she arrived back at Sam's, Ada and Celia were there. Ada was making bread and Celia was out back doing laundry. "Mornin' Miz Louisa," said Ada. "The boys are off playin' baseball and Laura's upstairs readin'."

"How are you, Ada?" asked Louisa.

"My children are alive and healthy, praise the Lord. But my cousin just lost a son to some white men. They didn't want colored folk workin' on the railroad with them. Beat 'em up so bad they killed 'em, three young men."

"I'm so sorry Ada. And I bet the white men that did it didn't get caught."

"You right about that, Miz Louisa."

Louisa unpacked her market basket and went out to the backyard.

Celia looked up from the laundry and said," I knew them. They were nice fellas."

"It's terrible Celia, I'm so sorry."

"I wish more people were sorry," said Celia as she rubbed Wally's shirt against the washboard.

"I do too, Celia."

Miz Louisa, I hope it's alright, I been keepin' up with the cleanin' and laundry on the mornings Mama comes, so Mama just has to take care of the marketin' and cookin'. The children don't need me much in the afternoon any more." She continued scrubbing.

"Whatever Mr. Sam, your Mama, and you work out is good. Would you like to work on lessons this afternoon?"

"I have to do laundry for another family this afternoon, but I would like a lesson tomorrow, if that suits you."

Louisa agreed. The next day she was impressed to see the progress Celia had made in reading, using the materials Mary had sent. Louisa saw that Celia needed to read more and more books now. She needed to be able to browse in a library and find books that interested her and were the right level. But Lynchburg had no public library, and if they had one, would surely not allow Negroes to use it, since everything in the city was segregated. Louisa decided to go through her own library and send some books for Celia back with the children, when they returned from Oak Hill. In the meantime, Celia was slowly working her way through Jane Eyre, which had too many unfamiliar words to be enjoyable at this point.

After Ada and Celia were gone the boys told what they had heard at school about Ada's cousin's son and two of his friends being beaten to death. "On the way home some of the boys were saying they deserved it," said Wally. "I told them that was a stupid thing to say. Then some boy punched me and I punched him back. Then Miz Lewis, up the street, came out and yelled at us, so we all ran away."

"Thank God for Miz Lewis," said Sam.

"I still don't understand why people hate Negroes so much," said Henry.

"I know we've talked about it, but it doesn't make sense," Laura said.

"It doesn't. But people hate anyway. Think about those white men workin' on laying the new railway," said Sam. "They probably didn't get much chance to go to school, so labor jobs are about all they can get. Now if young Negro men will take the jobs for lower pay, those white fellows might lose their jobs. It has happened."

"But these white men were working, right with the Negroes. That's what we heard," said Wally.

"It's important to many white people to feel that they are better than Negroes," Louisa said. "Lookin' down on Negroes makes them feel superior. They don't want to work with them, ride in the same train car, or go to the same church or school."

"Why don't they want them to vote, though?" Henry asked.

"What if they vote for leaders who will work for schools for Negroes that have enough teachers and books for every child to get a good education?" said Sam.

"Then Negroes would have opportunities for better lives. They would have choices," Louisa said.

"But some white folks want things to be like they used to be, when Negroes were only allowed to be servants, field hands, and laborers," said Sam.

"Now you two sound like Aunt Mary," said Laura.

"So those boys who said the three men deserved to be killed probably wish we still had slavery," said Wally.

"Maybe, but maybe they haven't really thought about it, and are saying what they heard someone else say," Louisa said.

That evening, when Louisa stood up to go upstairs to bed, Sam said, "Conversations like we had today go better when you are here, Louisa. In fact, everything goes better." Sam smiled broadly. Louisa felt the blood rush to her cheeks as she turned and walked upstairs. That night she had a hard time getting to sleep.

At the end of the week Louisa, Laura and the boys took the train to Danville. Louisa had told them all about their tiny cousins, so they were eager to meet them. Mary was arriving with the twins in two days. Peter couldn't get away from work and Sara didn't want to leave her mother for so many nights. Louisa had not heard from Sidney, but she assured herself that there hadn't been time for him to reply. So she was relieved to see him waiting with the buggy when they reached the station in Danville. But her relief quickly became disgust when she realized that he was drunk, and still drinking from a flask. How could he, with the children arriving?

Sidney greeted them by commenting on how tall they had gotten. "How will you all fit in the carriage?" he asked. "My wife will have to sit next to me, though she's hardly a wife any more. She has become all grandmother, and forgotten all about being a wife."

"That's enough, Sidney. You're embarrassing your grandchildren."

"Am I embarrassin' you, Laura? Henry? Wally?"

All three looked down.

Sidney took a swig from his flask. "Why don't you have some with me, Louisa, like Eliza?"

"No thank you, Sidney. Please put it away."

He did not, but at least he stopped talking and seemed to be concentrating on driving the horses.

Louisa tried to ease the awkwardness by pointing out birds and plants as they passed, but the ride seemed endless. When they arrived at Oak Hill, they sat at the dining room table and ate the supper that Lucy had left for them. Sidney was quiet and ate little. The children ran to the stable to see the horses after supper. When they came back they went upstairs, saying they were tired. Louisa started up the stairs too.

"Stop Louisa!" said Sidney. "I want to talk to you."

She followed him into his study and closed the door. "You have always been ready to help your daughters and your grandchildren," he said. "And you still are. But what about me? I need you to help me." He reached out to embrace her but she could not respond. He reeked of bourbon and had cheese stuck in his beard. She shrank away from him.

"What is this? You are my wife and I am asking for your help," he said loudly.

"And I will listen," she said a bit less loudly. "But not now. Not when you are drunk. I'll see you in the morning," and she went upstairs.

Laura was sitting on the bed in John's old room, waiting. "Why does Grandpapa get drunk?" she asked.

"It's hard to understand. I have some ideas about it but I still don't really know. I'm so sorry you all had to see your Grandpapa like this again."

"Are you alright, Grandmama?"

"I'm sad about it."

"You can sleep with me tonight if you want Grandmama."

"That would be very nice Laura."

The next morning the children woke early, eager to go riding. Louisa was already sitting on the veranda, drinking a steaming cup of sassafras tea. Wally explained that they wanted to take a long ride going east, and be gone all day. They could take food and water and be back by supper. Once Aunt Mary and the twins arrived, they wouldn't want to be gone so long. Louisa thought it was a good plan and suspected that they also wanted to avoid their grandfather for today. She asked

Lucy to put together some provisions and they left after a hasty breakfast.

Sidney arose shortly before noon and requested that Caroline bring water for a bath. When he appeared downstairs, clean and dressed neatly, he found Louisa in the library, picking out books for Celia.

"I apologize for yesterday, Louisa. But you don't know what I'm up against here."

"What is it? What's happening?"

"We're in trouble, Louisa. Four of the sharecropper families who were workin' the land I bought from John Stanton up and left. Sixteen fieldhands.

"Why, Sidney?"

I don't know. Shiftless, I guess. You just can't trust Negroes. I needed them to care for the crop and harvest it. If I don't get all that tobacco harvested and cured in time, I won't be able to sell it and make the mortgage payment on that land. They will foreclose on me. Damn it, Louisa!"

"Can't you find other sharecroppers? It seems like there are often folks in Danville who are lookin' for work."

"I thought of that, but haven't gotten to it. I'll go early tomorrow and see if I can find some folks who need the work. I have to pick up Mary and the babies at the train anyway."

"Sidney, if you get the help you need and can make the payment in the fall, would you consider selling the Stanton land?"

"That's absurd, Louisa. Why would you think such a thing.?"

"It seems like owning so much land and owing so much debt is overwhelming. Why not settle for less and not have to worry?"

"You clearly have no understanding at all of financial matters, because that is plain stupid. I want lots of land and more tobacco to sell. I want to be rich again. We may not have won the war, but we can still be rich and powerful."

"So that's what this is about?"

"Of course, Louisa. How can you not understand?" Sidney stood and looked at Louisa. She was silent. Sidney walked out. Louisa went back to looking for books for Celia. She felt the chasm between Sidney and her widening.

The next evening Mary and the twins arrived. Wally, Laura, and Henry were delighted with their little cousins, especially when Mary let them play with them on the floor. As soon as everyone had eaten and gone upstairs, Sidney called Louisa into his office. He had found two men in Danville who were ready to come immediately to work tobacco with their families. They would move into the vacated cabins on the Stanton land. Louisa told Sidney she would help them with provisions. She had also found out that morning that one of the families on the Stanton land had a cousin who wanted to come to work there with his family. When she told Sidney that she had said for the cousin to come ahead, Sidney was annoyed. "Why did you say that without asking me?" he asked her.

"I thought you needed more workers."

"Of course I need more workers, but it is not your place to hire them."

"It would have been foolish not to have taken advantage of the chance to get a family that was ready to come."

"You are deliberately being hard headed, Louisa. What is wrong with you?"

Louisa shook her head and went upstairs, hoping that Mary was still up. When she looked in Mary's room, she saw that she and the twins were sound asleep. And there was not a sound from Laura, Wally or Henry.

Knowing there would be extra laundry and cooking, Louisa had asked Sidney to hire Lucy's daughter Bella and her friend Jewel to work during the visit. Seeing Jewel again was going to be a secret pleasure. Sidney had agreed to hire the two girls, even though he complained that he needed them in the fields. He and Louisa argued over their pay. "It's as if you resent paying them at all," "Louisa said.

"I do resent it. If it weren't for the Yankees interfering with our property rights, I wouldn't have to."

"Oh Sidney, how can you still be thinking like that?"

It had been another of their conversations that led nowhere and only made them see how far apart they were. Louisa went to bed fretting about the distance between them. Later, when Sidney came to bed, he smelled of whiskey. He reached for her, but she pretended to be asleep.

Laura heard the babies first and went to Mary's room. She rocked Emett while Mary nursed Becca, and then they switched. Laura was entranced. When they went downstairs, Wally and Henry were in the dining room with Louisa.

"The twins aren't allowed on the veranda," Wally announced. "They might fall down the steps."

"What did you do with us Mama?" Mary asked.

"I only had one baby at a time, so it was easier to keep track of them," said Louisa. "As long as someone is in charge of each baby, we can probably be on the veranda. Do you agree, Mary?"

"Let's try it. Wally is in charge of Emett. Henry, you watch Becca."

"What about me?" asked Laura.

"You just had them both, upstairs." said Henry.

The days of the visit with Mary and all the children were full. Ellen's children rode, swam in the creek, read, and spent lots of time with Mary and their little cousins. Louisa and Mary had time to talk. Bella and Jewel worked with Lucy and Caroline and helped keep meals and laundry going smoothly. Sidney was busy with tobacco business most of the time. He continued to stay up late at night drinking whiskey and didn't get up until late in the morning. One early morning, when the older ones were out riding, Mary and Louisa sat on the floor in her room, playing with the twins and talking.

"I can see Papa is completely preoccupied with his business," said Mary. "How is that for you, Mama?"

"I have never been very interested in tobacco, you know. But you know that's not the most important problem we have. I'm afraid we have grown apart, so far apart I don't see how we'll ever find our way back together."

"I can see that, Mama."

"It makes me sad, Mary. We used to love each other."

"It makes me sad too. Is that why Papa is drinking so much?"

"It must be part of it. He's also still angry the South lost the war, and angry about how things are changing."

"I know. I remember."

"Now he's worried about finances too. Things are precarious because he overextended himself. He wants to be rich and powerful again."

"Ah yes, power. Will you be alright here, Mama?"

"I don't know. My pupils have moved on. If I could teach the sharecroppers' children, I'd have something I cared about doing here. But when I tried that a few years ago, we had a warning visit from the Klan."

"Mama! You didn't tell me!"

"They rode in on horseback carrying torches and left a note."

"Oh Mama!"

"They are active around here. I hear about their terrifyin' raids when I go to Danville. Their targets are mainly Negroes of course, but they also attack whites who, in their opinion, don't keep Negroes in their place. But just think, I actually put the families of the children I taught in jeopardy. I was so worried when I realized"

"And Papa probably wasn't very comforting."

"No, he was furious at me."

What will you do, Mama?"

"Right now, I'm living one day at a time."

That night, while Sidney was downstairs in his study, Louisa lay awake in their bed, the four poster Sidney was born in, made by an enslaved carpenter with considerable skill. She felt like she just didn't belong in it any more.

It was time for the children to go home. Wally, Henry and Laura decided to go with Mary and the twins as far as the junction of the South Side line and the line to Lynchburg. They took several books for Celia. There were too many people for the carriage, so they would have to ride in the wagon. "I don't know why everyone has to leave at once," Sidney grumbled. "We'll look like a family of poor white trash, all crowded in the wagon."

Louisa embraced them and kissed Becca and Emett. "Now you help your Aunt Mary with the babies all the way to the Junction."

"Of course we will, Grandmama," said Henry. "That's why we're goin' now."

"Hurry children, the train won't wait," said Sidney as he kissed Louisa on the cheek.

As the wagon moved off with the children waving, Louisa watched and kept waving until it was a speck. Then it was still. A few birds chirped. She walked slowly back to the house and climbed the stairs to the veranda. She entered the house and walked to the dining room, where she sat at her accustomed place at the table. After a few moments Lucy came and asked if she needed anything. "No thank you Lucy. With Mr. Sidney away for the day, we won't need any meals. I can take care of myself. You may go home if you like."

"Thank you Miz Louisa. I will see you in the mornin'. Should I bring Bella and Jewel for the day?"

"Yes, one more day to help clean up and wash the sheets and towels. Thank you Lucy. They are good girls."

"Thank you Miz Louisa."

Louisa heard Lucy walk through the pantry to the outside. Her footsteps crunched in the gravel. Then it was silent. Louisa sat listening to the quiet. She could almost hear Laura, Wally and Henry talking and laughing, the babies babbling, Mary's gentle voice as she soothed them, Sidney calling her.

Then it was quiet again. Louisa breathed in the silence. She stood and walked from room to room, feeling their emptiness. Finally she took refuge in the library and curled up on the sofa with Pride and Prejudice. She had always enjoyed solitude before. It gave her an opportunity to read, ride her horse, think, and write letters. What was different now was the chasm between her and Sidney. Thinking about that filled her with sadness again. She opened the book and lost herself in the story. After a few hours her stomach reminded her that it was time to eat something. She went out to the garden beside the kitchen house and picked some green beans, summer squash, and corn. While they boiled over the fire, she pulled a few weeds in the garden, remembering how she had labored during the war. Her vegetables tasted delicious, especially with the butter they had now. She cut off a hunk of cheese and some bread and her meal was complete.

After eating, she went to visit Sadie, bringing her a carrot. Deciding to go for a ride, she saddled her. She rode slowly around the fields, nodding and greeting the workers. She thought she recognized Jim's boys and Jewel, but it was hard to tell from a distance, since they wore hats, pulled down against the sun's heat. Seeing how young some of the workers were, she felt a pang of remorse. She followed the path to the creek, where a few children were splashing and playing in the water. She waved at them and they waved back. She rode back and spent the rest of the day lost in Elizabeth Bennet's struggle to find a balanced love with Darcy. At some point she fell asleep, because she awoke to find Sidney standing beside the sofa, glass in hand, looking down at her.

"When did you get back?" she asked, sitting up.

"I just got back and I'm hungry. Where's Lucy?"

"I told her we didn't need her today, since you were gone. I thought you would have dinner in Danville. You usually do when you're there."

"So you gave her the day off and I go hungry."

"I'll fix you something."

"I don't want bread and cheese. I want a nice hot meal." He took a swallow of whiskey.

"I'll slice some ham and scramble some eggs," she said on the way to the kitchen house.

"Go ahead then." In a few minutes he joined her.

"How was the ride with the children?" she said as she cooked.

"Alright. They are enthralled with Mary and the babies, you know. They barely spoke to me at all."

Louisa carried his plate and a cup of tea for herself into the dining room. They sat quietly while Sidney ate and Louisa sipped her tea. When Sidney went to his study, Louisa cleared the table, took her novel and a candle, and went upstairs.

The next day Bella and Jewel returned, as Louisa had requested. Jewel smiled at her and said," Miz Louisa, I been wantin' to tell you, I taught Bella here to read."

"And we both taught our sisters and cousins and friends," said Bella.

Louisa couldn't speak for a moment. Joy filled her throat.

"I can't tell you how glad I am," she said finally.

"I 'spect we gonna keep doin' it," said Jewel. "Those books you gave us are gettin' plenty a' use."

"I will see if I can get some more." said Louisa, wondering if she could somehow get her hands on old McGuffey Primers in Lynchburg.

"It would be mighty fine to have more books, Miz Louisa," Jewel said.

Lucy came down the stairs with a bundle of sheets. "Your readin' lessons is spreadin' around Oak Hill, Miz Louisa. But what these children need is a school. Why don't we have a school here in the county?"

"We ought to. The government of Virginia isn't putting enough money into schools now that the federal government is cutting funds for the Freedmen's Bureau. And Pittsylvania County is not making up for that."

The days passed quietly, for the most part. The new sharecroppers had settled in over on the old Stanton land and were working steadily. Sidney remained worried though, and spent the days riding around his acres of tobacco, checking on his workers, overseeing their labor.

Two weeks after all the children had left, Louisa and Sidney got a letter from Laura, thanking them for the wonderful visit. Laura also wrote, "Grandmama, please don't think because we are grown up now, that we don't need you. We all need you to come up here because we can talk with you. We can talk with Mr. Sam too, but it is better to be able to talk with both of you. I particularly need you because I am the only female in a house full of males, and there are certain things I need to discuss with you. When do you think you can come?"

Louisa laughed until the tears came when she read Laura's letter. She wiped her eyes and looked at Sidney, who was not smiling. "Laura has always been spoiled," he said. "Imagine summoning your grandmother like that."

"I'd like to go up next weekend. Will you please take a letter to Danville for me when you go tomorrow, so they'll know I'm coming?"

"Just like that, you decide to go up there? What if I need you here next weekend?"

"Do you?"

"Not for anything specific. I just want you to be here. This is your place! Here! With me!"

"I'm sorry if you don't like it, but it's really important to me to be with our grandchildren when they need me."

"I see. It doesn't matter what I want."

On Friday morning Louisa awoke before dawn, feeling a flutter of excitement in her stomach. She dressed quickly and put a few more items in the tapestry bag she had packed the night before. Then she patted Sidney's arm to awaken him. He reached for her but she slipped out of his arms when he breathed last night's whiskey in her face. Downstairs, she prepared tea and leftover cornbread and ate hurriedly.

Sidney came down, looking exhausted. "Just tea for me, Louisa. I'll have a real meal in Danville." He drank his tea standing up.

While Sidney readied the horse and carriage, Louisa went into the library to find Gulliver's Travels for Celia. She stood in the doorway and paused, looking for a long moment at the shelves full of books. Then she walked through the center hall and out to the veranda. Sitting down in her favorite rocking chair, she rubbed her palms on its smooth wooden arms. Sidney drove up in the carriage and she climbed in before he could help her. As they pulled away, Louisa turned around and watched Oak Hill disappearing into the distance, a silhouette against the rosy sky.

They rode in silence for a while. "Sidney," Louisa began, "Now that I no longer have Alexa, Max, and Robert to tutor, I don't need to come back on Monday."

"But when will you come back?"

"I don't know Sidney. It depends on the situation with the children and Sam. Whether they need me."

"I know you also want to stay for that Negro girl, Celia, you talked about. You have completely forgotten your wifely duties."

"I don't want to argue, Sidney."

They rode in silence the rest of the way to Danville, where they waited a few minutes on the platform.

When the train arrived they reached for each other and embraced.

"When will you return?" Sidney asked again.

"I don't know, Sidney," she said as she boarded. "I will write you."

The train pulled away.

Acknowledgements

First, I want to thank my writing group, who listened to sections of my novel and shared suggestions and encouragement with me for nearly two years as I was working on it. Susan Bellaire, Bob Rossi, Linda Jeans, Linda Dupuis and Susan Dean, I appreciate you all. Thanks also to my early readers Donna Gilton, Dan Feehan, and Lynda Tisdell, whose comments and support were invaluable. My husband Guy LaTour's shared interest in visiting African American history museums together in Virginia, Florida, and Alabama was an enormous help, as was his loving support.

The painting on the cover is by my grandmother Ethyl Emett Edwards and shows the James River in Lynchburg.

Finally I need to mention the rich background provided by both the nonfiction and fiction I read for this project. The titles follow.

Bibliography

History

The Narrative of the Life of Frederick Douglass, an American Slave, Frederick Douglass, 1845.

Lynchburg and its People, W. Asbury Christian, 1900.

The Souls of Black Folk, W. E. B. Du Bois, 1903.

Slaves in the Family, Edward Ball, 1998.

A People's History of the United States, Howard Zinn, 1999.

The Hemingses of Monticello, Annette Gordon-Reed, 2008.

The 1619 Project, Nikole Hannah Jones, 2021.

Four Hundred Souls: A community History of African America, 1619-2019, Ibram X Kendi and Keisha N. Blain, ed. 2021.

Of Blood and Sweat: Black Lives and the Making of Power and Wealth, Clyde W. Ford, 2022.

Fiction

Their Eyes Were Watching God, Zora Neale Hurston, 1937.

Kindred, Octavia Butler 1979.

Beloved, Toni Morrison, 1987.

Property, Valerie Martin, 2003.

The Known World, Edward P. Jones, 2003.

The Water Dancer, Ta-Nehisi Coates, 2020.

The Sweetness of Water, Nathan Harris, 2021.

The Love Songs of W.E.B. Du Bois, Honoree Fannone Jeffers, 2021.

About the Author

Pendleton (Penny) Hall grew up in Delaware with frequent visits to relatives in Virginia. She graduated from Randolph Macon Woman's College in Lynchburg, Virginia and received her MA from UNC at Chapel Hill. While in Lynchburg in the 1960s she became active in the Civil Rights Movement. After moving to Rhode Island she was a founding member of, and worked with, the South County Coalition Against Racism for over twenty years. She taught English and German in high school for 29 years. She has three adult children, ten grandchildren, and lives with her husband in Rhode Island.

Made in USA - North Chelmsford, MA
33482_9781960505613
11.17.2023 0507